MW00711547

...And Now Goodbye

...And Now Goodbye

Carole Kelly

Dream Catcher Publishing, Inc.

This book is a work of fiction. Places, events and situation in this story are purely fictional. Any resemblance to actual persons, living or dead is coincidental

Copyright© by Carole Kelly. All rights reserved.

No part of this book may be reproduced, stored in a retrieval system, or transmitted by any means, electronic, mechanical, photocopying, recording, or otherwise, without written permission from the author.

ISBN: 0-9712189-0-0

Library of Congress Catalogue Number: 2004114288

Published by Dream Catcher Publishing, Inc.
P.O. Box 14058
Mexico Beach, Florida 32410
Email: dcp@DreamCatcherPublishing.net

To Susan Thiel, my champion, without you no one would have ever seen my book, Paulette Linn for your silent push and hours of research, Dwan Hightower who believed enough in my story to take a chance, Louise Zivnuska my sister in my heart who never stopped believing in me, and finally, John, my husband, who lets me reach for my stars and is there to catch me if I fall.

Dedicated with love to my sister, Sharon J. Kelly.... I miss you still after all these years

"How do I love thee? Let me count the ways.
I love thee with a love I seemed to lose
With my lost saints, --I love thee with the breath,
Smiles, tears, of all my life! --If God choose,
I shall but love thee better after death."

Elizabeth B. Browning

...And Now Goodbye

Chapter One

Cordoba, Argentina – May, 1993

Roberto Bertinelli stood at the window, lost in thought. There was no way out. It was no longer a question of what he was going to do; that had been taken out of his hands. He had to tell her. He had been warned; if he didn't do it, someone else would.

The secret he had hidden from everyone for over twenty years would destroy them. Everything they had shared would be shattered. The worst part would be that he, who had spent all those years trying to protect and care for her, would be the one to stab her in the heart and break her trust. She would never forgive him and that knowledge was killing him.

Roberto winced in pain. His stomach knotted as perspiration dotted his forehead. Well, at least it wouldn't have to be tonight, he thought. His secret was safe for another few hours.

Then he saw the knife…there was so much blood, the ground was soaked with it. He was cold and tired. He didn't think he could carry her much further…the snow swirled around him, making him dizzy as he struggled to stay on his feet. Images - bloody wounds, a broken body, fire and ice - careened around in his head, bringing pain so unbearable that his body began to spasm and jerk as the scenes unwound like an old film, flashing single frames one at a time in slow motion.

Roberto struggled against the memories, pulling himself back, away from what he could never forget. Finally, his vision cleared. The view from the window came back into focus and he was surprised to find himself standing in his study. He did not remember coming into the room.

It was a beautiful evening in Argentina. The grass of the pampas was waving, like a great, endless sea stretched out to the horizon below him and he could hear the cattle lowing in the distance as they made their way across the trails. The light on the river was a burnished gold that shimmered like a million fireflies dancing on the water's surface. Evening would come soon. It was that time of year when the sun glowed royally on the horizon, only for a few trembling moments, before it started its rapid descent behind the mountains, leaving streaks of brilliant pinks and purples that bled into each other as the light faded, little by little, and evening became night. The creatures that were paused in silence, waiting for the sun to make its final course, knew that the land would soon be theirs. When darkness set in and all traces of light were erased except for the moon, strange staccato cries and wondrous songs would fill the air.

Roberto sighed. Usually he loved this time of day, but he could find no joy in it now. Tonight would come too soon and he wanted time to stand still. He wanted to hold the beauty of the day in his hands and not let it go. He wanted to stretch out the hours endlessly, so that tomorrow would never come.

***

When Julia entered the study, she saw Roberto standing at the window looking out at the deepening twilight. She knew she would find her husband here. Lately, he seemed to be spending more and more time in this exact spot. It seemed to her that he was entranced by the beauty of the sunset. But, sometimes she thought she saw tears in his eyes. He always turned away when he noticed her so she was never certain.

He still was as handsome as the day she first met him, she thought, even after all these years. Tall, dark and handsome! She smiled to herself as she realized how this phrase described him so perfectly. He was a wonderful man and she loved him deeply.

As she watched him, she was suddenly filled with an overwhelming sadness, which squeezed her heart and pushed down on her with a powerful weight and then was gone. Something was wrong, terribly wrong, but Roberto would not speak of it. There were times when she would look up to find him staring at her and the naked pain and sadness in

2

his eyes would hit her like a blow. He had lost weight and dark circles were stained under his eyes as if he had painted them there.

"Roberto, why can't you share it with me", she whispered.

All at once, he felt her presence and turned to see her watching him from the doorway. She still was so beautiful that she took his breath away. After all these years, her waist-length, midnight hair had just a few silver strands that only enhanced her beauty. She was tall for a woman, with long legs and a beautiful body, but her real beauty was found in her gentle soul and her tender ways. Time had etched tiny lines around her large dark eyes, but her face still glowed with youth and vitality. She was everything in the world to him, the love of his life and so much more. Words could not tell the joy he felt when she simply walked into a room. He looked at her and drank in her smiling image. He wanted to remember her this way, happy and flushed with excitement.

Today was Julia's 50th birthday and they were having a grand party this evening that would celebrate both her birthday and the wine harvest festival, *National de La Vendimar*. They had invited all their friends and neighbors, hired a local band that was renowned for its performance of the tango and cooked enough food to feed most of Argentina. Julia had been working feverishly with the gardeners, cooks and maids to make sure everything was perfect for their friends and the workers on the ranch. This was their party as far as she was concerned. The fact that it was also her birthday was secondary to her wish to say thank you to all the people she loved. The ranch and vineyard were more prosperous than ever and it could not have happened without all of their help.

"Julia, you look beautiful", Roberto whispered as he admired his wife. She was wearing a simple white, floor-length sheath that looked like alabaster against her olive skin and dark hair. It was a striking combination.

"Thank you Roberto. Your ability to shop for me and get just the right cut and size was extraordinary as usual. I love the dress, it's beautiful, and the look in your eyes tells me it is one I will want to wear sometime when we don't have so many people coming to dinner." She smiled as she saw the hunger come into his eyes. After all these years he could still turn her heart upside down and she knew it was mutual.

The dress was just more evidence of the way Roberto spoiled her. He had seen it in a shop while in Buenos Aires and had brought it back to her for her birthday. She never wanted for anything and he had such exquisite taste that she almost never went shopping for herself.

"Everyone should be arriving around 8:30, so you have some time before you need to start dressing", Julia said with a wink.

As she turned to leave the room, Roberto followed her with his eyes. "It's incredible that after all this time she can still fill me with longing just with a look and the sound of her voice," he mused aloud. But then with a gasp, the pain and sorrow of losing her blew through him like a river of fire, burning what was left of his broken heart - a heart that would be reduced to ashes by tomorrow. His house of cards was tumbling down. He had tried so hard to cover his tracks, to make sure that no one would ever find out. But he had forgotten one thing. It was something so inconceivable and something so final that he had never thought to prepare for it. That something was going to cost him everything and there was nothing he could do. It was over.

***

Victor stood in the shadow of the trees that surrounded the walkway outside the house and breathed in the evening air. God, how he loved it here in Argentina. He had taken a month away from the work that kept him moving between New York, Buenos Aires and, now, Japan. Being head legal counsel and Senior Partner for World Wide, an internationally known import/export company, as stimulating as it was, had its downside. Being away from Argentina for extended periods was one of them.

He would not have missed Julia's birthday for any reason. Both she and Roberto had been very good to him and they were the only people he could really call family since his parents had both died when he was fifteen. As a boy, he had become Roberto's vaquero after Roberto had found him wandering the pampas looking for horses to steal. It was a terrible time in Victor's life and Roberto had helped him work through his suffering and anger, helped him to accept the blow that fate had dealt him, taught him how to ranch and then sent him to school to study law. Yes, he owed them a great deal and Victor was a man that did not take his obligations lightly.

Roberto had called and said that he needed him to come home right away and since he had already planned to be present for the party, he just extended his vacation a few more weeks. He had worked at the firm for over 10 years, and except for a few days each year, he had never taken a vacation. The summons from Roberto had come at a good time because he was long overdue for some time off.

4

Victor hadn't asked Roberto what the problem was but he knew that there was something wrong. Roberto seemed extremely troubled and his physical appearance had changed. He was gaunt and pale, and his cheeks were prominent in his face. His eyes looked as if he were not sleeping well. He only knew that whatever Roberto needed, he would do whatever he could to help.

***

Julia was speaking to Carmen, her housekeeper, when the sensations of fear and danger hit her. She looked up to see Roberto watching her. She knew he recognized what she was feeling. How could he not after all these years? Ever since her fall, she had been plagued by these episodes. Julia turned away from Carmen and walked into the kitchen.

She could not let this happen, she told herself, not tonight. With all her strength she clamped her mind down on the fear and pulled herself together. Taking a deep breath, she returned to the party and her guests, giving a small reassuring smile to Roberto, who had been waiting for her to return to the room.

Roberto saw Julia's smile and knew that she was all right for now. When he saw the high color on her cheeks, he understood what the struggle for control was costing her.

Sometimes these periods of grief and fear would last for days and she would weep uncontrollably, never allowing Roberto or anyone near her. She would become distant and stay in her room, refusing all comfort, never bathing or eating. Only Carmen could get her to take some water during these times. Until one day, as if wakening from a dream, she would resume her life as if nothing had happened.

As the years went by and these lost-days happened less and less frequently, Roberto started to hope that they would never return. But, when he saw Julia's face before she left the room, he knew that he had been mistaken. He knew she would only make it through the evening out of the sheer strength of her will.

Roberto heard his name called and turned to see Victor approaching him.

"Compadre", he said, "you have a lovely wife, a magnificent home and me for your very best friend. You do not lack for much. Yes! You are a lucky man!"

Roberto smiled at the man he loved like a son. "Yes," he replied. "I am indeed a lucky man. My wife is beautiful and rare like a fine jewel. But, I believe you were flirting with her earlier. When I saw you two dancing, it seemed you held her a little too close. I realize a waltz is one of her favorites but I think you have taken advantage of our friendship."

Victor flinched as if he had been stung. "Roberto, believe me, I would never..,"

Roberto interrupted him, "I'm only joking Victor," he smiled, "you have always been a perfect gentleman and treated Julia with complete respect. I just wanted to take a little swagger out of your walk and I knew this would do it. Ha! Ha!" he laughed.

Clamping Victor on the shoulder, Roberto pulled him into his arms and gave him a giant hug. "It is good to see you again. You are no longer the little boy I met many summers ago out on the pampas. I believe you were trying to borrow a few of my horses, if I remember correctly," he grinned.

Victor smiled at the memory. Yes, it had been a long time ago and he revered this man who had done so much for him. "I only meant to keep them for a few days and you had so many", he replied. They both laughed. All at once Roberto shook as a tremor moved through his body.

"What is it Roberto? Are you ill?" Victor asked worriedly.

Roberto turned to Victor and grabbed him by the arm with a force that made him wince. "Do you love me, Victor? Can I count on you?" he whispered through clenched teeth. "Are you my loyal friend?"

"Yes," Victor said, confused by the intensity of Roberto's words. "You are like a father to me. There is nothing I would not do for you," he said simply.

Roberto looked away, moved to tears. It seemed he was always on the verge of breaking down these days. But, he knew if he did, he would not be able to stop the tears that threatened to burst like a damn from the crack in his heart. He could not give in to the pain. He had too much to do.

Looking at Victor again he said, "There will be a time when I will call upon you to help me in ways that you never dreamed. To make sacrifices beyond any you can imagine. I will put your love and faith in me to the true test."

Roberto's eyes blazed with a feverish light and his jaw was clenched rigidly as he said these words. Victor felt a chill pass through him as he saw the light fade from Roberto's eyes to be replaced by stark, agonizing pain.

"I need you to…" Roberto whispered but before he could say more he saw Doctor Cesar Fernandez and his wife Maria headed their way.

"Roberto, there you are", they called out. "We wondered where you might be hiding."

"Hello, you two", Roberto said with a broad smile and, in turning away from Victor, his mood completely changed. "I hope you have been enjoying yourself. You took my breath away when you were dancing the tango. You are both better than ever and I never tire of seeing you dance with such beauty".

Cesar preened. He knew he and Maria were excellent dancers but it was always high praise coming from Roberto. "You are so kind to say so. I'm just an old man still trying to win his lady's love," he said looking down modestly.

Maria snorted, "Humph! Old man, right! He almost bent me in half and I could hardly keep up with him. There was a time I could have danced him right off the floor, but no more. As for winning my love, he knows he has had that for over forty years."

Roberto and Victor both laughed as the two looked at each other lovingly. They were an amazing couple. Cesar had been the family doctor for years and a wonderful friend and confidant longer than that.

"Well, I see I can't impress you any more tonight," Cesar said with a large grin, "so I guess I will admit that I am a little tired. It was a beautiful party and Julia is as lovely and gracious as ever, but it is time for us to say goodnight. By the way, Roberto, have you given any thought to our discussion earlier this week?" Cesar asked.

"No, my friend, I haven't", he replied. "With all the preparations for the party, I haven't had the time, but I promise we will speak again later next week. Thank you for coming. I'm sure Julia was delighted to see you," he said trying to change the subject.

Cesar stood closely to Roberto and looked him hard in the eye for a moment with what seemed to be an angry expression, then he turned and took Maria's hand.

"Yes," he said smiling, "Julia was very happy to see me. If it weren't for the way that I love my lovely Maria, I might pursue your Julia. She just might like a man who can still do the tango!"

Roberto's face drained of color and Cesar stepped forward and took him by the arm. "I'm sorry, Roberto, under the circumstances that was

7

unforgivable of me. Please accept my deepest apologies. I know that Julia is the love of your life."

Roberto smiled as the color came back to his face. "No, it is nothing you said. I'm just feeling a little tired and edgy after the last few days."

Cesar continued to look concerned. Roberto tried again, "Please", he said "I am fine. I took no offense from your remarks."

With that, Cesar turned to Victor, who was still puzzled at what had just happened between the two old friends. "Victor, you've been a stranger to our home for too long. Please come by while you are here and have dinner with two old people who would love to have you".

"I will", he replied, "it would be an honor. I'll call early next week and we can schedule an evening together."

"And bring a lady friend if you want," winked Maria.

Victor laughed, "If you two are still trying to play cupid with Rosita and me, you can just stop. First, she is too young and I'm too busy for a relationship. My travel schedule makes it most unfair to any lady who might want to consider me for a partner."

"Well, the offer still stands", they chorused. "Don't forget your promise to call."

As the couple turned to leave, Roberto watched them walk away, then he turned to Victor and said in a soft halting voice, "Go now Victor, leave me. Enjoy yourself tonight. Find the lovely Rosita and dance. She has grown up while you were away. Forget about anything but enjoying this beautiful evening. We are so happy you are home. Go my friend, my son. Tomorrow will be soon enough to speak of other things, of regrets, to…," Roberto's voice trailed off.

Victor could see that his old friend had pulled back into himself and that he was no longer aware that Victor stood beside him. He decided he would stay nearby in case Roberto wanted to tell him what had him so troubled, so he moved discreetly into the shadows the moonlight had created on the lawn, but his eyes never left the man who meant so much to him.

***

Rosita Juarez stomped her feet impatiently. "Well where is he? I saw him speaking to Doctor Fernandez and his wife and now he has disappeared again. I think he is trying to avoid me. Damn him! Damn him!"

Julia smiled down at Rosita. She was wearing a tight red dress that accented every one of her luscious curves. During the past three years, Rosita had certainly gone from a little flat-chested tomboy to a beautiful woman. With her black hair and olive complexion, she had every unattached ranch hand and man for miles staring in open admiration.

But Rosita only wanted Victor. From the time she first laid eyes on him and developed a schoolgirl's crush, she had wanted only him. Her bickering with Victor was something that everyone was used to by now. She would antagonize him by pushing him with her taunts, trying to jump her horse one fence higher, shooting just a little straighter, running ever so much faster, and then, to add insult to injury, she would pull all kinds of terrible stunts for jokes. Placing burrs under his saddle was one of her favorites. They had been battling it out for years and Victor just thought she was a pain and a nuisance. He didn't realize that she did all of this to get his attention and to show that she cared for him.

Well, she now had the ultimate weapon. She had grown up to be a beautiful, desirable woman. Victor wasn't going to know what hit him.

Julia laughed to herself. She just wanted to be there when he got his first lesson. It was going to be a good one if Rosita had her way.

"Rosita," Julia said, "I'm sure that Victor is not avoiding you. It's impossible for anyone to avoid you in that dress". Raising her eyebrows to let her know she was joking with her, Julia continued. "Go have some fun. Let him find you. Stop worrying about Victor. There are so many men here who would love to have a dance with you. Victor just arrived today and I am sure he is trying to say hello to everyone. You're lovely. Go on and I promise you Victor will notice when he sees you dancing with all the other men."

Yes, Rosita thought, Julia is right. I have to act more grown up so Victor will not see me as a child. She turned and said, "Thank you. As usual you are right. He just makes me so angry and then I go and do something stupid. I will stop worrying and make it a point to dance with everyone!" she smiled wickedly.

As she turned to leave, she spotted Luke Molina and Ramon Calderon standing together talking. Swaying seductively from side to side, she wiggled up to the two men as they stared at her, like two deer hypnotized by the headlamps of a car.

"Hello, Luke. Hello, Ramon. Beautiful night isn't it?" she asked. When neither one of them answered, she continued, "I feel like dancing and I know both of you just love to dance. Don't you?" she smiled, leaning very close to them and giving them both an ample view of her breasts.

"Now which one of you handsome guys is it going to be? Let me see. Eeenie, meenie," she teased as she pointed first at Luke and then at Ramon, going back and forth between them. "Well, Luke," she said finally, placing her hand against his chest, "I believe this just might be your lucky night!" Then she grabbed him by the arm and dragged him to the dance floor. Luke was so surprised and love-struck, he just stumbled behind her and let her pull him.

Luke was handsome, tall and well built. With his wheat colored hair and beautiful blue eyes, half the women in Argentina were crazy about him. He had a way with women and did not spend many nights sleeping alone. Well, he had a way with most women.

When he first had the misfortune to run into Rosita, he had become a stammering pup, still wet behind the ears, mashing his hat in his hands. It was incredibly embarrassing to him and Rosita took every chance she could to either make fun of him or to make him miserable.

This was going to be one of those times, Julia mused. Rosita had thrown her arms around Luke and pressed her body as close to him as she could get. Luke's face was beet red and he looked like he was somewhere between being the happiest man on the earth and wishing he could just disappear.

Julia laughed out loud, and seeing Carmen watching her closely, took a moment to speak to her beloved housekeeper.

"I know you're worried, Carmen, but there really is no need. I am feeling fine now and everything is under control."

Carmen looked at her mistress and knew she was lying. Tonight, she knew, Roberto would have his hands full dealing with his hysterical wife. She hoped he could handle it since he didn't seem to be in the best of spirits these days.

Something was wrong. She knew that. They couldn't fool her with their play-acting. She had worked for them for eighteen years and she knew everything about them. Trouble was brewing! Bad trouble!

Carmen smiled at her lovely Julia, who was like a daughter to her, and turned away before Julia could see that Carmen was more worried this time than she had ever been before.

Victor looked away from Roberto, who had not moved or spoken, to see what the commotion was on the dance floor. A couple was dancing a very complicated tango, *orillero* style, while everyone else stood around the couple and clapped.

A very beautiful woman in a very tight red dress was executing a *molinete* and was the obvious focus of attention even though Luke's foot moves were syncopated and so quick they were almost a blur. As Victor watched, he had the feeling that something about the woman was familiar. As the dance ended, she turned to her companion and laughingly kissed his cheek.

"My, God!" Victor erupted. "It can't be that demon of sticker weeds and hornets nests, that infuriating little pest who I would dearly love to drop off a cliff! That can't be Rosita!"

Roberto laughed. Speaking softly to Victor he said, "Yes, that's your lovely little side-kick, Rosita. I told you she had grown up while you were gone."

"Well, what the hell is she doing dressed like that, showing off her legs, why that dress isn't long enough to cover anything! And would you look at how low-cut that thing is! Why, she is going to fall out of it! Her, her...well, everything is showing. My God! I'll kill the brat! I'll put my hands around her beautiful little neck and I will strangle her and I will damn well enjoy doing it," Victor growled.

"My, my, Victor. For a man who couldn't stand the girl and who couldn't wait to leave town so he would never have to see her again, and who I believe even told her he hoped she would drop off the face of the earth, you sound like a jealous lover!"

"Are you out of your mind?" Victor exclaimed. "I'm not jealous!!" By this time his face had turned a bright purple. "I couldn't care less! I just don't want her ruining her reputation. Look at the way the men are leering at her. Damn her, the little witch! She's not going to get away with this! She's got a lot of damned nerve sashaying around out there, acting that way! What the hell is she thinking!?"

Victor had forgotten Roberto and any promise he had made to himself and was still muttering under his breath as he stormed over to the dance floor. Roberto laughed and felt Julia's arm slip around his waist. Laying her head against his back, she said, "It look's like our friend has fallen for it," Julia said with a smile. "Rosita has finally found a way to make him notice her."

"Yes," Roberto said, "it's good for him to start thinking about love and having a family. I'm not sure Rosita is exactly right for him since they may kill each other during the first month of their relationship", he joked.

"Well, I hope he can find even a small piece of the love and happiness we have shared", Julia murmured.

Roberto didn't speak. He turned her toward him and embraced her, smelling her hair and the warm musk scent of her perfume. "Yes," he said, "we have been very lucky" he whispered, "Happy birthday, darling".

Julia leaned into his arms and, as she did, the demons she had been fighting all evening came back to her in a rush. She turned her frightened eyes up to his gaze and trembled. Roberto could see the manic change in her and knew he needed to get her to her room.

"Let's go say goodnight to our guests, shall we? Then you and I can go to our room and be alone," he said.

Julia bit her lip and nodded.

***

Luke stumbled out into the cool evening air and took a deep breath. It was hot inside and dancing with Rosita always caused his blood to boil. She was like a burning flame, hot and dangerous, and he was the helpless moth, caught in her glow, flirting and dancing around her fire, heedless of his ravaged wings.

He was so crazy about her that it left him weak and shaky when she was around. When she kissed him on the cheek at the end of their dance, he thought he might faint from having her lips so near to his. He knew one thing; he wasn't going to wash her lipstick mark from his face for a whole week. Wow! She had actually kissed him!

It was then, without warning, that Ramon hit him with his fist, hard against his jaw, and sent him flying to the ground. Luke was disoriented at first and didn't know what had happened, so Ramon was able to hit him again and this time his nose started to bleed. He thought it might be broken because he heard a terrible crunching sound when the speeding fist connected with his nose.

"What the hell!" Luke said as he scrambled to his feet and plowed headfirst into his attacker's stomach, knocking him off his feet. Jumping on top of Ramon, Luke began to pummel his face over and over again. Ramon struggled, pushed up with his arms and rolled away. Luke was in mid-swing and struck the ground hard with his fist. "Son of a bitch!" he yelped as he grabbed at his injured hand.

Ramon scrambled to his feet and before Luke could get up, he kicked him in the kidneys. Luke collapsed, face first, onto the ground as the pain ripped through his back and took his breath away. Ramon raised his booted foot over Luke's wounded hand and prepared to stomp down hard but Luke managed to grab him by the leg and flip him over backward. Ramon hit his head on the edge of the concrete patio and lay still.

Luke was up now, pacing back and forth, cursing, holding his hand; shaking it up and down, as the pain roared through his arm. His knuckles were swollen and bleeding and it looked like his hand might be broken.

"I'm gonna kill you, Luke Molina, if you ever touch my woman again," Ramon groaned through clenched teeth. Luke turned toward him and watched as he tried to sit up against the wall of the house while he held his head in his hands. Luke laughed out loud.

"Man, you're loco!" Luke shouted. "Do you hear me? You've lost your mind, if you believe that Rosita is your woman! There's only one man she cares about and that ain't neither one of us two cowboys. You know it, I know it and the rest of the damned world knows it. So, don't start trying to beat the shit out of me. I'm not the right guy. You want to murder someone? Go try your luck with Victor. You kill him and you'll be doing us both a favor, because as long as he's alive, you and I, old buddy, don't stand a flipping chance!"

"You heard me Luke. You better stay away from Rosita or you're a dead son of a bitch!" Ramon croaked.

"Ramon, you don't have the balls or the brains to ever bring me down. You better get your shit together and forget about Rosita. If I don't have a prayer with her, you damned well don't, so stop dreaming. And, don't you ever touch me again or I'll break you so bad that you won't be worth anything to anyone, much less a woman," Luke threatened. Then he spit onto the ground and turned and walked away. Ramon thought about what Luke said. Groaning, he placed his throbbing head in his hands. His head didn't hurt nearly as much as the knowledge that what Luke had said was true or that he was a damned fool for loving the little bitch!

Chapter Two

When Victor finally walked up the steps leading to his room, he was very intoxicated. Well, actually, he thought, he was rip-roaring drunk, as drunk as he could ever remember being. He was trying to avoid the damned walls as he lurched from side to side, but they seemed to keep moving in on him.

It was very late. He had stayed until the last guest had departed and continued drinking alone out on the terrace. It was a beautiful night but he didn't enjoy it the way he usually did. His mind was in turmoil.

As he stumbled again, he cursed all women and the trouble they created.

"Rosita!" he said out loud. Oh, how he hated that name and the woman who carried it.

"Damn it!" he exclaimed as he missed the stair and barely avoided falling down the landing.

Yes, it had been quite a fiasco! He was sure everyone in attendance was discussing his embarrassing behavior on his or her way home. He had made an ass out of himself!

The stairway blurred and swung from side to side. He eased himself down on the step to steady himself. Putting his head in his hands, he cursed his stupidity again.

Earlier, when he stormed over to Rosita, after watching her dance in a dress she was about to fall out of, he hadn't given her a chance to say anything. He just grabbed her by the arm, dragged her onto the dance floor, crushed her to him, and said through clenched teeth, "I believe this is my dance." She had struggled to get away but he just held her more tightly.

As he remembered it all, it caused him to groan again. She had pulled her chin up and said, "Well, well, well. If it isn't Victor! I guess this is one way to say hello to each other. But, could you let me go?" When

Victor did not respond she hissed, "Damn it, stop! I can't breathe. Let me go. What the hell is the matter with you?"

"I'm just here to save your reputation," he hissed back. "You're making a spectacle of yourself, and someone has to …"

Before he could continue, Rosita jerked her hands free and slapped him as hard as she could across the cheek. Victor's face grew red where she had left her handprint but he did not release his grip on her.

"Oh! So you're still into sucker punches," he growled, while he pulled her arms behind her back and pushed himself closer.

"What did I do?" she cried. "I haven't seen you in years and you walk up without even saying hello and drag me to the dance floor. What are you so upset about?" she said in a strangled voice.

"What am I upset about? I would think it was obvious. Here you are dancing that way, making a display of yourself, showing off that, … that body - … where did you get that body? It wasn't there the last time I was home," he said gently, as he lost his train of thought. She felt so good, all warm and soft.

All of sudden Victor remembered his anger, "You can't just work men up that way. You could get into trouble," he whispered pulling her closer.

"Oh, so you like my body," she murmured checking her anger by clenching her fists he held behind her back.

"Of course I like your bo… Hell no, I don't like your body! I mean of course I like your body but," he stammered, not sure what he was saying, "that is not the point. Where did you get that dress? It doesn't cover anything. Why couldn't you have worn something longer, something with a higher neckline? My God, you're about to fall out of it!"

Rosita was doing a slow boil by now, but Victor decided that her silence meant that she understood his good intentions and agreed with him.

"I knew you would understand when I finally explained it to you. Maybe you are growing up after all. Your dress and your actions just aren't appropriate and …"

Without waiting for more, Rosita kneed him with such force that Victor almost fell to the floor.

"You stupid, egotistical jerk!" she screamed. "You are the most pompous old fool I have ever known! I'm grown up now and don't you ever tell me what to do or what I can or cannot wear!"

The entire room of people turned in their direction and all paused as if in slow motion, while the music sputtered and spattered to a discordant halt. As all eyes in the room watched, Rosita marched to the nearest table and picked up what appeared to be the largest drink Victor had ever seen.

At that moment he was at a complete disadvantage since he was still unable to take a full breath. So he just stood there, like a stunned cow, while she threw the entire drink into his face and onto his evening clothes. The last thing he saw was Rosita running from the room before the alcohol started to burn his eyes like she had tossed liquid fire into them.

The drenching woke Victor up. As he mopped his face and tried to smile at the stunned guests, he could see Julia and Roberto laughing behind their hands across the room, he realized that Rosita was right. Man, was that ever hard to admit. He definitely didn't like the taste those words left in his mouth. But there it was. She was right and he had been wrong, wrong, wrong!

How could he have done something so stupid? He didn't know what had come over him. Never in his life had he done something so irresponsible. He would find her and offer his deepest apologies. He would admit that he was completely wrong.

As Victor pulled himself up from the step and his woeful recollection of the evening, he wondered what had happened to her. He had waited until everyone had left and had searched everywhere for her but she had been nowhere to be found. Well, he would go to her home tomorrow and straighten it out. He owed her that much since he had probably ruined her entire evening and embarrassed her to boot.

Lurching and stumbling, he finally reached his room. As he pulled and tugged his clothes off, sending buttons flying in his clumsy attempt to undress, he muttered aloud, "Rosita is beautiful and what a body! Whew! It's hard to believe she's the same girl."

Victor fell across the bed. He still had his socks on but he couldn't seem to reach his feet. Each time he tried, he would pitch forward and almost land on his head. So the socks would have to wait. He would just rest for a few minutes.

Closing his eyes, the room started to spin. "Don't let me be sick," he prayed knowing that tomorrow he was really going to hate himself. He threw one leg off the bed and placed his foot on the floor. Finally, the room righted itself and he started to drift away.

"Victor," a voice whispered.

"What the.." Victor jumped up, startled that someone was in his room. The room started to twist and turn violently and he sank back to the bed.

"Who is it?" he asked.

No one answered.

As his vision came back into focus, Victor saw a beautiful woman standing in the moonlight that was streaming through his window. That woman was stark naked!

"My God! I must really be drunk. Now I'm having hallucinations," he choked. But the apparition was moving toward him and Victor stopped breathing. It was Rosita. Rosita was naked in *his* bedroom and she was walking toward him. This had never happened in all the times he had drank too much. What the hell had been in those drinks, he wondered?

As the hallucination that looked like Rosita reached the bed, she leaned down and kissed him on the mouth. Victor decided that he was going to find out what was in the drink he had consumed in such large quantities tonight, and bottle a case of it to keep for those lonely nights on the road. This was great!

Rosita ran her hands down the length of his body and started kissing every square inch of skin.

"Please, please, please, don't let me wake up. Let this dream never end," he moaned.

He could feel the texture of her skin and the way her black hair brushed his body as she made her descent to his main area of torture. "That feels so good...."

With a start, Victor pushed her away and jumped to his feet. Staggering from side to side he yelped, "What are you doing here? My God do you realize what might have happened if you would have continued? Get your clothes on and get out of here before someone finds out you have been in my room!".

Victor was trembling all over. He had nearly taken her in his drunken stupor. With a gasp, he realized that he was standing naked facing Rosita. His sex was rigid, leaving no doubt as to his desire for her. Turning away, he grabbed his trousers and tried to put them on but he missed, tripped and fell to the floor. Scrambling back up, he tried again.

"Victor, stop it! Forget your pants and sit down before you fall and break your neck. Your face is so gray you're starting to worry me," Rosita said.

"I'm here because I want to be here," she said to him patiently, like he was a child who didn't understand. "I don't care if anyone finds out I've been in your room in the middle of the night without any clothes," she sing-songed. "Stop trying to protect me. I don't need it and I don't want it. Now let's go back to what we were doing before your conscience tried to come between us."

With those words, she pushed Victor back onto the bed and straddled him. Victor pushed her away again and scrambled over to the edge of the bed, where he attempted to sit up and get control of himself.

It was a tough decision. The devil stood on one shoulder reminding him that she was beautiful and desirable and *naked*. Yes, let's not forget naked, he told himself deciding he should make love to her. And he had been without a woman for too long, the devil continued. Yes he had, Victor agreed, looking down at his erection.

The devil had almost convinced him when the good guy on the other shoulder reminded Victor very gently that there was no way he could do something like this and still live with himself later. And that she was just a young woman and he was older and as such he should be able to control himself even if she was *naked!*

Standing up and staggering to the window he said, "Beautiful, sweet Rosita, don't give yourself to me. You should only be with someone you really love for your first time."

"But I do love you, Victor", she proclaimed, saying the words that she had held in her heart for so long. "I have loved you since I was a little girl. Why don't you want me?" she said as she started to cry.

Victor turned from the window and looked at her. She was sitting on the bed with her legs drawn up, her hair tumbling in a black mass of curls down her sides. He could see the tears shining on her cheeks. It was going to take all his resolve to send her away tonight.

"Rosita," he whispered as he walked to the bed. "I don't love you. I'm sorry. I can't love you, though God knows I wish I could. It would solve so many problems for me," he sighed under his breath. "You're a wonderful, beautiful princess who should be looking for her prince, not someone old and used up like me. You should never give yourself to anyone who can't love you the way you deserve. If I could change my heart I would, but I cannot. Please believe that I have tried. Making love to you would be wonderful and it breaks my heart to let you go. But I must. Go home, Rosita. Don't cry," he said gently. "Wait and give yourself to a man who will deserve your love. I'm too old for you and I'm

18

broken in ways that you can't know. You'll understand someday and you will thank me for letting you go. I'm very, very sorry" Victor sighed as he felt the weight of his words hit the girl.

Rosita didn't say anything; she just sat still on the bed for a moment then stood and started dressing. She was crying in great gulps and was heedless of the tears that fell onto the floor around her and down her body onto her clothes. Victor wanted to comfort her but dared not for fear he wouldn't be able to let her go.

When she finished dressing, she turned to Victor and, in a voice full of broken dreams and a broken heart, she said, "You *will* be very sorry for this someday Victor. I will live to see you sorry!"

As Rosita left the room, Victor knew that he would be sorry. He already was.

***

He stood in the shadows and all that was visible was the glow from his cigarette. As Rosita left Victor's room, he wondered how far they had gone. Did they make love? Did he touch her beautiful breasts? Did she like it? Did she cry and moan for more the way he knew she would if she were with him?

All these thoughts tormented him and twisted his heart with rage. Crushing his cigarette beneath his boot, he swore he would make them both pay.

***

Roberto gasped as Julia rode him. It was so erotic watching her astride him with her head thrown back, her hair grazing his thighs. He tried to reach out to touch her breasts but she stopped and pulled his arms up above his head.

"You are not to touch me! You know the rules. Don't touch me," she said forcefully.

She held his hands down as she continued to drive him mad. First riding him, then slipping off to nibble and lick various parts of his body, then back astride him, forcing him to lie still. It was such torture that he thought he might faint from the emotions and feelings running madly through his body.

Whenever Julia had one of these spells, she would tear his clothes from him when he reached the room and then they would make love so violently that he could never tell if she wanted to hurt him or just to have sex. There was no love in her actions, just wanton, delirious pain and passion.

As Roberto found his release, he cried out moaning her name. Never had his climax been greater than tonight. As his seed spilled into her beautiful body she bent over him and bit his lip so hard it started to bleed. Then she moved to his side, cuddling up to him as he wrapped his arm around her. Sleep was upon him but he watched her face relax and all the mania leave it as she drifted away. Only then did he close his eyes and allow his body to relax.

***

Roberto woke and he was afraid. Julia had not been in bed when he reached for her. Looking around the room he saw her standing in the moonlight on the patio. She had put on a white gown and it was awash with light from the moon. "Julia," he said.

As Julia turned, Roberto could see the tears falling down her face. She had been crying for a long time and her gown was wet. When she looked at him she had a look of such hatred on her face that Roberto cringed backward.

Did she know? Maybe she has found out, he thought. But the look was replaced with one of such sadness that Roberto knew that he was spared at least another few hours.

"Julia, Julia, come to me," he pleaded.

Unlike the other times, Julia actually turned to him and moved into his arms. "What is it, darling?" he asked.

"I don't know, Victor. It seems there is some danger. It sits right on the edge of my memory but I can't grasp it. Something is wrong; I am frightened but I don't know why. I feel like I've lost something - something very important to me and I'm searching for it. But, I can't quite recall what it is. I'm afraid to remember but I feel like I'm going to lose my mind if I don't", she whispered as she clung to him.

Roberto closed his eyes and choked back a sob. He was going to have to tell her. Where would he ever find the courage?

20

"Roberto," Julia continued, "why can't I remember the fall that left me this way? Why can't I remember my parents? I know the doctor told you that I would have to remember on my own, but why can't I even remember their faces?"

"Darling," Roberto said as he pulled her down to sit at the edge of the bed. "I want you to listen to me. No matter what happens, I want you to believe that I have always loved you with all my heart. I have loved you in a way that most men never have the joy of knowing. I have always wanted to make you happy. I cherish you and would give anything to take this pain away."

"Roberto," she sighed as she lay down on the bed, "I'm so sorry. I didn't mean to lay any blame for this at your feet. You're the most wonderful man and I don't deserve all the happiness you have given me".

"Hush, darling", Roberto said softly as he gently pulled her into his arms and lay down beside her. "Let's speak no more of this tonight. Tomorrow after we have rested we will talk. Sleep now, my love. Let me hold you in my arms and shelter you one more night."

Julia had already fallen asleep before Roberto finished his words of comfort. Roberto lay with his arms around her, looking at her sleeping face until dawn broke the next morning. Tears had drenched his pillow.

When the sun peeked over the horizon, he knew that his life with Julia was over. "Goodbye, my love, goodbye," he whispered.

Chapter Three
Hilton Head, South Carolina - 1993

Nancy D'Amato got up from her knees and shook the dirt from her smock. She had been weeding and preparing the soil around her prized flowerbed. She looked over at her husband Frank and saw that he had fallen asleep in the lounge chair.

It was a beautiful day in Sea Pines, in the low 70's, with a warm breeze blowing off the ocean; unusual weather for early April. In the past this would have been one of the days she and Frank would have ridden their bikes along the coastline or played golf. But now, since Frank had lost his sight, she would ride alone or play the course with someone else and it just wasn't the same.

She knew it was very hard for him to accept, since he had to be led everywhere. He was a handsome man with his share of pride and she knew he was humiliated when he stumbled or couldn't find what he had just set down and he had to ask for help. They called the disease Macular Degeneration and the doctor had told them that it was the leading cause of blindness in the aging population. I guess at eighty-six and eighty-three they could qualify as the aging population, she chuckled to herself. Frank usually said that they weren't just getting old any more. They were old.

Shading her eyes with her hands, she looked back at their home. It was a Cape Cod style with a gabled roof, cedar shingle siding and long sweeping lawns that led to the shoreline. There were palm and oak trees that framed the front on the street side and floor to ceiling, wall-length French doors on the back of the house that gave panoramic ocean views all the way to Tybee Island. There was a heated pool and, when their grandchildren were younger, they swam and played during the long summers when they came to visit. They didn't come much anymore. They were grown-ups with their own lives and didn't have much time for Grandma and Grandpa now.

Sometimes Frank would ask her to describe what she saw when she looked out at the day. So she would tell him about the ships, sailboats, and dolphins as they played in the surf, or about the new batch of sea turtles with their tiny bodies and little legs wandering, helter-skelter, toward the water and their new home.

Because it was a private beach, it was never crowded, so only once in a while did she have a story to tell about how the teen-aged volleyball game was going, or how some little boy or girl was coming with their sand castle. Mostly he was interested in the colors. She knew he missed them with a passion. So, she would try her best to describe the sunrise, or the colors of the sky before a storm or the magnificent sunset in the western horizon.

Nancy put her gardening tools in the garage and went to the back door of the house. She would go in and wash up a little, then bring some fresh iced-tea out to Frank. He wouldn't leave the chair without her if he wakened and she could hear him if he called.

Today, they had volunteered to work at the Family Circle Tennis Classic held in Hilton Head each April and, although Frank couldn't see, he loved to greet the guests and participants and feel like he was still a part of the event. Afterwards, they would go to Caligny Square and, following a brief stop at her art gallery, they would have dinner. She was having a small showing of her latest paintings and would need to make an appearance.

She had always been a fairly successful painter, working in oil as her medium, producing mostly portraits and landscapes. This time her work was very different and she wasn't sure how it would be received. Bah, she thought, I don't care what they think of me. Let them whisper that I have gone over the brink and embraced senility for all I care.

These were her most important works. She felt that deeply. They were visually dark and foreboding, the colors and faces filled with the pain and the horror that they each had lived through. She had to finally get it out of her system and these paintings had helped her purge some of her demons. They all could just lump it if they didn't like them!

Walking through the door into the house, she looked up at the portrait that hung over the fireplace mantel. She shuddered. She should have taken it down years ago, but Frank absolutely refused to have it removed. Maybe now that he could no longer see, she should ask Andrew, the young man who helped her with the heavy chores, to take it down and put it in the garage. It represented the worst tragedy of their lives and as she gazed at it, she felt the tears start in her eyes.

What had happened to their family and the others had almost killed Frank, their marriage and her. No, she thought as she made her decision, that picture was coming down. Enough was enough. It was a constant reminder to them and it was time to let it go. Frank had never fully recovered from the tragedy that had torn their lives apart and, even though it killed him to look at the painting, he had insisted that it stay right there where they had originally placed it, because he wanted to remember.

She didn't. Not anymore.

Chapter Four
Cordoba, Argentina –1993

Victor had awakened early in the morning to one of the worst hangovers he had ever experienced. After grabbing a cup of coffee from Carmen, he went to saddle his horse. He needed to think. Maybe a ride across the pampas followed by a short hike in the Sierras de Cordoba might help.

He was very troubled. Thoughts of Rosita and Roberto were pulling at him with greedy hands. He would have to speak to them both before the day was over. He was not looking forward to either encounter.

As he finished saddling up and started to mount his horse, Carmen called to him from the entrance to the stable.

"Victor, I'm glad you're still here. Roberto asked me to tell you that he would like to meet with you this morning around 10:00 A.M. Can you be available?" she questioned.

Victor pulled his hat further down across his eyes. The sun was like a million splinters working their way into his eye sockets.

"Damn it, Carmen, you don't have to yell!" he grimaced as he spoke. "Of course I'll be there! Tell Roberto I will return in plenty of time to meet with him."

With that Victor raced out of the corral, stirring up the dust into large billows.

"Looks like the devil is riding behind him this morning," Carmen mumbled. "No reason to take my head off! First Roberto and now him. Guess they think I'm just a servant around here jumping at their beck and call. Someone they can just yell at anytime they want." She continued to grumble as she went back into the house.

Carmen hadn't seen Julia yet this morning and when she asked Roberto about her, he had told her that she was still sleeping. Ever since she had come to work for the family, Julia would become ill several times a year. So it would be a blessing if she were wrong this time and Julia was getting better.

They were terrible times when they hit the family and they frightened her badly when she saw the way her mistress suffered.

She had even embarked on a pilgrimage to the basilica of *La Virgen de Lujan* to speak to the blessed virgin about Julia's illness. Praying with hundreds of other pilgrims had made Carmen feel that maybe her petition to the Virgin had been heard, but so far Julia had not received the healing she had prayed for so hard.

Carmen decided to go to her room for a quick prayer at her tiny altar. The angels needed to intervene. She could feel something bad was going to happen. She crossed herself as she knelt down to pray.

***

Roberto sat alone in his study tapping a large envelope against his knees. He was drinking straight whiskey and smoking a cigar. Carmen had already given him her most disapproving look before mumbling about a house gone crazy and people riding like the devil, while others were drinking and smoking before breakfast.

He opened the envelope again and looked at its contents. All the damning evidence was here. It would not take Julia long to put it all together and remember what had happened. Then it would all end for him.

He had contemplated keeping the secret and not telling her, but that would have been so cruel and selfish that he had discarded the thought. After all the evil he had committed, it was the only honorable thing left to do. There were no other choices. He had looked at all the options a hundred times, wishing there was another way.

While Roberto's mind was set to do this, his heart was in rebellion. Remembering a story that he had heard from his mother when he was a boy, he thought about the Garden of Gethsemane and how Jesus had prayed to his heavenly Father and asked that the cup of pain and death be taken from him. His Father had not listened and Jesus had been crucified despite his prayers.

God had not heard Roberto's prayers either and his doom, like the blessed Jesus, was just around the corner. The story said that Jesus had cried tears of blood. Roberto understood that kind of pain. He had been living it for the past few months, knowing this day was coming and that there was nothing he could do to change it. Unlike Jesus, Roberto was wicked and his punishment would be well deserved.

Knowing that did not make this any easier.

He had fashioned the life of the *Portena* of Buenos Aires even though his home was on the Pampas. They had attended the performances of the symphony and the opera, attending the two world cups and dining with the likes of Diego Maradona. He had wanted to give Julia everything and he had started to believe the lie his life had been. He had forgotten about justice. Justice, who wears a blindfold, but who finds you one day, when you least expect it, and makes you pay.

Today would be his first payment. The others would pale in comparison.

***

Victor returned to the hacienda feeling no better after his ride. The pampas area of Argentina was endless and beautiful. Once you left the stand of poplar trees that ringed the main house, and climbed down into the valley, you entered a sea of grass. In other areas, visitors to their country could find it frightening since there was nothing out on the horizon, just grass as far as the eye could see. Only an occasional windmill or a lone eucalyptus tree would break the monotony as the hot *pampero* wind whipped at the rolling wheat and thistle bushes. It could appear that you were out in the middle of the ocean, with nothing to direct you to shore and a sense that everything was unreal. It was said that some people went mad living on the pampas on land that appeared to have no boundaries as far as the eye could see.

The ranch, however, was located on the sides of a mountain, with views of the river and the endless rolling plains, so there was no lack of picturesque landscape and wonderful animals to hold your interest.

Victor looked up to watch a hawk gliding slowly on the wind. Today he hadn't found the peace that his rides usually brought him. He had not seen Rosita and this disturbed him. When he rode over to her home, he was told she was not there and they did not know when to expect her back. He was afraid that his rough rebuttal of her the night before could cause her pain. She was so young and she was not schooled in the ways the game of love and lust were played. There was no way she could understand his refusal to make love to her and there was no way that he could explain. The secret he carried he would never reveal and, if God were good to him, he would carry it to his grave with him.

With the ghosts of his past howling behind him, he had pushed his mare past her endurance and she was lathered with sweat. He would have to rub her down thoroughly and give her an extra portion of grain before he returned her to her stall.

He cursed himself for the fool he seemed to have become since returning to Argentina. He didn't know what was wrong with him.

As he groomed the mare, Victor continued to ponder his erratic behavior. He had always been especially proud of being able to handle his emotions but for some strange reason, he had totally lost control these past few days. He was unsettled, high strung and nervous. He was acting like a new colt that faces its first taste of the saddle. Yes, he was coming undone and he couldn't seem to stop it.

All the pain and the reasons he had chosen to leave Argentina, to work and live in America, were hammering at him. He should not have come back, damn it! Of course there was no way that he could have refused. Roberto needed him, he had said so.

These were the people he loved most in the world. Once, he had almost betrayed their love and trust and thus his self-imposed exile to another country. Now he was here and he needed to help Roberto and then get back to New York. It was not healthy to stay too long. There was a feeling of doom he could not shake. It felt like his world was shifting under his feet and he was sliding rapidly down to the edge of a cliff - a cliff that stood over a dark abyss.

Shaking himself loose from these thoughts, Victor finished rubbing down the mare and went to shower and change.

***

Doctor Cesar Fernandez placed the phone back down onto his desk and put his head in his hands. He sat perfectly still for a moment.

The urgent call he had been waiting for and dreading had finally come. With a sigh he stood and prepared the supplies he would need and started placing them in his medical bag. As he finished, he turned to see Maria at his office door.

"It is time?" she questioned.

"Yes, I am afraid it is. May God have mercy on all our souls," he said in a prayerful whisper.

28

"I'm so sorry, Cesar. Is there anything I can do?" she asked.

"No. Hopefully it will be over soon," he said as sadness and regret filled his heart.

Maria walked him to the door and they embraced. "Come home to me soon, my love. Come home to me soon," she said.

Cesar did not answer and turned and walked to the car with heavy steps. How he wished he could turn back time and somehow change the events about to unfold. He could not. It was all out of his control now. He would do what he had to do blindly, pushing his feelings aside.

***

Carmen was in the kitchen preparing *mate'*, a Paraguayan tea. Her hands were trembling.

Roberto had given her explicit instructions to prepare it with only one gourd and she was worried. What is about to happen, she asked herself?

The leaves of the tea, a relation to holly, were elaborately prepared as part of a ritual. The drinking from one shared gourd was particularly important and was usually done to express acceptance of that person. It was an extreme honor to share *mate*. Sometimes this ritual was performed, similar to a blood-brother oath, to solidify a pact between two people.

It was almost time for Victor to arrive and, since Roberto had said he wanted this tea for his meeting, Carmen was puzzled. Why would Roberto want to make a pact with Victor? The man adored both Roberto and Julia and would do anything in the world for them. Something was amiss and she was very afraid.

Julia found Carmen in the kitchen. She smiled at her old friend and said softly, "Do you know why Roberto is acting so strangely today? I asked if I might speak to him and he told me that he had to meet with Victor first." Without waiting for a reply she continued, "Well, this is very strange, and, as soon as he is through, I am going to demand that he......" Julia suddenly stopped speaking. She did not want to unburden her and Roberto's problems to her elderly housekeeper.

"Carmen, my goodness, what are you doing? Why are you preparing *mate`* this time of the morning? Are we expecting guests that I am not aware of?" she cried worriedly, looking around the kitchen at all the preparations.

"No, Miss Julia," Carmen said to reassure her. "We are not expecting guests. Just Victor and that husband of yours who asked me to prepare the tea," she grumbled.

Carmen liked to refer to Roberto as *Julia's* husband when she was particularly upset by something he said or did, so Julia let the comment pass. She was definitely going to take Roberto to task later this morning after he finished whatever foolishness he was up to with Victor.

"I will be in the garden. When Roberto is ready, please call me," she said as she left the kitchen.

Carmen made the sign of the cross and bent her head down to continue her work.

***

When Victor entered the study, he found Roberto sitting in the semi-darkness. He had closed the blinds to the light and pulled the heavy drapes across the windows so Victor could barely make out his shape sitting behind his desk.

"Good. You are here, my friend," Roberto said quietly. "Please sit. Carmen will be bringing us tea in just a moment."

Victor could tell that Roberto had been drinking by the slurring of his words and his stagger as he walked from behind the desk to stand in front of him.

"My son," he said as he placed his hands on Victor's shoulder. "This is a very dark day for all of us. Sins that were committed must be brought into the light for all to see and examine. Penalties and punishments must be dealt out. Ah, and you will be a witness to it all. Yes, you will see the evil and you will be sickened by it," he said drunkenly as he waved his hands around in the air, almost losing his balance.

Victor sat very still as he realized the extent of his friend's intoxication. Whose sin was he talking about? Fearing the worst, he wondered if Roberto knew his secret. Was that what this meeting was about?

Carmen knocked and entered the room. Without speaking or acknowledging either man in any way, she placed the tea on the table between them and left the room.

Mate, Victor thought seeing the tea. What in the world is going on, he wondered?

Roberto sighed as he staggered and fell into the chair in front of Victor. "Yes, it will all come out today. Things so awful and far worse than anything you can imagine. I am old and I am evil!" By the wave of his hand, he stopped Victor before he could speak and continued. "I need you, Victor. I need you to make a pact with me. Are you willing, knowing that what you will soon learn might cause you to hate and loathe me? I don't have much time so you need to make a decision quickly."

"Roberto, you have had too much to drink. You are rambling like a crazy man and not making any sense," Victor admonished his friend as his mind leaped around trying to figure out this turn of events. "You are one of the finest men I have ever had the fortune of knowing. You are honest, loyal and unselfish in all regards. There is nothing you could ever do, or anything anyone could ever tell me, that would make me change my mind. Certainly there is nothing anyone could say that would make me believes that you are evil!" he finished.

Throwing his head back, Roberto laughed harshly. "Yes, I was good. I was very, very good. Wasn't I? I even fooled you! I lived a lie and betrayed you and everyone else. But, most of all I have betrayed my heart, my life and my love…my beautiful, beautiful Julia," he finished in a moan as he doubled over from the agony of his confession.

"Roberto, what have you done? What is it? Possibly I can help. I can't stand to see you this way, it's eating you up inside. You need to tell me what is wrong!" Victor demanded.

Roberto looked at Victor and saw a man with a heart so true and a love so pure that he knew he had chosen him correctly. This man before him was strong like tempered steel. Yes! He had made an excellent choice.

"Victor," he said hurriedly, "come. We don't have much time. We must make our pact and you must give me your oath before Julia joins us."

Saying this, he poured the tea into the one gourd that they would share. "I need your oath," he said weakly. "Promise me that you will take care of Julia. That you will make sure no harm comes to her."

"Why," Victor exclaimed, "where are you going? Why can't you take care of her?"

"She will hate me and will never let me near her again after today," he said sadly. "Will you promise me?" he asked again.

"But I don't…." Victor started to say but Roberto shouted. "Promise me! I have no time left! Promise me!" Roberto's face had drained of color and in the dim light Victor could see the sweat beading his forehead.

"I promise. I promise I will let no harm come to Julia. I will take care of her for you," he said solemnly as he gave an oath to something he did not understand.

"Her mind is fragile," Roberto continued. "She might try to harm herself. You must watch her very carefully. Now drink after me so the pact between us is sealed."

Taking the tea in his hands, he took a drink and passed it over to Victor.

As Victor drank, Roberto sank back into his chair. "Good. Good. Now everything is in place. I will call Carmen and ask her to have Julia join us. Please do not leave me no matter what happens. I will need you here to help me. Remember your promise to me. Never forget it for a moment. I trust you with my heart and my soul."

As he went to the door to call Carmen, Victor suddenly felt his entire being shift and drop over the edge into the abyss. He lost his equilibrium for a moment and thought he might pass out. Lowering his head and holding the chair tightly the dizziness started to pass. Nothing was ever going to be the same. He knew that now. A feeling of doom covered him like a blanket.

***

When Julia started to enter the room, she found she could not see. After being outside in the sunlight, it took a moment for her eyes to adjust to the darkness of the room. As she hesitated at the door, she suddenly felt afraid. The room was too dark and something didn't feel right.

"Come in, Julia," she heard Roberto say. "Don't be afraid. It is time for you to know it all."

Roberto must have read her mind she thought, forcing herself to enter the room.

"Know what?" she demanded. "Why are you sitting in the dark? Have you been drinking? Why, it's before noon and...," she stopped when she suddenly realized that Victor was in the room.

"Goodness, Victor! You scared me out of my skin. What the hell are you two doing in here, sitting in the dark, drinking and God knows what else," she said angrily still shaking from her surprise.

"I asked Victor to join us. Please sit down, darling. I will turn on a light so that you will feel more comfortable. I have something I need to give you," Roberto murmured soothingly.

32

"I don't want it!" she said not knowing why she felt this sudden panic.

"No, no, I suppose you probably don't," he said as if speaking to a child, "but have it you will."

"What is it?" she whispered. "Why is Victor here? What's going on? I'm afraid, Roberto.....", she trailed off as she looked into the faces of the two men she loved more than anything in the world.

As Roberto turned on the light, he removed a large envelope from his desk. Returning to sit opposite her chair, he noticed she was trembling violently. The room suddenly turned ice cold as if a freezing wind had come blowing through the study. Roberto felt the final pieces of his heart crack and break into a million splinters as he looked into Julia's panic-filled face.

"I'm sorry, Julia. If there were any other way that I could spare you this, I would. Please remember, I loved you then and I love you now. It is no excuse, but it is the only one I have. Victor will be here for you if you need him. He has promised me."

As he finished speaking he placed the envelope on Julia's lap.

Julia stared down at the envelope and Roberto saw the color drain from her face as she looked at the evidence of his betrayal. Somewhere in the back of her mind he knew she knew something horrible was inside. He could see on her face that all of her sleeping memories were struggling to waken and soon would be shouting to be heard. Roberto shuddered and forced himself to sit on his hands to keep from rushing to her.

"No! No, I don't want it! Don't make me take it. Ple-e-ase," Julia moaned as great tears fell down her face. "I don't want it...," she trailed off as fragments of memory collided inside her head; she wanted something, someone wouldn't give it to her and she was crying because she was afraid. Why can't I remember, she thought as she noticed Roberto looking at her intensely.

The envelope was still lying on her lap and Julia was staring down at it as if it were a giant venomous snake that might leap up and strike her dead at any moment.

Victor couldn't stand it another minute. "Jesus, Mary and Joseph," he exclaimed to Roberto, "if she doesn't want the damned thing why does she have to take it?" he shouted.

"Be still Victor," Roberto said softly. "It must be done. There will be no real peace until this is finished. Open it, Julia," he commanded.

With trembling fingers, Julia tried to obey. She pulled the envelope toward her and after fumbling with the clasp finally managed to open the edge. Then, as if evil spirits had started to crawl out of the opening, Julia started to wail and writhe in her chair, dropping the envelope as if it were a hot piece of coal that had been placed in her hand. "No, no, no-o-o," she shrieked.

"Damn it Julia! Open it now!!" Roberto yelled at her with such force that Julia stopped her wailing and shrank back in her chair. Her face was so white that all you could see were the giant orbs of her eyes that stood out against her pale skin.

Moving as if in a trance and trembling like a giant wind was pounding her limbs, she reached down and picked the envelope from the floor. Flinching, she opened the envelope and removed what appeared to Victor to be old newspaper clippings.

"No, it can't be," she whispered as she opened her eyes and looked at the paper in stark horror. "Roberto, what is this…?"

As Roberto watched he saw Julia's mind remember as all the pieces clicked into place.

"But, it's not possible…," she groaned as the realization of what she was looking at started to hit her. "It can't be - you wouldn't do this. Tell me you didn't do this," she cried leaping up from her chair and sending the envelope and clippings scattering across the floor.

As the memories and the pain bombarded her, tearing holes in her soul and leaving knifelike wounds, she crawled on her hands and knees picking up each paper placing them in the envelope, struggling to catch her breath.

Suddenly, she stood and looked straight into Roberto's eyes and he knew she remembered it all – how he had harmed her, how he had lied. "I remember," she said quietly. "You bastard! Why? Why?" she begged. "Tell me why?"

When Roberto did not answer, she launched herself at him and started pounding him with her fists, scratching his face, and pulling his hair. "I hate you! I will kill you for what you have done!" she screamed.

Victor grabbed Julia from behind and held her twisting, squirming body up in the air away from Roberto. She had knocked him to the floor and he was doing nothing to defend himself. He was bruised and her scratches had left bloody marks on his face, yet he just lay there not moving. Victor didn't know what to do because she was so hysterical. The problem was resolved when Julia fainted in his arms.

"My God! What in the hell?" Victor erupted. "She wanted to hurt you. She has cut your face. Oh, my God," he stammered. His breath was coming in great gasps and he kept repeating his plea to God over and over as he bent over Julia's unconscious body.

Roberto stood and it took all the energy he had left to get to his feet. "Lay her down on the couch, Victor and then go and call Carmen. Dr. Fernandez should be here any minute. Have her send him right in when he arrives," he ordered.

As Victor gathered Julia in his arms and went to the couch, Roberto moved quickly through the room picking up the newspaper clippings, scattered around the floor. Once he had them all, he placed them back into the envelope.

Turning to Victor he said, "You must see that this envelope stays with Julia at all times. Do not let anyone see the contents and you must not open it unless Julia allows it. Promise me."

"I'm not making any more promises to you. You have just scared your wife half to death. She has fainted, Roberto, unless you haven't noticed. I think she wanted to kill you, she was so angry. Your face is bruised and bleeding, and you're worried about some damned envelope? What's wrong with you, man? Have you lost your mind? Forget about everything else right now and help your wife!"

She looks like she is dead, Victor thought, kneeling down beside the couch. Frantically he rubbed her arms and hands as he tried to restore her circulation.

So, Victor did not do as Roberto had ordered. Roberto was very pleased. Victor's only thoughts had been for Julia's care and safety and that was absolutely necessary if this were going to work out the way he had planned. Wearily, he went to the door to speak to Carmen.

She was standing outside the door wringing her hands in her apron, biting her lips and praying to every Saint she knew, when Roberto opened the door. She had heard Julia's cries and was torn between charging through the closed door to come to her aid, which was forbidden, or waiting frantically in the hall biting her knuckles. She had waited outside the door, but it had been all she could do to hold back when she believed her mistress was in some kind of pain.

"Go get Doctor Fernandez and bring him here. He should be arriving at any moment. Send him in immediately when he arrives," Roberto ordered.

"What happened to your face? Are you all right? What happened? Is Julia okay? You two haven't harmed her have you?" she asked as tears started in her eyes.

"No, Carmen. As you can see I am the only one who is harmed," he said trying to reassure her while touching the wounds on his face. "She has had a terrible shock and has fainted. Now hurry!" he commanded as he turned back to the room and closed the door.

Carmen, for once in all her years of service, did not believe Roberto. There was no doubt in her mind that Julia had inflicted the scratches on his face. She had heard her mistress' screams and heard her begging them not to make her do something. What it was, she didn't know. She would never forget those screams, they had chilled her soul. Julia was hurt. Somehow, someway they had hurt her. She was sure of that!

As she ran to the front door and threw it back, the doctor had his hand raised mid-air ready to knock.

"What is it?" he asked when he saw Carmen's hysterical appearance. Hopefully, he was not too late, he thought.

"It is my mistress, Julia," she sobbed falling into his arms. "Something bad has happened. She was screaming and screaming and when they finally opened the door, they told me she had only fainted. Please help her. Don't let anything happen to my Julia," she sobbed.

"Let me go, Carmen. It will be okay. Let me go and I will go there immediately. Where are they?" he asked as he said a prayer of relief and forced her to let him go.

"They are in the study," she said using her apron to wipe her eyes. "Come, I will take you there."

As Doctor Fernandez came into the study, he went straight to Roberto's side. "No, please," Roberto said, "take care of Julia first."

"Roberto," he said, "you're exhausted. When was the last time you slept? You need to rest. You're not superhuman, so stop trying to act like it." Dr. Fernandez stood over Roberto looking like an army general who expects to be obeyed by one of his troops.

"Please, my friend, a few more hours will not matter. Please make her comfortable. She was far more upset than we imagined. I will rest later, I promise."

The doctor did not like it, but he turned and asked Victor to carry Julia to her bed. There he left Carmen to help undress Julia so that she could be more comfortable. Finally, he gave her an injection of a heavy sedative and posted Carmen by the door in case her mistress wakened and needed her. Taking a deep breath, the doctor squared his shoulders and started down the stairs to the study. Julia would rest. Roberto would need him now far more than Julia.

Chapter Five
Washington, D.C. – 1993

David Grant sighed and took his glasses off, rubbing the bridge of his nose with his fingers. It was dark now and the streetlights were on. He should go home. He was exhausted. His wife, Lainie, never complained, but he knew she got tired of holding dinner for him night after night.

This time though, he had really thought they had found something solid, a lead that would pan out. But just like all the other times, it had rambled on to a dead end. No one knew anything, no one saw anything, everyone had lost their memories and they were back to square one, chasing another shadow.

There were rumors going around again that the man he had hunted all these years was dead, but his gut told him no. And, usually, he trusted his gut. But he was worn out by the chase. He was sick of having his hopes dashed time after time. After twenty years, he was bone tired.

Flipping his notebook closed on his desk, he pushed back his chair and stood up. He was tall and blond and he kept his weight down by playing handball three times a week at the local gym. But he was getting older now and it was getting harder and harder to whip all the other guys in the office. Some of the young ones had come pretty close lately and he knew he was about to lose his status as "king of handball". They were a great bunch of guys and they had stood by him, helping when they could, as he waged his war on someone they could not find. But when it came to sports, they were like a pack of rats waiting for the ship to sink so they could desert, he thought. They teased him now and called him "old man" at the end of each game – games that he barely won anymore – as he staggered to the shower, groaning and limping. Yes, he was going down and the whole group couldn't wait to pay him back for all the years he had rubbed it in.

Thank God he still had some of his looks or they would be merciless in their heckling. Because of good genes he still had a full head of hair that was turning gray just at the temples. His eyes were a deep color of blue and before Lainie, well, if he were truthful since Lainie, women had always thrown themselves at him, much to the dismay of his younger cohorts.

Thinking of Lainie made him smile. He had had no interest or desire for any woman for a long time before he had met his wife. She had somehow pierced the veil of pain that had surrounded his body for so long, a veil that had made him immune to any and all who tried to enter and touch his heart. Everyone but her had failed. Since they had married, he could truthfully say that he had had no attraction for any other woman. He loved only her, deeply and totally and he didn't want or need anyone else.

Lainie thought he was obsessed with this case and, although she never said it, he knew that she wished he would let it go, and she was not alone. Everyone at the bureau had told him to give it up and he knew they were right. Most of his work had to be done in his off-hours, since the case had been formally closed over fifteen years ago. So nights and weekends he usually spent in the office.

He wanted this guy so damned bad it made his teeth hurt so he kept tracing down leads, going without meals, ignoring his wife, and working so late that sometimes he fell asleep at his desk. But he was tired now. He had reached the end of his rope and he couldn't do it anymore. Besides, everyone told him that the search was hopeless and it would just go down as one of those crimes that would never be solved and that he needed to accept that the trail was too cold and the scent was gone. Yes, they were right, he thought wearily as he shrugged into his jacket, turned off the light and locked the door.

As he left his building and headed for the metro station that would take him back to his home in Alexandria, Virginia, David felt a sense of relief. Twenty years was enough. It was time to go on with his life. He would tell Lainie tonight about his decision and he knew that she would be pleased.

It was Friday night, and if she didn't get called out on assignment, maybe they could walk to Old Town. Maybe even go on one of those "lantern lit" tours that Lainie was so fond of and, if they were real lucky, maybe even see a ghost or two, as the tour guides claimed they sometimes did. They could have dinner, go dancing, sleep late in the morning... yep, he thought, the possibilities were absolutely endless. That is, unless she got called out.

Lainie was the anchorwoman for the nightly news on WTTG-TV, Channel 5 in Washington, so she wasn't scheduled to work on weekends unless there was a big story breaking. Then, no matter what, nothing was going to keep her home. Her days of field reporting did not die easily and she still loved digging out the facts and getting the next headline ahead of everyone else. Besides, with the way he worked, David admonished himself, she never had any real reason to say no.

How long had it been since they had spent a weekend together, he wondered? Too long, that's all he knew. Now that the kids were out of the house, there was no reason they couldn't make this a very romantic evening. If he hurried, they could start as soon as he got home. The mental picture of what he had in mind for his beautiful wife caused him to smile. Feeling energized and not a bit tired, he laughed and then broke into a run for the next train.

.

Chapter Six
Cordoba, Argentina – 1993

Julia woke with a start and wondered where she was. Her mouth was dry and she needed something to drink. She had been having a violent nightmare. Her gown was drenched with sweat and she was happy to have wakened from the terror she could now barely remember. As she tried to get her bearings, she looked around the room.

Carmen was asleep in a chair by the door. Only a small light was lit on a table next to her so the room was draped in darkness. What was Carmen doing in her room? Where was Roberto?

In a rush, the memory and the pain washed over her. Closing her eyes tightly, she willed herself to let go of the thoughts that tormented her with flashes of things forgotten long ago.

Roberto! Evil, evil, Roberto! She had given herself to that monster many times, over and over. Wantonly, she had desired his embrace and brought the snake to her bosom. Yes, she had coupled with Satan. The shame and rage shook her as her body began to tremble from all the memories cascading around in her head.

Stop! She commanded herself. She had to stay calm. She had something she had to do! He thought he could drug her and keep her here like a prisoner. Keep her here so that she would not be able to fight him. He was wrong! She would show him!

Pulling herself upright in bed she tried to move her legs over the side. The exertion caused great beads of sweat to form on her body and her heart began to beat rapidly against her chest. Swooning, she lay down again to get her breath. Finally, pushing herself up, she managed to place her feet on the floor. Her legs would not hold her and she crumbled. Catching the sheets as she fell, she was able to break part of her fall.

Gasping with her effort, she lay with her face on the cool tile floor. Carmen shifted in her sleep but did not waken. Good! She had to get out of the room and downstairs before Carmen noticed that she was not in bed.

Sliding her body along the floor, she inched her way over to the nightstand. The evidence was still lying there in the envelope. Pulling it down from the table, she held it against her heart. Tears that came from her eyes surprised her.

She had thought that she could never cry again, that there were no tears left in her body. Trying to forget the pictures hidden behind the envelope cover, she lay down on the floor again. She had to conserve her strength. Put the memories away for a while.

When her heart had slowed and she could control her trembling, she reached inside the drawer and removed the gun. She was so weak she coul hardly lift it. Making sure there were enough bullets, she clutched the gun to her breast.

The drugs in her body pulled at her, willing her to sleep. Fighting their control, she continued to crawl across the floor a few feet at a time using her elbows and forearms. When her heart threatened to pound out of her chest, she would stop and lie down on the tile floor to rest.

Reaching the door, she opened it slowly so the noise would not waken her housekeeper. Crawling out, she closed it behind her. She was weak with relief. She prayed that the angels would help her do what she had to do and that no one would stop her.

Pulling herself to a standing position, she waited while the room spun sideways. Lowering her head, she rested it on the stair banister and hoped she wouldn't be sick. She needed to gain the strength to climb down the stairs without falling. If her luck held, she would find him in the study.

****

Roberto was lying on the couch when Julia opened the door. Wet strands of hair were plastered against her face - a face without color. Her nightgown was so sheer he could see her naked body. She was trembling so hard that her hand that held the gun was jerking up and down from the effort to hold it still.

"Julia," Roberto whispered as he tried to sit up. Even in this condition, he marveled, she still was the most beautiful woman he had ever seen.

"Yes, it is me - your lovely, obedient wife. The one you cherished with all your heart. The one you vowed to protect and never betray. Did I get any of that wrong?" she asked, hissing out the words.

42

"No. No, you didn't get it wrong," he said quietly.

"Well, I'm here to make sure you never harm anyone again. I'm here to end it all," she said as she trembled even more violently while the sweat poured off of her body. Raising her empty hand to swipe at her eyes, she said, "I am going to kill you!"

"Julia, listen to me. Don't waste your bullets on me."

"Oh," she smiled coldly, "they won't be wasted, I promise you. I plan to place every one in the middle of your worthless heart so that you can carry them to your grave and then on to hell."

Roberto did not doubt that Julia would do just that even though she was distraught and weakened by the drugs. He had taught her to shoot and she was able to find the bull's eye with every single bullet. Julia was a beautiful woman and she needed a way to protect herself when he was away in case one of the ranch hands was tempted to take his admiration of her too far.

Victor stood up from his seat in the corner of the room. "Julia," he said very softly, "give me the gun. Don't do this." Still speaking very softly, he slowly advanced toward her.

Julia threw back her head and laughed shrilly. "Victor, I should have known that you would be here! Still protecting your dear friend? Your patron? A man who has loved you like a father?" she sneered.

"Julia, put down the gun. Don't do this. Please?"

"Don't come any closer, Victor or, I promise you, I will place a bullet in you and you will never walk again without help," she said as she aimed the gun at him. "You would want him dead, too, if you knew what he had done."

"Julia. Stop!" Roberto cried as she waved the gun erratically around the room. "You don't have to shoot me and for God's sake you don't want to shoot Victor! He is only trying to help!"

Taking a deep breath and letting it out very slowly, he said in a very soft voice, "I am dying".

Julia stood so still that Roberto wondered if she had heard him. "It's true, Julia. I am telling the truth."

Julia turned her face away and looked out the window into the night. The moon was full and looked so beautiful shining across the wide expanse of lawn. Why do I see the moon, she wondered? I'm sure I am dead. Do you continue to see the world the same when you are dead? She had certainly left her body. She could see the room below her and hear perfectly what everyone was saying. Isn't that what happened when you died?

As she continued to watch the cast of players, from her place far above the room, she heard the woman named Julia, a woman who looked amazingly like her say, "You're lying! If you think that your lies will work you are wrong! I'm going to kill you for what you have done. You're not dying! Satan never dies and neither do any of his sons and you are a true son of Satan!" she screamed.

"No, Julia," Roberto said as he tried to reason with her. "You're wrong. It's true. I only have a few more weeks to live. I have very little time left. You can speak to Cesar. He has known for months. He will tell you that I speak the truth."

Victor was so shocked that he couldn't move. Looking over at Roberto he could see that it was true. His face told the story of the kind of pain that would have broken most men. How long had he been suffering this way? Why hadn't he realized that Roberto was ill?

Victor grabbed the edge of the wall and doubled over. Suddenly he felt like he couldn't breathe. It was too much to bear. The pain of losing this man was too horrible. He couldn't stand the thought that Roberto would suffer and waste away and then die pitifully wracked in pain. He had seen the destruction before when others he had known had died a similar death. It was not fair that a man so vital and full of life could be diminished this way.

No, he choked. No. Let there be some mistake, he prayed.

Julia had turned to stone. She looked like a wraith, which had one foot on this side of the vale and one out in eternity, ready to make a leap. You could almost see through her, her skin was so transparent.

"You are dying," she whispered as she lowered the gun.

"Yes," he replied. "I'm sorry. Please forgive me, Julia. I'm so sorry."

Cutting him off, she screamed, "Forgive you? I will never forgive you! I hope you suffer badly and die in terrible agony. It will please me greatly when you are finally dead and I can throw dirt on your coffin. I hate you more than I thought I could ever hate anyone!" she choked.

Turning away, she staggered, caught herself, and slowly walked out of the room, closing the door very softly behind her.

Roberto blanched at her words and crumbled before Victor's eyes. His body sank back onto the couch. He curled into himself, drawing his legs up to his chest and then he lay down.

44

Julia's words had destroyed any will he had to fight the pain and it immersed him now, chewing at him like a ravenous wild animal.

Victor rushed to his friend's side, "Roberto, we can find the best doctors to care for you. Please don't give up."

Placing his hands weakly on Victor's, Roberto said softly. "To all things there is a season..." he paused, "a time to live and a time to die. It is finally my time. You will find out the evil that I have done. Please believe that no matter what you learn, I did love you truly. You are a wonderful man.

'There is so much I want to say but now I won't have the time. The pain eats like a burning flame through my body. I have tried to wait, but my body is screaming and all thoughts of anything else are torn from my mind. I can only see and recognize the pain now. I'm sorry but without Julia there is nothing left to fight for and I've known for a long time that there is no hope. There is no cure." He paused for a moment to get his breath, which was ragged with pain.

"The drugs that I will need," he swallowed as he forced himself to continue, "will take away the pain for awhile but they will also take away my mind. And so it will be that I will not know you or my darling Julia at the end. I will die alone. Just me, my sins, and the torturing pain I have come to know so well. You must prepare yourself and you must help Julia to get through this. Don't stay with me and do not allow Julia to see me this way. I would spare you this if I could. I know that you love me and I will hold that thought in my broken heart until I leave this world," Roberto gasped as he finished. He was exhausted. These words had taken all his strength.

As Victor looked away so that Roberto could not see his tears, Roberto gasped, "Victor, please find the doctor for me. I am ready for him now. I need him."

***

Victor was tired. He was as tired as he could ever remember. Stretching his arms, he started massaging his shoulders as he walked out onto the balcony that ran along the front side of his room. Yes, it had been a very long and difficult night.

Cesar had come into the room as soon as Victor called him. Together they had walked Roberto to a guestroom on the main floor. Roberto had

45

refused to be carried but the effort of moving had cost him dearly. He was racked with pain by the time they helped him into bed. Victor could still see the tears in the old doctor's eyes as he prepared the drugs that would numb Roberto's pain so he could sleep.

Murmuring softly while he worked, Cesar, in one breath, would admonish Roberto for waiting so long to call and, in the next, reassure him that he wouldn't leave his side until it was over.

Roberto had smiled weakly when the doctor had promised that he would make sure that he didn't suffer any more.

"Ah, but I will suffer," Roberto had said. "You may take away the pain but you can't take away my sins. The sins that I carry are like a great weight on my heart."

Cesar had commanded him to be still as tears fell down his cheeks.

Victor had waited in the shadows of the room choking back his own tears. It was as if there was no oxygen left in the room.

Roberto had called to Victor as he started to drift away under the power of the medication Cesar had given him. He said, "Victor, my son, let me go. You must let me find my peace now. Don't keep me here. My sins march out against me. The pain torments me night and day. What I have done to Julia is what is really killing me. Don't cry for me...", his voice had slurred as he finally found blessed relief.

Victor could hear the sound of great, beating wings as Roberto finished speaking. Looking around, he thought he saw a vision of the angel of death waiting patiently at the foot of Roberto's bed. Forcing himself not to run, he walked swiftly from the room. He couldn't stay. He was afraid he would start howling like an animal because he could not contain his grief.

He had to deal with Carmen next. When she learned that Roberto was dying, she tore her clothes and ripped at her hair, running out into the night and throwing herself onto the ground. He could not console her.

Luke and some of the other men had come and carried her back into the house. He could still hear her crying and moaning.

The ranch hands had come with candles of grief and had placed them by the hundreds, in every available space, all over the hacienda. Now, other than the occasional sound of someone weeping, there was a hush over the ranch that was unnatural. It was as if the night creatures were told the news, by the whispers of the wind, and out of respect held their songs and remained silent.

When he had asked about Julia, he had been told that she had not spoken to anyone since she had left the study. Victor had gone to her room and found her sitting at the window staring out at the night. When he approached her, she had turned and looked at him without any expression on her face and asked, "It is true? He is dying?"

Victor had forced back his emotions and had told her, "Yes, it is true". Never saying another word, she had turned away and continued to stare out of the window. She had the envelope clutched to her breast.

Victor had wondered again what it contained that could cause this woman to hate the husband she had adored for so many years. Calling one of the other maids, he had left Julia in her care.

Victor looked out at the night as he felt the tiredness push in on him. There was a great deal to be done if the ranch was going to continue working uninterrupted during the next few months. He would need to call tomorrow and extend his time away from his practice in New York. Julia was going to need someone to take control until she was feeling better.

Cesar had told him that Roberto would not live long. The cemetery plot and funeral arrangements needed to be prepared. Victor didn't know how he was going to get through the next terrible weeks but he had promised to be here for Julia and he would not break his promise.

As Victor prepared for bed, his mind went back to the first time he had met Roberto, in 1961. Victor's family had owned a ranch twenty miles west of Cordoba closer to San Juan. *El Sauce*, Roberto's ranch, was huge in comparison.

Victor had loved his home. He was the only child of an Indian mother and an Italian father thus his black hair, chiseled features, high cheekbones and dark complexion. In Argentina he was known as a *Mestizo* because of his European and Indian mix.

The only real things he could claim from his father were his gray eyes and height. His father had been a large man standing 6' 2" and weighing over 200 pounds. Victor was 6'4" and more slender at his 200-pound weight, but they said you could see his father in the way Victor walked and in his mannerisms. He had idolized the man who had sired him and adored the woman who was his mother.

His father had emigrated from Italy in the early 1940s, met and married his Indian mother who gave birth to their only child, Victor, in 1945. They had been a happy family and he had only fond memories of his childhood.

When he was fifteen, tragedy struck. Both of his parents and many of the workers on their farm perished from an illness that was now known as Argentine hemmoragghic fever. Even though he had fallen ill, he had somehow survived.

He had stood by silently while they poured fuel on the bodies of his family and all the others he had grown up with and loved. He was too weak to protest so he had watched helplessly while they torched everything including all the buildings that made up his home. They said it was the only way to kill the deadly virus so others would not die.

Afterward, refusing all help, Victor had wandered the pampas shooting only the game he needed to eat to stay alive. He lived on the lonely plains and avoided all human contact. Sitting by the campfire at night, he would curse the fate that had taken everyone and everything he loved and left him alive and alone.

Everyone wanted him to go on living as if nothing had happened. They didn't realize that his father had been his legs and his mother had been his arms and both of them had been his heart. Without them, he was emotionally crippled. Thus it was that he never knew what day it was or if he had slept the night before or if he needed to eat because he couldn't remember the last time that he did any of these things and he didn't really care.

Occasionally, he would remember that he needed something the land could not give him, sometimes a hat, a saddle or once for a new bunk roll after he had slept on a nest of fleas and no matter how much he washed his gear, he couldn't get rid of them. So he would steal a horse and sell it to a trader he knew who never asked any questions. His anger at what fate had dealt him left him with no conscience to tell him this was wrong.

One day, while he was trying to steal a horse, he met Roberto. He was trying to lasso a particularly feisty mare he had cornered when Victor had realized that a lone horseman was sitting, silently watching him. Horse thieves were dealt with harshly, so he had prepared himself for the worst.

Roberto had walked his horse slowly over to him and said, "Let's go home now. It's almost time for supper. I think you have worked enough today."

Something in the man's eyes, compassion, gentle kindness, he wasn't sure, burst the dam that he had built around his ravaged heart. He wanted to go home. Wherever that home was.

The teenaged boy that he was then had ridden silently back to the hacienda with the man who would from that day forward treat him as his son. Never questioning, never accusing, always caring, Roberto gently nurtured him back to life. Victor was 48 years old now and the images of that day were as clear and poignant today as they were that day in 1961.

Roberto had saved his life, and after a time of healing, he came to be happy that he was the recipient of his kindness. He had learned that life was good and that he could go on.

Roberto had brought Julia back as his wife after an extended trip in 1973. She was thirty years old but appeared much younger. He could still see her standing at the door of the hacienda, looking disoriented and a little afraid.

She was tall and very thin with short black hair but most of all she was very, very beautiful and she took his breath away when he was first introduced to her and he had looked into her huge, dark eyes that dominated her face.. She seemed dazed and a little shy around the people she met and in awe of the beautiful home and the surrounding land, but that had changed as time went by and she adjusted slowly and naturally to her new life. Everyone at the ranch loved her for her gentle ways and loving disposition.

Roberto obviously adored her and they had been very happy over the years in spite of the fifteen-year difference in their ages.

There were so many wonderful memories. What had caused it all to end? Roberto lay dying and Julia didn't seem to care. How could that be? What in the world could Roberto have done?

As the questions floated around in his mind, Victor knew it was time to rest before he collapsed. To shut his mind down, he took a long hot shower and then gulped a glass of water with two sleeping pills.

When he traveled to the Orient, he sometimes needed something to help him adjust to the time changes so he could sleep when his body thought he should be awake. Tomorrow would be soon enough to face the sorrow and pain again.

***

She floated above the room watching the woman who had her name. Julia. Somehow, she was linked to this woman. She wondered how.

Where was the white light she had been told to expect? Why was she still here? Maybe she couldn't leave. She remember hearing, she couldn't remember where, that sometimes your spirit could not leave this world until you performed a good deed - like the movie "It's A Wonderful Life". The angel couldn't leave and get his wings until he saved someone.

How had she remembered that? Some painful memory was trying to break through. She could see the woman below start to twist in her chair by the window. She pushed the hurt away and decided she would wait until she figured out what she was supposed to do.

The word "forgiveness" kept popping into her mind. She was sure that had nothing to do with her. She hoped that whatever she was supposed to do was revealed to her soon. She was tired of this life and didn't want to stay here. She didn't like these people very much

***

Julia opened the envelope and laid out the newspaper clippings on her bed. She traced the faces of the grainy images with her fingertips. When the feelings became too intense, she folded the papers up and placed them back into the envelope. A little at a time, she told herself. It's too much to bear all at once, so I will do it a little at a time.

***

Rosita knocked gently on Victor's door. She knew it was late but she had just heard the news about Roberto and wanted to offer her condolences to Victor. It was well known that the two men had a special bond. She knew Victor must be devastated.

There was also the need she felt to speak to him again about their relationship. It didn't matter that Victor didn't love her now. Over time he would learn to love her, she was sure of that. They were perfect for each other in so many ways and many couples started out a marriage with one or the other wondering if they could learn to love their mate.

Her own mother had told her that when her marriage was arranged by her family, she did not believe, at the time, that she would ever learn to love the boy she was forced to marry. And as everyone knew, their love was legendary in the pampas of Argentina. Rosita's love for Victor was so great that she was sure they could work it out if he would only try.

There was no answer to her knock, so Rosita opened the door and called Victor's name very softly. Getting, no reply, she tiptoed into the bedroom and found him sleeping soundly.

Sitting down gently on the bed she looked at his face. The moonlight created shadows and planes against his cheekbones and lips. He was such a gorgeous creature.

Placing her fingers on his skin, she felt the powerful outline of his jaw. As she skimmed her fingers across his lips, he murmured as he kissed them. A bolt of fire lit up her body. All at once she was inflamed with desire. God, she wanted him so much.

Trying it again, she tentatively placed her fingers full on his mouth. This time his tongue lapped at them hungrily. Moving off the bed, she pulled her dress off over her head. She was naked underneath and her body radiated a heat that flushed her skin. She had large breasts, a tiny waist and long legs. That she was beautiful was something she had always known. She had waited all these years for him and had saved her virginity. Tonight she was prepared to give it to him.

Climbing gently into bed she placed her dark nipples on his lips. Victor lapped at them, sending jolts of electricity through her body. When he started to suckle them, whispering how much he loved her, she was lost. Taking her breasts in each of his hands, he sucked and licked them noisily. Touching her everywhere at once, he ravaged her body with his hot touch and his mouth.

His mouth was what she would always remember she had thought at the time. When I look back at tonight later in my life, I will remember how he drove me wild with his mouth.

All the desire Victor had held in check for so long, all his grief, all his love and his pain were mixed up in his wild passion for her. He poured it all out, telling her how he could not live without her, pleading with her to never leave him, fondling and caressing her like a wild man. As he drove her wild with desire, she bucked and writhed on the bed.

When she opened her legs for him, he entered her violently, kissing her face and eyelids. She cried out from the pain but he did not hear her. He was lost in the feelings of her body around him. He rode her savagely, sucking and nipping her neck and breasts, taking great handfuls of her hair and holding her head up to kiss her more deeply, all the while murmuring how beautiful she was. She screamed his name as she climaxed.

Still Victor did not stop. Turning her over onto her hands and knees, he plunged into her again and again. Holding her hips tightly with his hands he promised his life to her, promised to protect her, told her she was all that he ever wanted. As she rode to the top of the giant wave, she climaxed again with a huge shudder that ran back and forth through her body. Only then, because she was so tight and hot and her muscles were clamped around him so tightly, did he find his release and pour his juices into her. Crying her name over and over he held her to him and plunged himself into her as far as he could. Tears and sweat mingled with his kisses as he proclaimed his undying love. Slowly his voice got softer and he fell asleep still deeply imbedded in her young body.

Rosita lay stiffly on the bed, trying not to move; her mind in turmoil. What had she done? He had taken her innocence and nothing he could say would unbreak her heart. He had tried to warn her but she hadn't listened. Now it was too late.

As she tried to move away from him so she could leave the bed, she felt Victor harden inside her body.

As he took her again with manic passion, she tried to fight the feelings of desire that tore through her body. She could not. He was a magnificent lover and her body betrayed her as she fought for control.

Soon she was begging him to take her, pleading with him to ride her harder. When she finally climaxed, she felt an explosion of raw sensation so powerful she started to weep from the emotion she felt.

Victor found his release only seconds after her as she bucked against him, scratching and biting, throwing her head violently from side to side. As Victor eased back into his drug-induced sleep, he whispered her name over and over.

Rosita muffled her sobs as she turned away. He didn't know, she told herself. He wouldn't remember tomorrow what she would never forget. Each time he had called her name – each time over and over and over..........

Julia! He had called her Julia!

Chapter Seven

It had been two weeks, two long, long weeks since that morning. That morning when he had awakened feeling cleansed and released from the demons that taunted him night and day.

That morning when he felt that he could go on, that life could be good again, that he could do all that he needed to do and would not fall under the burden of his grief.

He had sung the words to "You Were Always On My Mind" as he went to the shower. The song had become one of his favorites after hearing it on the radio while driving to the airport one evening in New York. The words had touched something deep in his soul. They were so powerful that he could listen to the song over and over again. Because of this song, Willie Nelson was now one of his favorite singers and he had collected all of his recordings.

Bellowing the words - fortunately for anyone in hearing distance he had a beautiful tenor voice - he vigorously scrubbed himself under the cold shower. Victor felt wonderful. He wasn't exactly sure why, but he believed it had something to do with the wonderful dream he'd had the night before.

But all of that was before he had dried himself and walked back into the bedroom and seen the sheets. The bloody sheets! The sheets that held all the tell-tale signs that someone had lost their virginity. Either that or he was bleeding.

This was the first time he could ever remember wishing that he had a bloody bullet wound somewhere in his body that could explain the condition of his bed. No, wishful thinking would not change what he knew to be true. As bits and pieces of the night drifted back to him, he sat holding his head in his hands. His earlier euphoria was replaced by what appeared to be the start of a massive headache.

Rosita! Yes, it was certainly Rosita. She had found a way to get to him and he had probably loved every minute of it. Yes, he was certain that he had enjoyed himself based on what he could remember.

What he could remember, however, did not bode well for Rosita. For instance, he did not remember being gentle with her. In fact he seemed to remember that he had shown no mercy for her tender uninitiated maidenhead and had taken her like a rutting bull. He must have hurt her terribly. God, what a mess this was!

Rosita was from a very devout Catholic family. Making love to Victor outside of marriage would be tantamount to a mortal sin in her family's eyes. Unless Rosita went to confession, promised it would never happen again and received absolution, she would not be able to take Holy Communion. If she failed to take Holy Communion, this act alone would alert her family that something terrible was amiss. Her reputation would be ruined and Victor would be to blame.

Groaning, he stood and started pacing the room. He knew there was only one answer. He would have to marry Rosita as soon as possible.

Most of Argentina was deeply Roman Catholic and Rosita's reputation would be ruined if he did not do the right thing. He would not see her dishonored. They would have to wait until after Roberto's death and funeral but it should be done immediately thereafter.

**

Later that morning Victor had called Rosita. When he finally reached her to ask if he could meet with her, he had felt so shy and nervous it had reminded him of the first time he had asked anyone on a date. Rosita had seemed to be very pleased that he had called and suggested that they meet at her house since she was a little tired from being up so late the night before.

There was an awkward pause on the phone after she said this and Victor had started to stutter his apology but couldn't find the words. As the silence lengthened, Rosita finally laughed very gently and said that it was all right, he had no need to apologize and that he should just come over for some coffee - she was sure he could use some.

When he arrived, Rosita led him into the breakfast room and poured hot, Argentine coffee into a cup in front of him.

Visitors to his country often said that the coffee served here could take the enamel off your teeth it was so strong. Victor was used to it and missed it very much when he was in America where he was forced to eat out so often due to his lack of culinary skills. It was hard to get a decent cup of coffee much less the strong Argentine brew that he loved.

It was a beautiful morning and the bright yellow kitchen was warm and cozy. There was a small fire in the kitchen fireplace that took the chill off the room. Rosita was dressed in a beautiful ice blue robe and she was breathtaking.

Victor watched her under his downcast eyes as he sipped his coffee. She did not look like he had abused her too much. Although, he told himself, the parts of her he had enjoyed and possibly bruised and torn were areas that were well covered by her robe. Blushing profusely from his thoughts, he noticed she was watching him quietly with no emotion on her face.

Victor didn't know how to start so he sat there twisting his napkin in his hands and averting his eyes from her face. She looked at him, he looked at her – he looked away, he twisted in his chair and she folded her napkin again for the third time. Finally, Victor couldn't stand it any longer and blurted out that he was sorry for what had happened but he was prepared to do the right thing by her and that he wanted to get married immediately.

Rosita sat quietly staring into his eyes until he looked away. Then she stood and walked over to the kitchen counter that looked out at the rear garden. After standing still for a few moments, she took a small wet cloth and began to wipe down the counter tops. As far as Victor could tell they were already immaculate and he wondered why she was washing them. Was this something she would normally do or was this something the housekeeper would take care of?

After a few moments, Rosita came back to the table and sat down. Looking at Victor she asked him one question. That question still bothered him. Not just the question but how he had reacted to it at the time. She asked him if he loved her. She went on to say that she would marry him if he could tell her now, to her face, that he loved her.

Victor couldn't speak. What could he say that would make her understand? Looking down at his hands he twisted the ring that had been his father's. His mother had given it to his father on the day they were married. This ring, and the one that matched it that his mother had worn, plus a few other pieces of jewelry were all that he had left of them. In times of stress he would always twist the ring and it always seemed to comfort him. Today there was no comfort.

He had never thought that he would marry or that he would give anyone his mother's ring. Staring at their token of love and remembering how they had adored each other, he knew he would never find that kind of love for himself.

But, he could have a good life with Rosita and in time they could find some happiness, of that he was sure. It didn't matter that he didn't love her. Many people married who didn't share the soul searing romance and love for which so many - he excluded himself of course - longed. He just had to make her see the logic of his thinking.

"Well...I know that we made love", he said in a small conspiratorial whisper, looking around to see if anyone might be listening. "I...I...want to make it right."

"Yes", she said "we did do that - several times, if I remember correctly. But, that is not what I asked you, Victor. I asked you if you loved me."

Rosita sat there very quietly for a very long time looking straight at him. Victor began to get angry.

"What difference does that make", he demanded loudly. "We will be married and we will grow to care for each other. I will be good to you and I will never betray you for another after you are my wife. I am a wealthy man and you will not want for anything."

"So, you do not love me. Is that what you are trying to say?"

Victor looked down at his hands again and began to twist the ring around and around his finger. He couldn't lie to her. She would know if he did and he couldn't make himself say the words she wanted to hear.

"Victor, weren't you the man who told me not to give myself to anyone who doesn't love me? I have already violated your advice by being, ah........intimate. Shall we use the word intimate so you will stop blushing? Yes, intimate is a good word, I think. But, surely you are not advising me to marry someone who does not love me?"

"Yes," he said. "That is exactly what I'm trying to tell you to do. It's entirely different now that we have been together and we need to talk about the wedding and start making plans. Of course, we need to wait until after Roberto's..." he stopped not wanting to say funeral in the same breath he said wedding.

"Victor, thank you very much for your lovely offer. I'm sorry but I will have to decline. Thank you for taking the time to come by to see me today but there are things I need to do and so I must say goodbye".

Victor was stunned. What had she said? She didn't want to marry him? Well, that was completely out of the question now that they had been together. Of course they would marry. What was she thinking? He was considered to be quite the catch by some women. He was good looking, some might even say handsome. His ego was talking to him rapidly as he tried to assess the situation.

But, before Victor knew what had happened, Rosita had walked him to the door, kissed him gently on the cheek and said goodbye.

Two weeks had passed and Victor had sent her dozens of flowers that she refused to accept. All of his many phone calls went unanswered.

Victor was mildly amused by this. She was playing hard to get and he liked the challenge. He had hurt her and she needed a way to make him pay. That was all right. He understood her need to feel vindicated in some way.

In fact, he was starting to like the idea of being married to the little wildcat. He would keep his barrage of flowers and phone calls going and soon she would soften. Of course she would marry him. He didn't doubt it for a second.

***

Victor's thoughts of Rosita were the only ones that had made him laugh during the past two weeks. Each day Roberto had grown weaker but the pain seemed to grow stronger.

Cesar was forced to increase the medicine to compensate for his suffering. As a result, Roberto lay wasted and unconscious most of the time. Once in a while, he would waken and look around the room. Whispering Julia's name, he would drift back to sleep as tears seeped out around the edges of his eyes. He was never left alone. Victor, Carmen and Cesar took turns keeping a vigil beside his bed.

Sometimes, when Victor sat in Roberto's room and he saw how the pain ravished him even in his sleep, he would pray that God would take him now. As quickly as those thoughts would come he would be filled with guilt for praying for his friend's death.

Other times he wished he had the strength to take a pillow and place it over Roberto's face and end his suffering. Roberto was so weak it would only take a moment. No one would ever know. He was torn by convention but he knew he would never let one of his animals die this way.

Of course, he couldn't do it. He didn't have the courage. Besides, it was a mortal sin. At least, that is what he tried to tell himself as he sat helplessly by and watched, day after day, the toll the disease was taking on his friend.

As for Julia, she continued to refuse to see Roberto or to speak of him. When Victor had approached her about funeral plans, she had stared at him blankly and then turned and walked away. For this reason, Victor had been left with the arduous and painful task of making all the funeral preparations without her input.

Traditionally, Roberto Anthony Bertinelli would be placed in the tomb of his uncle, Gino. It was situated in the cemetery of the Cathedral Inglesia in Cordoba.

The body of Roberto's uncle had lain on an altar in the main floor of the tomb waiting for the next death in the family. Upon Roberto's death, it would be moved and placed on shelves that lined the walls in a room underneath the floor of the main vault. There his uncle would rest through eternity next to his beloved Isabella, his wife, and Angelina, their daughter who had died alongside his wife during childbirth. Roberto's body would stay on the main floor of the tomb until Julia died and there her body would remain forever since there was no other family.

However, this funeral and burial would not be performed under the traditional rules. Roberto had made it well known to Victor that he wanted to be buried on the hill that overlooked El Duce River, beneath a stand of trees that gave him a view of the Sierras de Cordoba and the pampas below. It was a short walk from the main house and one of Roberto's very favorite spots to picnic and relax.

It was a beautiful place, and Victor shared his friend's distaste for being buried in a building made of marble in a cemetery where hundreds of other buildings that looked like small churches sat side by side, filled with the dead.

Of the 34 million people in Argentina, 85% were of European descent and 93% were Roman Catholic. For this reason, Catholicism was the official state religion. However, it was permeated with ideology. Most of those unsupported beliefs surrounded spiritualism, or the supernatural, and an almost manic fixation with death.

It was customary for the Argentines to hold homage and memorials on the anniversary of the deaths of their loved ones. As such, it was not uncommon to have families honoring their dead and even believing that the spirit of the person who had passed on still walked the earth. They

58

would leave trails of food from the cemetery to their homes so that their loved ones could find their way back. Cemeteries, themselves, could be very strange and scary places and he and Roberto had agreed that they never wanted to be placed in one of the tombs.

Getting special dispensation from the church in order to bury Roberto's body on the *estancia* had taken some work.

Roberto's huge wealth and donations to the Cathedral Iglesia, built in 1572, had made it possible. Father Vladimir would have to consecrate the land but he had assured Victor that this would not be a problem.

The *El Sauce estancia* was 70,000 hectares large and employed over 1000 people, so it was a vast holding. Yearly, Roberto donated to both the Mothers of the Plaza de Mayo, and the church, a sum that would be considered huge even for a man of his great wealth.

So it was that Roberto's body would be taken to the *Cathedral Iglesia* in Cordoba for his mass. Then transported back to *El Sauce* for burial and a requiem mass for all the workers on the *estancia*.

Roberto had petitioned Ciro Duarte, a man who had lived on the *estancia* for years and was gifted in all manner of carving, to carve and build the casket. This again was one of Roberto's wishes - to be buried in something grown from the earth and not to be placed in some steel container.

All preparations had been made. Victor hoped that Julia would approve once she emerged from the madness that had taken control of her.

Each day she looked worse. She had lost a tremendous amount of weight and her color had changed from her normal dusky rose to a white that looked as if her skin had been bleached. She was not sleeping and could be found drifting silently from room to room at all hours of the day and night clutching what she referred to as "the evidence" against her bosom.

She spoke only to Carmen and when she spoke, which was not often, she did so in whispers. Other than her daily bath, she took no care of her personal appearance.

Carmen was doing her best to care for her mistress but Julia continued to waste away, growing more ghostly each day. Everyone feared for her sanity and prayed that her grief, or whatever it was, would not kill her, too, and cause them to lose both Julia and their Patron at the same time. No one feared it any worse than Carmen. She could not reach Julia no matter how she tried. It was as if she didn't hear or see anything around her anymore.

***

Rosita opened the door and smiled at the delivery boy from the florist in Cordoba. He was holding a huge bouquet of blood red roses and he didn't look happy. She knew they were from Victor and she was almost tempted to accept them this time. No, it was too soon, she cautioned herself. She needed to wait a little longer.

Turning to the delivery boy she smiled and said, "I am sorry. Please accept my apologies for the long ride out here, but I cannot take this lovely gift. Please tell the sender that they are truly beautiful, but unfortunately I cannot accept them."

The young man, who had brought at least one dozen bouquets of every color and description to this house almost every day of the last two weeks, finally lost his patience. No longer willing to be the quiet and dutiful messenger, he said, "Why don't you give the guy a break? He is obviously sorry for whatever it is he has done and is trying to show you with these flowers I keep bringing and you keep refusing. I am really glad that I never made you mad at me!"

Rosita laughed. "My dear young man," she started, although he was not much younger than she was, "you don't understand. This is customary when a man is courting a woman. We cannot give in too soon or the chase won't be as satisfying for the man. You are much too young to understand now, but someday, when you fall in love, you will understand the rules of courtship," she said smiling gently.

"I'm never going to fall in love and let some girl drive me so crazy that I throw all my money away like this guy does. It's damned embarrassing," he said as he started back to his car.

"I'll see you next time," he called over his shoulder. "As love-sick as this guy is I'm sure I'll be back either tomorrow or the next day. Hopefully, you will be able to change my attitude about women by accepting at least one of the bouquets he will send you."

With that he got into his car and mumbling under his breath, she heard him say, "Although I doubt it the way the past two weeks have gone."

Rosita laughed again and turned back to the house. As she walked up the steps to the door, she tried to analyze Victor's motives for all the calls and flowers.

Maybe he really did love her? Maybe it meant nothing when he had called her Julia.

Julia's old, for goodness sake, he couldn't possibly love her, she argued with herself. Sure Julia's pretty, but she isn't young and she isn't beautiful like me, she continued with her argument. This is not my ego talking, she told herself - just a fact that anyone could see was true.

Julia loved Roberto and even though she would soon be a widow, and a very rich widow at that, Victor was not her type. But, it was true that Julia and Victor were closer to the same age than she and Victor, she reminded herself. Yes, she thought, but older men like Victor seemed to like to have young, vivacious and beautiful women for their wives. Look at Roberto. He was nearly fifteen years older than Julia was and they'd had a wonderful marriage. Yes, but there was over twenty-five year's difference between her and Victor, she reminded herself. Well, it just didn't matter, she thought, stopping her argument with herself.

But, the real question that came up, as Rosita continued her musing, was this - why hadn't Victor told her he loved her?

Well, she offered to herself as a way of explanation, Victor obviously had never been in love before so he wouldn't know if he were in love or not. All at once Rosita knew that had to be the answer. The reason he couldn't tell her was because he didn't know! Why hadn't she figured it out sooner?

All doubts about what to do left Rosita as she came to this realization. The way Victor was pursuing her meant that he did love her and that he did want to marry her! She had never been happier than at this moment!

Rosita decided that she would wait a short time longer and then she would suggest that she and Victor have a candlelight dinner at Rosa Negro in Buenos Aires. This had been her favorite restaurant since the night Victor had taken her there for her eighteenth birthday.

That had been a wonderful, exciting night, she remembered. She was in Buenos Aires with her parents, staying at the *Alvear Palace* Hotel, enjoying a shopping spree for her birthday. Victor had arrived unannounced at her door on the night of her birthday, wearing a huge grin, and announcing that he was there to take her to dinner. She had never been allowed to go anywhere without a chaperone, so when her parents told her that she could go without them, she was delirious with joy. She knew they had all planned it as a surprise by the way her parents were beaming and giving each other the eye. She had been so excited that she had hardly been able to get dressed.

He had bought her a wrist corsage of white lilies and Rosita had dried it and still had it lying on her dressing table in her bedroom. She wondered how Victor would feel if he knew that. Men were so blind; they usually didn't realize what a small thing like flowers could mean to a woman. At the tender age of eighteen, she thought it was the most romantic thing that anyone had ever done for her.

They had taken a taxi from the hotel to the restaurant. They had been thrown from side to side on the wild and reckless drive. It was enough that the driver was speeding and disregarding every corner, but he also did not have his headlights on. All in all, it was extremely frightening, but somehow exhilarating, as the driver sped through the night, ignoring the screeching brakes and car horns that blared at him at each intersection.

Rosita had found herself thrown into Victor's arms time and time again as he tried to save her from being thrown onto the floor. It was very sexy! However, she had to admit looking back at that night, she hadn't looked so great when they had finally arrived and the driver skidded to a halt and she had flown up out of the seat onto the floor, despite Victor's attempts to hold her back. Her dress was pulled half way up her body, her hair had fallen out of its pins and hung over her eyes in her face and she couldn't even see to pull herself up.

Victor had just taken all her pins out and let her hair down telling her the whole time that it was such beautiful hair that she didn't need to worry and should just wear it down. Helping her rearrange her dress, he had offered her his arm and they had walked regally into the Rosa Negro.

After dinner he had allowed her to have champagne with him to celebrate her birthday. The bubbles tickled her nose and at the time she didn't think it tasted all that great but it warmed her with an inner glow that she loved. He had given her a beautiful pin in the shape of a butterfly with dark Jade stones for wings.

Victor had said that the stones were the same shade of green that were highlighted in her eyes when she was angry or the sunlight was reflected in them. Teasing her he had said that he had seen her angry enough times so that it had been no problem picking just the right shade.

She had been spellbound. She had fallen deeply in love that night and it had not changed during the last three years. Each night, following their date, she would fantasize about the day she would become his wife and wonder at the strange tingling in her body when she thought of him.

However, something very strange happened following that evening. She had assumed that Victor would start courting her and during the next year would ask for her hand. Much to her surprise, she thought, remembering the hurt again; she didn't see him very much during the next several months. When they did run into each other he was cool and distant, as if he had something very important on his mind and couldn't be bothered with her. Then about six months later she was told that his firm had promoted him and moved him to New York. They said that he would only visit Buenos Aires occasionally and she had cried for weeks. She had not seen him again until Julia's party.

She had suffered greatly after he left and she didn't want to think about the betrayal she had felt. He was back, he was in love with her and he wanted her to be his wife. That was all that mattered. It was all going to work now. All her dreams were finally coming true!

He would need her now. Victor would be hurt by Roberto's death and she would be there for him. She would comfort him and help him heal. He would not be alone. He would have a woman that loved him, who would stand by his side in the face of all adversity. Their love would unite them and they would stand stronger for it. Then, someday, they would raise a family together and she knew that this would be what Victor wanted most of all, something that was a part of him, a family.

Humming to herself, Rosita went to the phone. She needed to start the work on her wedding dress and accessories. She would not tell her mother and father until after the funeral and she and Victor had finished making all their plans.

They would be so happy for her. She smiled brightly as the phone was picked up on the other end.

"Senora Matrice, this is Rosita. I am going to need a dress. A very, very special dress......

***

Carmen peered out from under her eyelids. Julia was standing at the door to Roberto's room.

She would come every night, when she thought everyone was sleeping, and stand quietly at the entrance to the room but she would never go in. Carmen would pretend to be asleep each time.

Like all the other nights, Julia stood in her nightgown and robe, absently stroking the outside of the envelope she held to her chest. Her face showed the emotions that tore at her as she fought with herself.

Go on. Go into the room, Julia, Carmen said to herself. *You may wait too long. Go on into the room*! She said it over and over trying to will Julia into the room and to Roberto's bedside.

Julia placed one foot into the room and glanced over at Carmen to make sure she was sleeping. Carmen closed her eyes tightly and waited a few moments before peeking out again.

Julia stood in the same position at the entrance to the room staring at Roberto's bed where a small lamp, sitting on a table by the window, offered the only light. Carmen could see her squinting into the semi-darkness trying to see.

Slowly Julia's face changed. Her mouth twisted as she tried not to cry. Blinking her eyes very rapidly, she attempted to force the tears back into them. Shaking her head from side to side, as if to clear the thoughts that tumbled inside, she turned and left the room.

"Damn! Damn! Damn!" Carmen muttered. She had thought for sure that Julia would come in this time. Roberto was not going to last much longer and Julia needed to make her peace with him. Whatever Roberto had done, she could not let him die this way.

Carmen had prayed on her knees until they were raw from the tile floor she had knelt on, but still Julia did not find any peace and would not come to her husband's deathbed.

Roberto continued to linger past what the doctor believed would be the date of his death. Carmen was sure that Roberto lingered because he was waiting for Julia.

"Father," she prayed, "I know he suffers greatly, but let him live a little longer so they can say goodbye."

***

Whew! That was a close call, the woman thought as she followed the woman named Julia outside into the darkness. For a moment there she had almost been pulled down into Julia's body and she certainly didn't want that! Julia had a horrible life and she wanted no part of it.

Yes, she knew the whole story, although God knows she wished she didn't.

Julia's husband was dying and he had betrayed her horribly. He had even committed crimes that were punishable by prison sentence or death.

64

She had seen the pictures that Julia stared at for hours on end and those pictures had torn her apart! Why, she had almost cried herself! It was just pitiful!

What she could do to save this family or Julia was beyond her. She had pondered it over and over as she floated above while Julia wandered from room to room or once in a while when she slept for a few hours.

No! She never wanted this woman's life. It was just too sad.

As much as she thought about it, she could not see what she could do. Couldn't the angels see her plight and give her another assignment that wasn't so difficult?

"Forgiveness?" Why did that word keep popping into her mind? Was she supposed to tell Julia to forgive Roberto? Never! She could never do that.

Why she didn't even know the man and it would be hard for her to forgive him much less someone like Julia who had been shattered by what he had done. "Forgiveness?" Forget it!

Hey, you angels out there, are you listening? You'd better come up with something better than "forgiveness" because it is not going to happen in this family.

Chapter Eight

Julia was standing in the entranceway of the hacienda, staring at the closed front door, when Victor came down the stairs for breakfast the next morning. She was dressed in a beautiful navy suit with a long jacket and short skirt. The jacket was buttoned to the neck and she wore a beautiful pair of baroque pearls as her only jewelry. The pearls were Mikimoto and had a slight pinkish hue that accented the suit beautifully. Victor remembered when Roberto had given them to Julia on their fifteenth wedding anniversary. Julia was running her fingers back and forth on them while twisting them in her hand. In the other hand she carried a small handbag and white gloves.

She was tall at five feet ten inches but in her Via Spiga pumps she was over six feet tall. Her hose were translucent and with her short skirt, her legs looked very long.

The Argentines attached particular value to their appearance. Up to now, Julia had been no different. She always devoted careful attention to how she looked and meticulous grooming was an intricate part of her. It was inconceivable to her or any Argentine that they would not be impeccably groomed and dressed. The past few weeks had been a definite aberration.

Julia was ravishing! Even with no make-up, he thought as he looked her up and down, she was beautiful.

"Good morning, Julia," he said.

She never moved or gave any indication that she had heard him, so Victor walked in front of her and took her hand. A tremor went through him, a subtle shot of electricity. Victor dropped her hand and started rubbing his palms together.

"Julia, what are you doing? Are you going somewhere? Is this why you are dressed to go out?" he questioned her. No one had seen her in anything other than her robe and gown for the past two weeks, so he was slightly worried about her state of mind.

"I want to go to town. Can you summon Alejandro for me?" she asked in almost a whisper.

Julia had her face turned toward him but she appeared to be looking through him at a space somewhere right behind his head.

"Julia, come with me. Let's sit for a moment. We need to talk."

Hesitating for only a moment, she turned and walked over to a small sofa situated in front of a massive stone fireplace in the living room.

Victor sat down and faced her. Julia laid her handbag and gloves on her lap and sat clenching and unclenching her hands.

"Julia, do you believe that I care for you and would never harm you in any way?" he asked.

"That is not my name," she said quietly.

"What? What is not your name?" Victor asked totally confused.

"Julia," she responded.

"Julia, what?"

"Julia is not my name," she replied in a conspiratorial whisper.

"What is your name," he asked cautiously.

"Elizabeth."

"Elizabeth is your name? It is not Julia?" he asked to be certain he had heard her right.

"Yes."

***

The woman who drifted above them was very upset.

Now what is Julia doing, she asked herself.

It's obvious that she's trying to take my name now. Well, it is just ridiculous. The lady with all the problems down there is named Julia! I'm up here and I'm Elizabeth, not her! All I want is to earn my wings so I can get out of this world. And, now this happens!

It's getting far too complicated and confusing!

How did Julia figure out my name? Why does she want to use it? Doesn't she like her own name anymore?

The lady above knew she was going to have to start paying more attention. Obviously, she had missed something. It must have slipped past her when she wasn't watching.

Victor reached over and took both of Julia's hands into his and a jolt of fire leaped through his fingers.

Julia looked down at their entwined hands and lifted her head with a jerk to look into his eyes.

My God, she is beautiful, he thought. Does she feel it to? This is dangerous, he reminded himself, but he did not let go of her hands.

"Elizabeth? Is that what you want me to call you? Elizabeth?"

"Yes," she murmured.

"Elizabeth, where are you going when you get to town?"

"To Church," she answered simply.

"You want to go to Church?"

"Yes."

"Elizabeth, I can ask the priest to come here if you would like. Then you won't have to go to town."

"No, I need to go to Church," she said emphasizing the word go.

"Why, Elizabeth? Tell me why," he said as he struggled to keep from calling her Julia.

"To pray for forgiveness."

"Julia, I mean, Elizabeth…," he started but words failed him. The sadness in her eyes pierced his heart. "Elizabeth," he choked, "what can I do to help? I will drive you if you would like me to."

Julia would not answer. She just sat there quietly staring back at the door.

"Then I will call Alejandro for you," he said as he stood and walked to the back of the house.

***

The woman above was surprised. There was that word again.
"Forgiveness"
"Forgiveness"
"Forgiveness?"
What did it mean?

***

Cesar sat with his wife Maria in the small living room of their home. It was early for a fire since the day had not started to cool as it usually did when evening advanced, but Maria had laid a fire anyway knowing that Cesar would want to talk. Staring into the open flames seemed to help him speak when he was troubled.

When he called to say he was coming home for a few hours, she knew he had something on his mind, something other than Roberto's death.

As Cesar sat in his favorite chair facing the fire, he placed his feet up on the ottoman and stared at the small cassette tape in his hands. Maria sat beside him in a smaller version of his chair working on a needlepoint table runner. He noticed it was a scene of the Blessed Mother with Child. She had been working on it faithfully as a gift for the altar of the church.

"I could destroy it and never give it to her," he said indicating the tape he held in his hand.

Maria did not answer.

"It would be better for everyone if I did," he tried to convince himself.

Maria said nothing.

"You know she has been wandering around the house for over two weeks in her nightgown and robe. She refuses to see her husband who is dying and carries that damned envelope clutched to her chest the whole time as if someone were going to try to steal it. Now Victor tells me that she doesn't want to be called Julia anymore since that is not her name! The whole household thinks she has finally gone mad."

"Really," Maria said, speaking for the first time. "And what does she say her name is?"

Cesar did not answer.

"Cesar, my darling, what does she think her name is?"

Sighing he said, "Elizabeth".

"Ah"

"Marie, don't 'Ah' me, please! I know what you are thinking but no one needs to know about this tape. What Julia has in her envelope is enough to condemn us all. Why drag all of this other mess out in the open? You know this will put me in a terrible position. What she has is bad enough but this tape will seal my fate. We are getting old now and if this all comes out I shudder to think about what might happen."

Marie sat silently working on her sewing.

"I know, I know. I swore I would give it to her. I promised him and I did it while he was lying on his deathbed," he mumbled to himself.

Pushing his hands through his hair he stared at the tape that he had placed on the small table next to him.

Finally, after several moments he said, "Okay. Okay! You're right. The truth must be told. I must accept the consequences whatever they may be. I will do exactly what I promised Roberto."

Maria smiled to herself. She loved this man so much and she was very proud of him. He never disappointed her. He had made a terrible mistake and now there would be a price to pay. They would face it together the same way they had all their married life.

Laying down her sewing and reaching down to the table next to her she said, "Darling, could I interest you in a nice, hot cup of tea?"

***

He was rubbing kneads oil into his saddle and, as he worked, he thought about her again. He had seen her leave Victor's room several weeks ago. She had been with him a very long time and his gut had twisted and turned, as the jealousy ate away at him.

He'd had her face in the cross hairs of the scope of his rifle when she sneaked out of the hacienda early the next morning before the sun had risen. It would have been easy to shoot her. She would have never known what hit her.

He hadn't been able to pull the trigger.

She had turned her face to him, as if she could see him watching her. The pain in her face and eyes had struck him like a blow to his chest. Throwing the rifle down, he had been filled with revulsion for himself. He had lit a cigarette with trembling fingers, cursing himself vehemently for what he might have done.

He had to get hold of himself! Somehow he had to get control. He repeated to himself over and over until he felt some sanity return. He couldn't go off the deep end over her.

What had happened that night, he wondered? Every time she was with Victor she left crying. Did he physically abuse her? That thought left him weak. He would kill him if he ever hurt her.

When he had ridden out to her house a week later, he had expected her to be sad and depressed. Instead, she was excited and kept smiling that way she always did when she knew a secret that no on else knew. He had ridden away devastated by her happiness.

He knew he was obsessed but he couldn't help himself. He also knew now that she loved Victor and nothing was going to change that. He had to face it.

He didn't care; he just wanted to be with her. No one could ever love her the way he did. He would just have to make her see.

***

The woman above had watched Julia throughout her meeting with Father Vladimir Frederico. At one point she had watched in horror as Julia had taken the envelope out of her handbag and handed it to the old priest.

After looking at the old newspaper clippings he had stood and paced the floor of the chancellery. It was obvious that he was shaken by what Julia told him and by what he had seen.

Julia sat still as stone looking at her lap, gripping her hands together so tightly her knuckles were white, as he continued to walk back and forth.

Finally he had knelt at a small altar for a few moments, crossed himself and stood. Moving to sit in front of Julia, he spoke to her very softly.

He was saying things that the woman above didn't want to hear. She tried to yell at Julia and tell her not to listen but Julia didn't seem to notice. She just sat there with her head bowed as the priest gave her his advice.

The woman finally decided to start humming out loud so she would not have to hear what the priest was saying.

Hmm, hmm, hmm, she sang louder and louder.

***

It was late when Julia arrived back home. The sun was setting behind the mountains as the Mercedes pulled back into the courtyard.

She was tired. Her time with Father Vladimir had left her shaking with exhaustion. He had spent several hours listening, as she poured out her story, then he had counseled her and offered his advice.

After leaving the old priest, she had gone to the chapel to pray. She made herself light a candle for Roberto as Father Vladimir had suggested. Her hand had trembled so badly that she had been unable to light it. She kept dropping the matches or, when she did manage to get one lit, she would shake so badly that the flame would go out. Finally, after several unsuccessful attempts, she managed it.

Sinking down in front of the altar, she knelt and prayed for a long time but still she felt no peace. Her love and her hate were twisted up inside of her as they waged war upon each other. She could find no peace, no solace. She kept searching for the answers, but to no avail.

Finding no help from her prayers, she finally stood and went over to a pew to sit down.

Julia ached inside. She felt like a blind woman groping around inside of herself. Touching the walls of her heart, she constantly tripped and stumbled as she searched for a window to open. If only she could find just one and let the breeze in, to cool the fire in her chest. If only she could let the sun in, to shine a light, so that she could finally see. But her heart stayed dark and she could not find the window for which she was searching.

It wasn't until she walked out of the church and into the cemetery that she realized that Roberto would soon be lying dead along with all the other souls whose tombs lined the small avenues she walked.

She wondered what it would feel like to die. Would it hurt? Do you feel a great blast of joy that you no longer have the earthly travails or do you weep because life has been taken from you?

All of a sudden, a great fear swept over her.

She knew she could never forgive Roberto for what he had done, but would Roberto forgive her?

When his soul left his body would he wander alone and lost, never finding his final rest, because he could not forgive her for deserting him at his final hour? Would the pain of her ultimate betrayal keep him wandering the earth as one of the walking dead?

This thought brought waves of fear over her body. Chills ran up and down her arms and she rubbed them trying to chase the thoughts away.

The terrible way Roberto was suffering and dying might help him atone for the sins he had committed. But what if he wasn't able to forgive her? Would he haunt her for not allowing him to die in peace?

Julia was still worrying about all of this, as she stared out of the car window, when she realized that the car was not moving and that they were stopped. She did not know how long they had been in front of the hacienda. Alejandro was sitting patiently behind the wheel of the car waiting for her.

"Alejandro, I'm sorry," she said. "I am not myself these days and I find my mind wandering and before I know it I'm completely lost in my thoughts. Thank you for being so kind as to wait until I finally find myself again. I am ready to go into the house now."

Smiling very kindly, Alejandro left the driver's seat and went around the car to open her door and help her out. As he took her hand he said,

"It is nothing, Senora. I am only here to help. Do you remember when I was sick from the fever and you sat by my bed for three days nursing me? You would not leave my side and you kept telling me very softly that I would soon be well? "

"Why, yes I do," she said finding herself embarrassed by his words.

"Well, I may be an old man, but I will never forget. I will go wherever you need to go and I will do whatever you want me to do and I will wait for as long as you ever need me to wait. Never, never worry, Senora, while I still breathe, I will always be there for you."

Julia was astonished. Alejandro was a man of few words and she did not believe he had ever said more than two or three to her in all the years she had been at the ranch.

She was deeply moved. A small ray of light suddenly burst through a tiny crack inside her. Blinking back her tears and without saying a word, she nodded once and stepped from the car because she found she could not speak.

***

When Julia got to her room, she stepped out of her heels and left her handbag and gloves on the dressing table. As she walked to the balcony doors and opened them, she did not realize that for the first time since Roberto had given it to her she was not holding the envelope. Even when she slept she kept it in her hands and held it against her chest. If she woke and could not find it immediately, she would panic.

Staring out at the night sky, she listened to the rustle of the leaves as the trees bent gently in the wind. There was a full moon and the clouds shrouded it in layers, partially hiding its glow. "A magic night," she said softly. "That is what Roberto always called a night like this. A magic night."

There was a time, it seemed like a lifetime away now, when a night like this would be a night of beauty and passion for her and Roberto.

They would bathe together with candles surrounding the tub. Then the water fight would start and they would squeal and giggle like children as they splashed and slung the water at each other. Julia smiled as she remembered.

After a time, Roberto would have her kneel in front of him and he would wash her hair. He always told her this was one of his favorite things to do because he loved the shape of her head and the silkiness of her long hair. Stroking his long fingers through her hair and vigorously massaging her scalp, she would sigh as tiny chills rushed up and down her body.

As the water would start to cool, they would sip their wine, murmuring of their love for each other. Sometimes the words were only spoken with their eyes as they trailed their fingers through the soapy water, regarding each other.

Finally, he would pull her over on top of him as he sat with his back against the tub. As she moved on him he would lather her body with soap. Slipping his hands up and down following the motion of her body, he would stroke her skin until she was wild with desire. Gathering her to him they would move against each other in a dance as old as time. It was a dance that was immortal and at that moment they had believed that they were too. As they finished she would lie in his arms, drifting, as her body relaxed.

Only after the water had cooled and their skin had turned white and wrinkled would Roberto dry her and wrap her in an oversized Turkish robe. He would carry her to the rocking chair that sat in front of the fire. Settling her in his lap he would rock her in his arms. Holding his lips next to her ear he would whisper beautiful words so sweet that she would sometimes weep from the joy of loving him.

She would try to stay awake but somewhere, sometime while he was holding her, she would slip away. The next morning she would find herself lying in his arms in bed but would have no memory of when he carried her there.

Magic nights. They had shared many.

Julia wondered how she would survive now and whether or not she really wanted to. There was almost nothing left of her now except some bleached white bones that were scattered out on a barren desert.

What would happen to her when he was gone? Each day as he slipped from this life she felt herself disappearing little by little. Because she was such a part of him would she just fade away when he took his last breath? Would she be sucked away with him in the vortex that would be created by the force of his soul leaving his body? Julia shivered.

A cool wind blew over her and she shivered again. It was time. Julia turned and left the balcony. She knew what she had to do.

***

Julia entered Roberto's room and didn't bother to look to see if Carmen was asleep. It just didn't matter now. She hoped she wasn't too late.

She almost lost her nerve as she stepped over the threshold. Taking a very deep breath, she forced herself to walk over to the bed. What she saw there made her flinch and start to turn away.

"Oh, Roberto," she whispered, "what have I done? I didn't realize. I should have been here to help care for you. I'm sorry, I'm sorry."

As she stared down at the man she no longer recognized, feelings of grief and pity made her sway on her feet. Reaching down she took his hand into hers and instantly Roberto opened his eyes.

"Julia," he breathed out her name with a sigh. "Oh, Julia, Julia. I knew you would come. I prayed that you would come. Thank you, thank you."

"Shhh," she said softly. "I am here now. I will not leave you. Don't worry. Just sleep and know that I'm here."

Roberto closed his eyes and relaxed. Julia pulled a chair close to the bed. Laying her head down on his chest and holding his hand to her lips, she spoke of their life together.

"Remember when...," she started and it went on from there.

She spoke of the fun times and the crazy outrageous things that they sometimes did. She didn't mention anything about what she had just recently remembered, or the newspaper clippings, or the pain of it all. She went back to happier days, days when they thought that the sun would always shine on them and the wind would always be at their backs.

When she starting recounting a particularly funny story, about the time they had gone skinny-dipping and Father Vladimir had interrupted them, she turned and saw a smile on Roberto's lips.

So on and on she went, filling the room with their memories. Passing through the many years they had shared, she created images of them that seemed to live and move in the room. A shy young girl, a mature handsome man with a constant smile, they courted and flirted with each other. And still she went on, her gentle voice weaving a tapestry that was the fabric of their life together.

Roberto had started to stroke her hair, running it through his fingers as she spoke and sometime during the night her voice was replaced by his soft whisper when she fell asleep lying across his heart.

He spoke as he had so many other times when he had held her in his arms, telling her of his love that would never die. That she should be strong and know he would always be there for her. All she had to do was to call his name. That he hoped she would be able to love again and what he had done would not harm her in a way that wouldn't allow her to find happiness. That he would miss her and how much it meant to him to hold her one more time.

As his whisper became faint and his voice grew hoarse, he continued to speak far into the night, letting his words mingle with the memories floating in the room, while his beloved Julia slept.

It would be their final love song, for sometime in the hours between midnight and dawn, the Spanish call it *madrugada*, Roberto Anthony Bertinelli died.

Chapter Nine
Cordoba Argentina – 1993

It was a death house.

A house of mourning.

Wreaths draped in black hung on every door and all the ranch hands and staff wore black armbands as an expression of their grief.

Julia had stayed with Roberto until they had come for his body. She did not cry.

Listening quietly while Victor spoke, she agreed to all of his plans for burial and funeral masses. She thanked him for his kindness over the past several weeks in taking care of all the arrangements and apologized for her actions saying that she could not have done it better.

Dressed in black and wearing no jewelry or makeup, she greeted all the guests at the door as they arrived night and day to pay their respects. She calmly accepted their warm words and saw to everyone's comfort.

The crush of people in and out of the hacienda would have daunted even the most courageous at a time like this, but somehow everyone was fed, offered something to drink, shown to their room, and settled without any disruption.

Julia seemed to be everywhere at once and never seemed to sleep.

Everyone, Victor included, expected her to either weep hysterically or to drift farther away from reality to madness. She had fooled everyone when she didn't do either, everyone except Carmen.

Carmen had told Victor about Julia and Roberto's last night together. She had cried when she described how the lovers had talked into the night settling the matters between them.

"Julia will be fine now," Carmen had assured him. Much to his surprise, Carmen had been right.

Victor, however, was not all right. When he had learned of Roberto's death his first reaction was one of relief - relief that Roberto would not have to suffer any longer. Then the panic attacks had started.

"You will never see him again," a small voice inside his head would say. "You will never be able to go to him for advice or help when you are troubled. You will never be able to call him just to hear his voice, when the pressures of being in New York get to be too much," the voice taunted. "You never told him the truth. You never told him how you betrayed him," his conscience reminded him over and over.

Victor had just started to realize that there was going to be a lifetime of "never again" and wishing that he could see Roberto one more time. The feeling of panic that had come to him when his parents died came back to live with him again.

When the attacks came, his heart would beat very rapidly in his chest and he would begin to sweat. Fear would shake him and he could not stay inside. He began to walk long distances, sometimes sitting outside far into the night until he became calm again and could return to the house.

Julia never questioned his absences, seeming to understand when she saw him slip out of the house to return sometimes hours later. Silently, she would continue her vigil, caring for their friends, neighbors and ranch hands.

***

Roberto's funeral was held three days after his death, on the third day of June.

It had started to rain the night before and continued into the next morning as they prepared for the drive to the Cathedral in Cordoba. It was a gray and over-cast day, which only made the sadness of saying goodbye to someone you love harder to bear. It should be ordained, Victor thought as he sat in the limousine opposite Julia, by someone, somewhere in the universe of Saints and Godly beings, that the sun would always shine on the day you laid someone you love to rest. At least during the hour or so at the gravesite.

But it rained. And then it rained some more. It was as though the sky had decided to mourn Roberto too, on this day when the cortege of limousines and automobiles, with their headlights glowing, made their way to the Cathedral Iglesia.

The ride took a very long time. The procession moved very slowly and no one in the limousine spoke. Everyone stared out at the gray skies and the gray rain falling across the gray landscape, lost in their own sad thoughts.

The mass was even longer and more sorrowful. At one point, Victor started to panic and was ready to leave the church. Without looking at him, Julia placed her hand in his and his heart calmed.

It was a beautiful ceremony but Victor had to struggle to contain his sorrow and distress. He was confused by Julia's actions and it worried him that she showed no emotion during the mass. Holding her back perfectly erect, she was stoic throughout the long ceremony. She knelt and stood using her rosary beads at all the appropriate moments as she followed the priest's commands, but it was done by rote. She swayed only a little when she went up to the coffin to say goodbye to Roberto. It seemed everyone in the church was crying as they watched her but Julia's eyes were dry.

Victor knew how she had suffered, had seen her waste away, so it was possible that she didn't have any tears left to cry. But he knew her too well and it just didn't feel right. She was going through the motions and handling everything just a little too perfectly. Remembering his promise to Roberto, he decided to watch her carefully.

Then, somehow, they were back in the limousine driving back to the *estancia* for the requiem mass for all the workers and finally for the gravesite ceremony.

It was late by the time they gathered at the graveside and it was raining harder now. The wind had started to blow sheets of rain sideways as the small group of family and very close friends stood by the grave trying to shield themselves with their umbrellas. It was no use. Everyone was cold and wet by the time the ceremony ended.

Julia would not leave the grave until Roberto's body was completely lowered and the gravediggers started to shovel dirt onto the casket. Only Victor and she remained, everyone else having decided they didn't want to watch this part of the burial. Victor did not want to stay either, but he was not going to leave her here alone as it was starting to grow dark. It had been a very long day and he could see, by the dark shadows under her eyes, that she was drained and ready to collapse.

Julia stood by the grave and stared down at the casket. As she watched, the dirt the gravediggers threw fell into large clumps across the spray of lilies that she had laid on top of the casket. Rivulets of mud started running down the pure white of the petals, streaking them with brown veins. As the rain hit the flowers, it caused the lines of mud to wiggle and squirm like worms crawling, this way and that and the image caused her to turn away. She had suddenly felt sick and could not bear to look any longer. Turning to Victor, she told him she was ready to go home.

As she and Victor walked back to the house, Victor held her arm so she would not stumble while he tried to keep the umbrella in a position that would give her some shelter from the storm. At one point, as they struggled against the wind, he thought that Julia might be crying but he could not be sure since the umbrella did not shield them and they were both getting soaked to the skin.

***

Carmen was waiting for them when they returned.

"Victor, I have laid a fire in your room and your bath is ready. I will have a tray brought up with hot tea and it will be waiting for you when you are finished bathing. Hurry now and get out of those wet clothes. I don't want you to catch a cold," she said, glad that they were back and out of the storm.

Victor smiled at her motherly ways and went to do as she asked. He was very cold and a hot bath sounded like heaven after the day's events.

"Come now, Julia," Carmen said. "Let me help you get settled and out of your wet things. There is a hot bath waiting for you, also and I have laid out your heavy robe for you. Would you like something stronger than hot tea to drink?"

"No, Carmen, tea will be fine but I would like you to wait until later to bring it up. I want to relax in the tub for a while. I need some time alone to think."

"Of course. I understand. A good soak will help. Take all the time you need and let me know when you are ready for something to eat or drink," Carmen said.

***

As Victor soaked in his tub, Julia stood in her room with her arms wrapped around her body staring at the fire. Water was dripping onto the floor from her clothing and she was shivering uncontrollably.

***

The woman above watched and waited.

80

***

It was almost an hour later when Carmen decided that it was time to check on Julia since she had not called and asked for her tea. Climbing the stairs to her room, Carmen hoped she would not be intruding.

No, she told herself, Julia needed someone to take care of her now to help her through the next few weeks, until she was able to accept her husband's death. Grief was a terrible thing and she was going to make sure that Julia was pampered and sheltered until she could cope with her loss.

When she entered the room she realized that it was empty and that Julia had not bathed.

Carmen panicked. Where could she be?

Victor had finished drying himself after stepping from the tub and had just put on his robe when he heard the pounding at his door. Carmen was there telling him that Julia was not in her room and that she had searched the house and could not find her. They both realized at that same moment where she might be.

Throwing his clothes on Victor raced out into the night. Damn, damn, let me find her. Don't let her hurt herself, he prayed as he ran.

He found her on the grave. She was pulling up great hunks of earth and tossing them aside. Her face was smeared with mud and you could hardly see her kneeling on the earth in the darkness. She had lost her shoes and her nylons were torn in giant holes that stretched across her legs. The rain was pounding down and the fresh dirt was flowing off the grave in a muddy river.

"Roberto," she wailed. "Don't leave me. Please, don't leave me. I'll be good. Come back. Don't go. I forgive you. I forgive you. Please don't leave me here alone."

"Julia," Victor said, "come, Julia, don't do this."

Julia turned and said, "Oh, thank God you're here, Victor. Help me! He can't breathe. Help me get this dirt off of him!"

With those words, she began to scratch and tear at the dirt with more vigor. Victor grabbed her from behind, dragging her away.

"Stop it, Julia! He is dead!" he shouted. "Do you understand? He won't come back! He is dead!"

Julia erupted in his arms, fighting and scratching him. "Let me go! You don't care; you want him to die! I have to help him! He can't breathe under all that dirt!"

She struggled so hard that Victor could not hold her and she ran back to the grave. When Victor tried to approach again, she turned and flung a handful of mud into his face. Temporarily, he was blinded. Scrubbing at his face with his hands he tried to get the dirt out of his eyes.

Once he could see again, Victor grabbed her again, pulling her away from the grave and onto the ground, and this time he slapped her. Julia fell backwards, stopped struggling and just lay there. Falling down beside her he tried to still his heart that was pounding madly in his chest.

"Victor," she said hoarsely, "you don't understand. I am no one. I have no life. He took it all away from me and now he has left me here without a life. I don't know who I am. I can't live without him." She was crying now.

Victor stood and helped her to her feet. Holding her tightly in his arms he said, "Julia, Julia. I will help you. I will be there to help you learn to live again. Come with me. We must go back to the house. You are cold and wet. You will get sick. Please, Julia, please," he pleaded as he tried to get his breath.

Suddenly Julia jerked back from him, pulling herself away from his grip. "That is not my name," she screamed! "That is not my name! Don't call me Julia!" With those words she ran toward the cliffs that were several hundred feet behind the grave.

Victor was stunned at first and it took him a moment to gather his wits and run after her. He caught up with her just before she got to the edge. He tackled her around the ankles forcing her to the ground. She fought him with all her strength, scratching his face with her jagged fingernails. Then the mud started to slide down the edge as it broke away from the ground. Grabbing her, he dragged her on top of him pushing himself backward, scooting quickly away from the cliff until they were out of danger. Julia was fighting and screaming words he could not hear because of the pouring rain.

She wouldn't stop. He couldn't control her. He was afraid she might do herself harm so he hit her under the chin, knocking her unconscious.

Straddling her body, he checked to make sure she was breathing, then he sat down in the mud and the rain, pulling her limp form into his arms. Crying her name over and over, he kissed her face, rocking her back and forth finally letting go of all the grief he had kept locked up inside. He cried for Roberto - like he was a little boy again on the day he stood by his parents' pyre – and he cried for Julia. Then he cried for himself, letting his tears mingle with the rain.

***

When Victor arrived back at the house, he shouted for Carmen to open the door for him. When she did, she was astonished. Victor was carrying Julia, who was unconscious in his arms, and they both were covered with mud from head to foot.

Taking the stairs two at a time, he yelled at her to get another bath ready and to place more logs on the fire in Julia's room. Turning on the shower in her room he stepped inside fully clothed, carrying Julia with him.

As the mud sluiced from their bodies, Julia slowly opened her eyes. She looked up at Victor for a moment and then she closed her eyes again. The water did most of the work getting the dirt off of them, warming them both as well. She did not try to move out of his arms. She just let him hold her.

When Victor felt she was warm enough, he helped her stand and started removing her clothes. When she was naked, he lifted her into the tub that Carmen had filled.

Stripping off his own ruined clothing, he toweled and pulled on a bathrobe while keeping an eye on Julia so that she did not slip down under the water.

Carmen just stood by helplessly as her mistress was stripped and then as Victor toweled his naked body before covering himself with his robe. It was as if she weren't in the room.

"Go get me some whiskey," he commanded. "Bring two glasses and also make some hot tea. Hurry!"

Carmen stopped gaping and rushed to do what he ordered.

Julia sat in the tub with her face turned toward the wall and would not acknowledge Victor in any way. He took her hands in his and realized that her nails were broken to the quick and caked with mud and blood. He washed them gently, cleansing them with soap and rinsing them in the tub. Julia did not make a sound but he knew that what he was doing must hurt terribly.

He washed her body and her hair, paying special attention to the numerous scratches and cuts she had on her legs and feet. He spoke to her gently like she was a child when he moved this part of her or that part to wash a particular area of her body.

Victor's hands trembled as he ran them up and down her skin. She would have a large bruise on her cheek and chin from where he had hit her. He hated the thought that he had inflicted any pain on her.

She was so beautiful.

He had only seen her naked once before on a day, several years ago, when he had found her swimming in the pond. She hadn't known that he was there and he could not take his eyes off of her when she left the water to lie down in the sun to dry her body. He should have gone away, but he didn't. He watched her, mesmerized by her naked body and the tiny droplets of water that sometimes clung to her skin or fell and rolled gently down her breasts or thighs. He watched until she had finally dressed and then he turned away, moving silently back into the trees.

He had kept those images of her through all the lonely years in America. Images that kept him awake at night. Images that created a desire for her that no woman had ever been able to replace. Victor had betrayed Roberto and Julia. They had trusted him, but in his heart were feelings they didn't know about and would have been horrified by if they had discovered them. It was a hopeless situation, one he couldn't control, so he had left them and tried to exorcise his desire for her by staying away.

She was much thinner now. He could see her ribs beneath her skin and it hurt him to see how she had suffered.

As if she could read his thoughts, Julia put her hand up to Victor's face and pulled him down to her. She kissed him fiercely, moaning for him to make love to her. He kissed her back and his whole being came alive, as he half lifted her out of the water so that he could get closer to her.

Then he came to his senses. Pulling himself away, he looked at her face and saw how feverish her eyes were.

"No, Julia, it is not me that you want. You would hate yourself and me if we did this. No. Let me finish your bath and then you can lie down in your bed and rest."

Victor was shaking all over, but somehow he finished her bath. When Carmen arrived with the whiskey he made Julia take a few sips to help her sleep. Then he lifted her from the bath and dried her. Taking the gown from Carmen he helped Julia slip it on and then he drew back the covers and helped her into bed.

Victor did not once think that Carmen might find it odd that he was bathing and undressing and dressing her mistress. He was going to take care of Julia and everyone else could be damned if they didn't like it.

Taking a chair from the room, he placed it near Julia's bed and took her hand in his.

"Carmen, could you bring me some bandages and ointment for Julia's hands. I need to dress them before she sleeps. Then you can go get some rest. I will stay with her and I will call you if I need you."

"Are you sure you don't need to rest yourself?" she asked a little upset that he thought he should be the one taking care of Julia.

"I will not leave her until she is better. Go now and bring me what I need."

Julia would not look at him or speak but he noticed the tears as they squeezed out underneath her closed eyelids.

***

Several hours later, Victor was jolted from sleep by Julia's cries. He had fallen asleep in the chair he had placed by her bed. She was thrashing back and forth, twisting her bedding around her body.

"Roberto, please, please, give them back. It's all that I have. I'll do whatever you ask but don't take my babies," she cried.

As Victor reached his hand out to comfort her, he realized that her skin was too hot and that she had a fever. Taking her from the bed he pulled her into his arms and onto his lap.

Gently, he touched her face and pushed her hair away from her damp forehead.

"Shh.... It's okay. I'm here, don't be afraid. Shhh, sleep now. Try to rest," he said as he tried to calm her.

"My babies, my babies," she moaned.

Victor replied the only way that he could. "Shh, your babies are fine. They are all safe. Be still and rest. They're okay. Try not to worry."

"You promise?" she whispered.

"Yes, I promise," he replied and, as he said it, he felt her relax.

As soon as Julia went back to sleep, Victor placed her back on her bed and went to the door. He called for Carmen and she answered immediately. She was sitting outside the door, as he knew she would until she knew for certain that Julia was better.

"What is it Victor? What is wrong? I heard her crying. Is everything all right?"

"No, she is burning with fever. Bring me some ice and I will try to bring her temperature down. I'll need your help to control her for she won't like it when we place the cold towels on her body."

Carmen left and returned with a large bucket of ice water. Then she helped Victor remove Julia's gown and all the extra covers from the bed. Carmen could not help but notice that Julia seemed so pale and thin lying there on the large bed.

Victor did not seem to notice Julia's nudity and went straight to his task.

Placing several towels in the cold water he squeezed the excess out and began to place them on her body. Carmen had to use all her strength to hold Julia's hands so that she wouldn't throw off the wet towels.

Julia's skin erupted in chills as she shivered violently from the shock of the cold water against her hot skin. Moaning and crying out, she tried to move away from them.

When the water grew warm, Carmen would replace it, making sure it was ice cold, but nothing helped. During the next twenty-four hours her condition worsened. Finally they called Cesar.

There was nothing he could do. He told them that only time would tell if she would survive the deadly fever. Victor and Carmen were doing all that they could do. Julia would need fluids and they were told to try to make her drink at least small sips of water at a time.

Cesar wanted to move her to town to a hospital but the rains had caused so much flooding that the main roads were impassable.

For three more days Julia's fever continued to burn through her body. She no longer moved or resisted the cold baths and just lay there flushed and silent on the massive bed in her room.

Victor allowed no one to assist him with her care following Cesar's visit. Even Carmen was sent from the room. He called her only when he needed something brought to him.

On the seventh day of her illness, Cesar demanded that Victor let him in so he could judge for himself how Julia was doing. Victor was haggard looking. His hair hung limply into his face and his eyes were hollow from lack of sleep. He had not shaved and it was obvious that, when he did sleep, he slept in his clothes they were so wrinkled.

"I see she is no better, Victor, and I am afraid for her. She will not be able to fight this fever much longer because her heart is growing weaker.

86

You should go rest and let me care for her now. You have done all that you can do," Cesar said.

Victor did not speak and stood with his back to the doctor. After a moment he whirled around and cried out, "No! Get out! Get out now! She's not going to die, too. I will not let her die! Leave me alone! No more death! No more!" he exclaimed as he violently pushed Cesar away.

Staggering and almost falling, Cesar shouted, "You are mad! You cannot save her, only God can save her. You're out of control and not thinking clearly. You must rest! Let me do what I can for her. There is nothing more you can do!"

"Nooo!" he roared. "Get out! I will break you with my own hands if you don't leave immediately! I can make her live; I will make her live! I will not let her die! Roberto left me in charge, Cesar, not you, and you have no dominion here. He made me swear to take care of her and I will. No one is going to stop me! So, get out!"

Victor's face was a mask of fury causing Cesar to back away from him as he moved away from the bed. Grabbing the doctor's arm, Victor pushed him out of the room, then slammed the door and bolted it.

Cesar was trembling as he stood outside the door and tried to compose himself.

"Let him be, Doctor," Carmen said from a chair in the corner of the hallway. "He can do no harm. As you said, only God can save her. If anyone can pull her through, Victor will. Let him be. It's in God's hands now."

Cesar nodded and crossed himself.

***

Rosita had been to the *estancia* everyday for the last week begging Carmen to allow her to see Victor. Each day Carmen had told her that it wasn't possible since he was caring for Julia and that Julia was very ill. She couldn't stand it any longer. She was going to see Victor and find out what the hell was going on. What was he doing taking care of Julia?

She had just heard the exchange between the doctor and Victor from her hiding place down the hall behind the guest bedroom door. She had slipped upstairs when Carmen had forgotten to latch the front door after she had ushered the doctor in. Going up the back staircase, they had not noticed her when all the commotion with Victor started.

She was going to wait and she was going to find out what was really going on in that room.

***

The woman above could feel and see the light now. She must have made the angels happy for she could tell that she was going to leave this world. There was the sound of beautiful music that made her heart sing and a bright light that warmed her to her very core. She was walking to that light now and she was filled with happiness.

***

Victor had opened the door for Carmen to bring him coffee because he knew the doctor was right. He had to keep his strength up. As he sipped the warm brew, he noticed that Julia's breathing had become shallower. Looking down at her pale face he was suddenly afraid that she might be dying.

Throwing the cup against the fireplace, he grabbed her from the bed and held her body up in the air in supplication.

"Please, God," he begged. "Please don't take her, too. Please, hear me. Don't take her from me. Let her live. Don't take her."

Pulling her close to him, he held her naked body against his chest and began to spin crazily in circles.

"Julia, Julia," he pleaded. "Julia, live for me. Don't give up."

As tears fell from his eyes, he continued his crazy dance.

"I love you so much. I never told you. I had no right, but I love you and I will care for you. Don't leave me. Please try to live. Whatever it is that has broken your heart, we will face it together. You have to fight this. Do it for me. Please, please......"

Finally, when he could cry or stand no more he staggered to the rocking chair and sat down placing her in his lap. Cuddling her to him, he rocked her back and forth calling her name. As he kissed her face and her lips, he remembered what she had said to him before the fever caused her to lapse into unconsciousness.

"What about your babies? What will happen to your babies if you die? Who will take care of them?" he asked hoping that somehow these words would reach her through her fevered sleep.

Then he told her all about his love. He poured out the story of his betrayal of Roberto and how he had longed for her whenever she was near. He spoke of the pond and how he had watched her swim naked and how he had desired her and could not get her out of his mind. He talked about the pain of knowing he could never have her and how that pain and the pain of his betrayal had forced him to leave Argentina and start a new life in New York, where he still wanted her every day.

Speaking softly with his lips against her ear, he told her that he had loved her since the first day he saw her standing in front of the hacienda and Roberto had introduced her as his wife. There was so much inside him and he confessed it all knowing that if she died, he could not let her go without telling her the truth.

Julia didn't hear.

But, Rosita did.

She stood in the doorway of the room watching Victor as he kissed Julia and as he declared his love for the woman who had been another man's wife.

Rosita stumbled from the room and almost ran into Carmen at the foot of the stairs as she tore the front door open and slammed it behind her.

What in the world was she doing upstairs? How did she get into the house, Carmen wondered as she started up to see if Victor needed her.

Victor never saw Rosita standing in the room and never heard her leave. All he could do was hold Julia and make his peace with her. He did not know that it would be almost three full years before he would see Rosita again.

***

The woman turned away from the light, someone was calling her. She would have to go back. She understood now. He had said the only words that could make her come back to this life. So with a sigh she let go and Elizabeth and Julia became one again.

Chapter Ten
Chicago, Illinois – 1993

Brian was sitting at the bar, usually his favorite spot at Mario's on the corner of Dearborn and Goethe. He had started coming here when he moved into his apartment across the street. Mario, the owner, was a great guy. He was a big, burly, ex-hockey player with a heart of gold, who was awesome to behold. Brian was six foot two and in good shape, but he felt small next to Mario.

The restaurant had become a sort of home-away-from-home for Brian while he had been studying for his MBA, and later when he was hired as an analyst at the prestigious investment-banking firm of Hart & Newman.

Tonight, however, he was not eating his favorite dish, Ravioli Aurora, which was sitting in front of him. He hadn't even noticed when Claudio had brought it to him. He was not watching the NBA play-offs with the Chicago Bulls and Michael Jordan – his favorite basketball team - which was being projected on television monitors strategically placed around the room, and the major reason everyone was at Mario's tonight screaming and cheering their team on.

But…, he was nursing his third beer.

Mike, the bartender, had tried his best to strike up a conversation but he had finally given up when Brian kept ignoring him.

Brian was in trouble. He knew that for certain. He just didn't know what he was going to do about it.

He had just finished his MBA program at Northwestern last June. It had been grueling, but all his hard work had paid off and he had graduated tops in his class. After graduation, he had taken several months off and had gone backpacking through the Bob Marshall Wilderness in Montana with two of his best friends, Rick and Ted. He had really enjoyed the trip and the weekend he had been able to spend with Alexandria when he visited Missoula before heading back to Chicago.

When he returned he had had his pick of jobs and since he had grown to love Chicago – it didn't hurt that the Bulls and Cubbies were both here – he had accepted the coveted position that all his classmates had wanted at Hart and Newman. He had been at the firm for eight months but, just lately, the dreams had come back.

He would wake up in the night with his heart pounding, screaming the words, "No, No!!!" over and over. He would be drenched in sweat and he would break down as the memories reeled through his head like a horror movie. Everyone, all the doctors, his parents and grandparents, had always told him that what happened wasn't his fault and over time the nightmares would gradually go away. He figured that it was all the pressure of his current dilemma that was causing the dreams to reappear.

Everything was just great at work and he was living a charmed life, until he flew out to Milpitas, California to perform due diligence for an IPO that was planned for the late summer for a new technology company, eMicro. Part of that responsibility was to review the books and records, the manufacturing processes, the inventory records and the controls in place at the company. He had found the problem when he was going over the sales records, the shipping documents and the accounts receivable.

It appeared that the sales data were inflated. After following up on some of the shipping documents it seemed eMicro might be shipping to warehouses - some of the locations seemed odd - thereby inflating their sales in order to look better when they went public. It also looked like the figures were doctored in other areas as well, like the month-end cash balances. He was having a difficult time reconciling the bank records with the company books.

During his MBA program, Brian had studied the late 70's collapse of the record industry when some companies had been accused and indicted for "shipping Gold" – a term that was used when an album sold over one million copies - to falsely inflate their sales and increase the demand for albums. Instead of real sales, these albums were shipped to warehouses in order to make it look like a band or artist was hot in the market. So, he was very familiar with what eMicro might be doing.

When he had approached the senior partner, Barry Newman, who was heading the offering for the IPO, he learned that Barry had gone to college with the CEO of the company, Al Hansen, and that they were old and fast friends. Then he had been told to back off.

Well, if he remembered correctly, Mr. Newman's exact words were, " Brian, we're a young firm and you have a wonderful future here at Hart &

Newman. This IPO is a big deal for us and it will put us over the top. Believe me, we won't forget how you helped us. But…, Brian, we don't want to hear any bad news. Don't go questioning everything, just get the job done! And Brian, don't talk about this to anyone else, just make sure you have enough to support what you report and don't go digging any deeper that you have to. The market is right, we need to move quickly, so get it done fast, my boy!"

Brian had not been convinced by his boss' words and thought about going to Robert Boland, a junior partner in the firm and his mentor, but after what Newman had said he was afraid.

He knew that if the information he was uncovering proved to be correct and became public, it could, at a minimum, wreck eMicro and could even lead to criminal action against some of Hart's own management. If it came out *after* they went public, who knew how far-reaching the effects of the inevitable SEC investigation would reach?

Brian was new to the company and it was hard to say no to his boss, but if he left his concerns out of his report and just went along with it and then it all blew up in their faces, what would happen to him and his future? He could see everyone pointing the finger at him if anything went wrong. They would all deny any knowledge of what he had told them. He was the analyst. It was his job, they would say. He just didn't know how he was going to protect himself. His dad could probably help but he wanted to try to work it out himself if he could.

But, what could he do?

Brian stared down at his fourth beer.

Life just sucks some times, he thought, and this is damned well one of those times.

Chapter Eleven
Cordoba Argentina – 1993

Julia was fighting her way through the swirling water, trying to reach the surface. She could not see clearly because the water was so murky, almost like a fog, and she was so tired that she did not believe she had the strength to make it to the top. She had seen Roberto on her journey through the haze and the fire and he had told her many things. She was the only one, it seemed, who could undo some of what he had done and, to do that, she would have to live. So, Roberto had sent her back.

As she struggled up out of the darkness, she gulped a breath of air, opened her eyes and found herself staring at the sleeping face of Victor. Disoriented, she closed her eyes for a moment because she thought she might still be dreaming. But when she opened them again, he was still there and he looked terrible. His face was covered with black stubble and his eyes had dark circles under them.

She was lying in his arms in the rocking chair and she was naked except for a light cover. The question was, why? As she turned to look around the room, Carmen left her chair by the door and came to her.

"Oh, Julia, I am so happy that you are awake," she said with tears in her eyes. "We were so worried." Then she placed her hand on Julia's forehead and finding no fever, she smiled at her. "Victor is exhausted," she whispered. "Let's try not to wake him. He would not leave your side so he has worn himself out."

Remembering that she had been ill, she asked, "How long…?"

Anticipating her question, she whispered, "Over a week has passed. Victor has not left your side the entire time. He has watched over you from the first moment and wouldn't let anyone else care for you."

Julia nodded her understanding and tried to slip quietly off of Victor's lap but she was too weak to get up. As she tried to gather the strength to move again, Victor bolted upright in the chair.

"What? What is it?" he demanded.

Then he noticed Julia face and saw the slight smile on her lips and realized that she was awake.

"Julia, Julia, thank God!"

Touching her face he said, "Your fever is gone. You're going to be all right."

"Yes," she smiled weakly, "and it seems that you may have had something to do with that from what I have been told."

"No, you did it! You did it!" he shouted as he stood, grabbed her up and spun her in the air while she shrieked and tried to hold the blanket over her nakedness.

"Victor, put her down this instant! Have you lost your mind? She has been ill! Put her down now!" Carmen demanded, stomping her foot to emphasize her feelings.

"Oh, I'm sorry. You're absolutely right. Here, Julia, let me help you lie down" he said.

After placing Julia carefully on her bed, he grabbed Carmen up and started dancing around the room, holding her off the ground, as he twirled and yelled at the top of his lungs

"You haven't been sick, old woman. So you will dance with me instead. We did it! We did it! You, Julia and me, we did it! Oh, and Carmen, all those prayers you said, they certainly helped. Yes! Yes! Yes!"

"Let me down, you maniac! Let me down! I'm getting dizzy!" Carmen screamed.

Victor dropped Carmen down on her feet and said, "Well at least give me the 'high five', and don't pretend you don't know how. I spent too many days teaching you and you know how to do it, so get going, old girl!"

Carmen was out of breath from his exuberance but she couldn't keep from laughing. His joy was contagious.

"Okay, but if I do, you have to promise me that you'll get out of here, go clean up and lay down and rest."

Victor agreed, did the "high-five" with Carmen, grabbed Julia back up, kissed her soundly on the mouth, and, still whooping loudly, left the room. They could still hear him as he went down the hall.

"Well, if you don't have a relapse from that little display of irrationality it will be a mystery to me," Carmen said as she tried to act as if she hadn't enjoyed every minute of it.

Julia smiled. It felt good being with the people she loved. Maybe she could be happy after some time went by. But first, she needed to get her strength back, she thought closing her eyes. There was a great deal to do.

***

He had found Rosita waiting outside his door when he returned to his room last night and now, this morning, he was packing.

It was a miracle.

She had told him she was going away and wanted to know if he wanted to go with her. There was a fierce glow to her face and flames seemed to shoot from her eyes as she spoke. He had stood before her wondering if he was dreaming.

"Me?" he asked. "You want to go away with me?"

She had assured him that she did and that he needed to decide immediately because she was leaving first thing in the morning.

He was so excited he didn't even ask her where she was going. It didn't matter. He would go anywhere with her.

She smiled when he said yes and he knew that she had known all along that he would go.

He couldn't believe his luck. She wanted him to go with her. Only him! That was all that mattered. He loved her so much and now he had a chance to make her love him too. Closing his suitcase he rushed out the door.

***

It was several more days before Julia felt well enough to leave her room. She had asked Victor and Carmen to give her time alone after reassuring them that she wouldn't do any harm to herself. Other than accepting her meals from Carmen, she stayed in seclusion.

On the third day after her fever broke, Julia went to the kitchen and found Carmen and Victor having coffee. It had stopped raining and the sun was pouring through the windows.

Victor and Carmen felt her presence and turned to look at her at the same time. Carmen yelped and dumped her coffee across the table while Victor stared at her dumbstruck.

"My God, Julia, what have you done!" he exclaimed.

Julia did not answer. She was dressed in black, baggy slacks and a white shirt. With no makeup she looked like a young man standing there. She had cut all her hair off completely to her scalp. The cut was not professional so some areas of her scalp showed through while other areas had black tufts of hair standing at various lengths every which way. It looked like an animal had attacked her and chewed big holes all over her head.

"I didn't like it anymore. I didn't want it anymore," she said softly trying to break the dead silence in the room.

Victor jumped up and started helping Carmen wipe up the spill as he tried to recover from his shock.

"Well, it looks just fine and if that's what you wanted to do, well that's just fine. It was just a little surprise to us..." Carmen trailed off not knowing what else to say. What she was thinking, however, was that it looked absolutely horrible and that she wasn't sure she was up to too many more surprises.

Going to the counter to get another towel to finish soaking up the mess she had made, she grumbled under her breath, "Yes, that's just fine, just fine!"

"Victor," Julia said, interrupting their sideways glances at each other, "I have asked Cesar to meet me here this morning around 9:30. Could you please join us? If you can, we will meet in the study," Julia asked.

"Today? Are you sure you are strong enough? You're just getting back on your feet after your illness."

"I know, but some things need to be addressed as soon as possible and it is important or I wouldn't ask you. It's time I explained my behavior. I'm sure that you have many questions. They will all start to be answered today."

"Julia, you do not have to explain yourself to me..."

"Yes, I do, Victor. I will see you at 9:30." Julia said as she smiled weakly at them both and then rushed from the room.

"My God! Did you see her? What did she use on her hair?" Carmen said loudly.

"Shhh! Be still! She will hear you. I don't know what she did or why she did it anymore than you. I agree it looks pretty awful but it will grow out. It's not the end of the world," he said in a hard whisper.

"No, but you have to agree it's pretty strange that she chopped off all her hair. Do you think she's okay?"

"I hope so. I hope so," Victor sighed, agreeing silently that Julia did look terrible.

Thinking that it might help to change the subject, Victor asked, "By the way, Carmen, have you seen Rosita lately?"

"No, not since the other night when she came by and demanded to see you. I told her no, like I had all the other times she asked for you, since I knew you had your hands full caring for Julia."

Carmen did not tell him that she had seen Rosita in the hall before Rosita had run out and slammed the door, or that she had obviously been upstairs listening to something that had upset her, before she made her mad dash from the house.

"Hmm. That's very odd," he said stroking his chin. "She hasn't answered any of my calls and, now that Julia is better, I need to speak to her on a rather urgent matter."

"Well…, I heard…," Carmen paused for effect, "that she left and moved away."

"What! What do you mean she left and moved away?" he demanded.

"Well, I don't know if it is true, but that is the rumor. She packed up everything she owned, went to Buenos Aires and left the country. I heard someone say that they thought she might have gone to America. I hear her parents are very upset."

"What in the hell is the matter with everybody!" Victor yelled, slamming his fist down on the table. "Rosita knew we had to make plans. Important plans! Now she has left without telling me where she has gone and when she'll be back? And as for Julia, she looks like she was just released from prison right before they finished shaving her head in preparation for her execution! Now… I have to get ready for some meeting where Julia is going to explain everything to me. Well, damn it, somebody had better explain everything to me because I'm out of my depth right now! Hopelessly out of my depth and going down quick - not that anyone I know seems to notice, or to care for that matter. Humph! You women are all going to be the death of me," he shouted as he glared at Carmen and stormed from the room.

"My, my, my, aren't we a little upset. So…, what is this about him and little Rosita? Heh? What plans were they making?" Carmen said softly. Then Victor's description of Julia's hair cut caused her to start laughing.

"I just wish I could be a fly on the wall in that room when they meet. I would love to have someone explain everybody's behavior to me! Yes, I would," she said emphatically as she finished wiping up the remainder of her spill.

*****

Rosita was with him on the airplane, seated in the first class section, as they left Buenos Aires. They had arrived at *Aeropuerto Internacional Ezeiza* for the early morning flight on *Aerolineas Argentinas* to New York City. Her family had made a huge fuss when she had told them that she was leaving and she felt terrible because she couldn't tell them the real reason why. They didn't believe it was because she had received a wonderful job in the United States, as she had suggested. They knew she wanted to get out of Argentina in a hurry and they were worried about her.

Previously, she had toyed with the opportunity to go to New York and work and had discussed it with her parents at length. Of course, after Victor came home, there was no way she would have accepted anything that would have taken her away from Argentina. Now, overnight, she was going.

Damn him! Damn him, she thought for the hundredth time. Now she had no choice. She had to go. It was also Victor's fault that she had to take someone with her. Someone she didn't love.

Look at him, she thought, as she glanced out of the corner of her eye at the man seated next to her. He is sitting there delirious with happiness. He hasn't stopped smiling and groveling since we left. He has no idea how I really feel... men are such fools!

As he turned to her and smiled, she forced herself to smile back. Ugh, she hated this play-acting but she needed him now, so she was going to have to try hard not to let him see how she really felt.

Victor had ruined her life. But, she knew how she was going to destroy him. It would take time, but one day she would make him pay. Him and his darling Julia!

*****

Julia placed her fingers on the bruise that ran along her jaw line. It was still deep purple in color but it was starting to fade along the edges to a greenish yellow. Yes, but it was very attractive, she joked to herself. She still couldn't sleep on that side of her face because it was too painful.

She supposed that it had been necessary for Victor to hit her, but she didn't like it.

She glanced over at him. He was seated in the room waiting for Cesar to join them and he was staring at her. Quickly looking away from him, she resumed her pacing back and forth across the room.

Too many men had hurt her and betrayed her, she thought. Feeling the bruise again, she winced and promised herself that no man was ever going to hurt her again. Tapping the envelope against her leg, she continued walking as her thoughts turned to Cesar.

There was so much she had to do, tough and painful decisions to make, but first she was going to confront him regarding his complicity in the crimes that Roberto had committed.

Roberto was gone now. "Ah," she murmured to herself as she paused in her stride; the knowledge that this was true was so painful that it felt like a giant, invisible hand squeezed her heart. "Roberto is gone now," she made herself repeat it in a whisper, "so there is nothing that I can do about him."

Cesar, however, is a different matter, she thought. He is damned well going to tell me everything. Then I will send him from my home –he will be dead to me from this day forward. If I see him on the street, I will look through him as if he didn't exist.

She hadn't decided what to do about the authorities. They would have to be told, she thought. Crimes like this could not go unpunished and Roberto and Cesar had both gotten away with it for too long. So many years they had lived as if they were above the law. Suddenly, Julia felt the beginning of a headache that was starting at the base of her neck.

As Julia rubbed her neck and continued pacing, Victor watched her. She was dramatically thinner since her illness and with her new hairstyle, vivid bruise that ran down the entire side of her face, and fingernails that looked like they had gone through a shredder, she looked terrible. Grimacing, he thought about the part he had played in her appearance.

Damn it, he thought, I shouldn't have hit her. Every time she ran her fingers across her jaw, he thought he saw condemnation and blame in her eyes.

She hadn't stopped moving since he came into the room and, if she continued her march back and forth across the Oriental carpet, she was going to wear a big hole in it. He wished she would just sit down somewhere; she was making him nervous. Squirming in his chair, he wondered again what this meeting was all about. Maybe Cesar was bringing over Roberto's will. He and Julia had searched through Roberto's papers and they hadn't been able to find it.

There was a knock on the door, then Cesar entered the room, Julia stopped her pacing and turned to him,

"So, Cesar, you are finally here," she said.

"Yes, I am here," he said tiredly, setting the expression on his face so she would not see his alarm as he regarded her new coiffure.

Victor was amazed at the difference in Cesar's appearance since he had last seen him. He seemed to have aged overnight. A man of average height with a full head of white hair and a beautifully trimmed beard – he usually carried himself proudly, with an aristocratic flair. Today, however, he was stooped and walked with a shuffle. It appeared that he had not slept for several days, for heavy bags of flesh hung under his eyes. Normally, he was meticulously groomed, but now he was rumpled and disheveled, his shirt wrinkled and partially hanging out of one side of his trousers. He had been drinking and the smell of alcohol followed him as he walked gingerly into the room.

"I asked Victor to join us today, Cesar, so he can hear first hand of your treachery," Julia said loudly, getting right down to the reason she had called them together.

Cesar sat down in a chair near the desk and did not reply.

"You will not leave here today without telling me everything, Cesar. I mean everything!" she said louder.

Cesar put his head down but still he said nothing.

"Do you hear me!? I demand to know the part you played in this!" she screamed.

Cesar looked up abruptly and then shrank back in his chair as if she had struck him. His face was pale and he was trembling. Victor's head was whirling since this was not what he had expected when Julia asked him to join her.

"Yes, yes, I understand. You want to know it all. I understand," Cesar said, his voice quavering.

"And you, sir, are going to tell me the truth! No more lies!" Julia stood over his chair and placed her hands on the arms. She began to shake the chair violently back and forth while she said through clenched teeth, "Roberto's gone now, but you're not and I want some answers!"

Cesar stared at Julia, white-faced with fear, as Victor jumped up from his chair and pulled Julia away.

100

"Julia, stop it! You are scaring him to death. Get control of yourself!" he told her sharply.

"Oh, shut up, Victor!" Julia said flinging her arms out at her sides. "What do you know about my control? I'd like to kill him, so believe me, I am showing far more control than you can possibly know. And, as for you, old man," she said turning away from Victor and back to Cesar, "don't even think that I will be moved by your trembling and shaking in your chair. It won't change one thing for me. I don't have any pity for you. Do you understand? You didn't care if I was afraid. You didn't care how much I cried or begged. Did you?" she yelled even louder.

Overcome, Cesar bent over at the waist and started to swing from side to side with his arms wrapped around his body, moaning, "I'm sorry, I'm sorry. I didn't know. Not till years later. I didn't know what he had done. I didn't know. It's the truth, I swear it."

Walking away from him, Julia stood at the window watching the sunlight as it played among the branches of the trees and created patterns on the lawn. She had thought that if she could hurt him, punish him in some way, then it would take away some of her pain. It didn't. Watching him only made her more miserable and maybe he was telling the truth.

"I remember you," she said softly with her back still to him. "You were there and you helped him."

Pulling out a handkerchief, Cesar blew his nose. Sitting quietly for a moment he said, "I loved him. He was like a son to me and I owed him my allegiance..."

"Owed him!?" Julia interrupted flinging herself away from the window to face him again. "You owed him? What was I, just the payment of a debt! What about the others? Did you owe him their lives too?" she said through clenched teeth.

"You don't understand. I didn't know about you or the others when I helped him. I swear it before the Blessed Virgin."

"I remember. I remember that you helped him and you lied," she repeated very softly again.

"Yes, yes I did. May God have mercy on my soul. But, I'm telling you the truth. I didn't know what he had done! "

Victor was completely forgotten. Thinking that maybe it might be more appropriate for him not to hear any more of this conversation, he tried to discreetly leave his chair and go to the door. But that didn't work; Julia saw him.

"Victor, sit down," she said. "This is very important. I need you here. I can't do this without you. Please," Julia said as her voice broke.

"Of course I will stay if you wish," he said as he sat back down wishing he knew what the hell was going on.

"Thank you," Julia whispered.

The room became still and they sat that way for a while - each of them posed in the various areas of the room. A room that was changed from a moment before, by the coming together of the three of them and what had been said.

The betrayer, the betrayed and the unwilling witness sat alone. There was only a thread that held them together. A fragile thread, but a thread none the less, by which they were all inextricably bound.

After some time had passed, Cesar broke the silence.

"I know there is much that you want me to explain to you," he said in a small voice. "However, I ask that you please listen to this tape first."

Reaching into his pocket he pulled out a small black cassette tape. "Before Roberto died, he gave this to me and asked that I give it to you when you were strong enough." Smiling a little, he said, "I do believe you just might be strong enough now."

Pausing a moment, he continued, "In addition, I was to ask that Victor be present when you listen since it will be very painful for you, Julia, and Roberto did not want you to be alone. After you listen, maybe you can come to understand why Roberto did what he did and possibly you may be able to forgive him a little. As for me, there is no excuse and I don't ask for your forgiveness. I have known about the crimes that he committed, and how I unwittingly helped him, for some time now and I did nothing because he was so ill. For the part I played I am deeply sorry. For all the pain I caused you and the others, I will feel the burden of that on my heart for the rest of my days. I am here for you and I will do anything you ask to help make it right."

As he handed the tape to Julia, she asked, "What is it?"

"It is Roberto," he replied, "in his own words before he grew too ill to speak. I ask that you please listen with an open heart if you can. Now, with your permission, Julia, I will leave you and go home to Maria, who is anxiously awaiting my return. I will only be a phone call away and I will come to you immediately whenever you are ready. I will answer any and all questions that you may have of me at that time."

Julia sat very still looking at the tape in her hand, twisting it back and forth. Then she slowly nodded her consent and Cesar stood, with his head bowed, turned and left the room.

"Ah, Victor," she sighed as she sat in the chair behind the desk, "I don't know if I am strong enough for this. Will you stay with me while I listen?"

"Julia, why don't you wait a few days? Take some time, get your strength back. Even I am feeling unsteady at the moment."

"No," she sighed. "There will never be a good time. I believe that today is the day that I must hear the truth. I can't go on without knowing why Roberto did these things to the others and to me. I will set up the tape player."

Moving to the corner of the desk, she picked up the envelope that she had been carrying around with her and gave it to him. He noticed that her hand was trembling.

"Are you sure, Julia?" he asked looking at her face that was taut with grief.

"Yes," she said abruptly as she turned and began to busy herself getting the tape player ready.

The envelope held old newspaper clippings as he had expected. At first he did not understand what he was looking at and how the headlines he was reading and the pictures he was seeing had anything to do with Roberto or Julia. Then he saw the picture of her; she looked almost the same as the day he first met her.

He looked back at Julia and met her eyes. Something stirred in him. What was it? Looking back at the pictures, a named leaped out at him?

Elizabeth!

"Oh...no...," he said out loud. Then in silence, he thought, could Roberto have been responsible for something this horrible?

Victor raised his head and looked up at Julia's face again. Tears were sliding down her cheeks and he knew it was true. As he reached out to take her hand, she turned away and pushed the play button.

Chapter Twelve
Cassino, Italy – 1944

Click

"I was born in 1927 to Alfonso and Marguerita Bertinelli," Roberto said softly, the strain of speaking evident in his voice. "I am sixteen years old when my story starts and at that time, Italy was deeply immersed in war. My older brother Ricardo had been killed one year before in the conflict in North Africa under the direction of Erwin Rommel, Hitler's "Desert Fox". My parents were determined that they would not lose me too, so I was forbidden to enlist on any side. There were several sides to choose from, it later turned out.

"As you will see as I tell my story, there was much that I did not know and, because of this, the things that formed me were made from a child's perspective and made with too little knowledge about the events and tragedies that eventually shaped my life. I will tell my story through the eyes of the child that I was at that time. It would be a time when my life as I had known it would end and my innocence would die.

"Initially, Italy was pro-German, thus pro-Hitler, and had proclaimed their loyalty to the Third Reich. Benito Mussolini, *Il Duce*, was the dictator of Italy and a Fascist and, as such, was a particular favorite of the Nazis. As a child I did not understand the persecution of the Jews that was directed by Mussolini at Hitler's request. I only learned of this much later.

"I had a particular hatred for the Allied forces since I believed that they had been responsible for the death of my brother in Africa. So, it was with horror that I heard that Italy had surrendered within twenty-four hours of the first Allied attack on Sicily in September, 1943. By the time the news reached us, the Italian armies had deserted or yielded without a struggle and Mussolini was arrested by his own countrymen and placed in a small mountain resort in Abruzzi. The Nazi's would later overrun the resort with glider troops and kidnap *Il Duce* in a light airplane. But the

104

damage was done and Mussolini would never recover his direction of fascism in Italy.

"When I heard the news of our surrender, I ran home from the vineyard to talk to my parents. Finding them together, I had hurriedly told them how I must go and fight with the Germans. My mother didn't say anything, she just pulled her black apron up over her head, placed her fists against her eyes and started to cry. My father fixed me with a murderous look, but I was so caught up in my excitement that I didn't notice. When I continued to try to explain why I had to go, my father stuck me across the face, something he had never done. Then, he pulled me to him in a smothering embrace and begged my forgiveness. As he rocked me back and forth he said, 'We have given enough. One son is enough. You will not go. Let them kill each other, I don't care! We are simple wine makers. No, you will not go. Promise me!'

"And so I did. From that day forward, I never spoke to either one of them again about Italy's humiliation or my burning desire to fight against the Allied soldiers.

The enemy, who had invaded our country, consisted of Americans, British, Canadians, French, New Zealanders, South Africans, Poles, Indians, Brazilians, Greeks, Moroccans, Algerians, Senegalese, a brigade of Palestinian Jews and even a handful of Italians.

"Those Italians, who had betrayed our country and taken the side of the Allies during the invasion, I considered to be traitors. Looking back now, I realize I should have known that we could not win a war against the force of the Allies and that by surrendering, Italy may have done the only wise thing it could have done.

"However, Germany's answer to our surrender and betrayal was swift and horrible. Soon after the announcement of an armistice, Nazi headquarters ordered the immediate disarming of the Italian troops. Later we learned that Germany took approximately 640,000 Italian prisoners, the majority of which were shipped to Nazi internment camps.

"As the Allies advanced to Naples, the Germans, taking vengeance for our defection, destroyed the city. When the Allies finally entered Naples, the population was half-starved and the port and everything within three hundred yards of it was demolished. I tell you this now, but I did not know of this until years later.

"My home was in Cassino, just east of Anzio. The Germans had massed their troops in our town because of its location along the Liri and Rapido rivers. We were directly above the narrow valley leading to

Rome. To take all of Italy, you had to take Rome. The invasion of Anzio, on January 22, 1944, brought the Allies to our front door. They did not obtain the foothold they needed in Italy, because of their failure in Anzio, so they wanted and needed Cassino. The Germans were told to hold their position at all costs, so our small town became a war zone of its own.

"I was sixteen and my country was deeply embroiled in a war that it would lose, no matter which side won. I was filled with hatred for the enemy and I felt embarrassed and guilty that I could not go fight for my country like my other countrymen. And, in spite of all of this, I was in love.

"She was fifteen and tall for her age. We had been promised to each other from birth, as was the custom among families in Italy. My family and hers owned vast vineyards and this marriage would consummate the joining of our lands and fortunes. It was a long awaited union and one that greatly pleased both our families.

"She was beautiful and had long black hair that looked like silk. Fortunately for us, we were both very happy about the arrangement between our families and longed for the day when we would finally become man and wife. It was another custom in our village to marry early, so when she became sixteen, we would be wed.

"The day the Allies invaded Anzio, she came to speak to me while I worked in the vineyard, placing heating pots near the vines so they would not freeze. It had been a bitter winter so far and showed no signs of getting better.

'I am afraid, Roberto,' she said. 'We're between the two sides and we are going to be crushed. The Germans hate us since we have surrendered and as long as the Germans are here in Cassino the Allies will stop at nothing to gain our city. What are we going to do? I'm so afraid,' she moaned.

"She was standing at my side shivering in her coat so I took her in my arms and held her trembling body.

'Hush now, sweetheart. We will make it through this. The fighting will move away and we will go on as we have always done. Now tell me, have you finished your wedding dress?' She had been painfully sewing her dress by hand and although I had not seen the dress, since it was forbidden until our wedding day, my mother claimed it to be the finest gown ever made.

'No, not yet,' she said, 'but don't try to change the subject. You're just as worried as I am, so don't treat me like a baby.'

'But you are a baby!'

"The words were barely out of my mouth when she pushed me, knocking me backward into the mud. 'I am not a baby,' she exclaimed, 'and don't you say that I am. Why I'm almost sixteen years old!'

"As I fell, I grabbed both of her legs and pulled her down on top of me and began to tickle her through her coat. As she squealed I told her, 'You're my baby and I love you even if you are only a tiny infant barely out of her diapers.'

'Why you, you...' she said at a loss for words. 'Diapers? I haven't worn those for a very long time and I'm old enough to have babies of my own in diapers!'

'Yes,' I said as the image of her carrying our child swept over me. 'Yes, you are and you would have beautiful babies. Let's hope they all look like you,' I finished as I yanked her into my arms and began to kiss her passionately.

"She kissed me back with a fervor that took my breath away. 'Let's do it this time, Roberto. Let's make love, please. Make me your wife, now, here in the vineyard among the burning pots. Take me and make me yours.'

"I was caught up in my desire for her. Always she was the one who pulled back and stopped us when we became too excited. She was still a virgin and insisted that she wanted to be one when we married.

'No, not here,' she said. 'I changed my mind. Let's go to the barn. No one is there now. It will be warmer in the hay. Come on hurry,' she said.

"As she tried to drag me behind her, I stopped. 'No, no. Wait a minute, young lady. You're the one who has always told me that you wanted to wait until we were married. Why are you ready to do this now? Why today?'

'Roberto, come on, please. I know you want me, so don't stop now. Come on,' she insisted still dragging me by the arm.

'Tell me what is going on,' I demanded.

"Turning to me, her face pinched from the cold, she said softly, 'I'm afraid. I want to know you before anything happens to us. I want to be one with you. Don't you feel the danger around us?' Pausing for a moment, she took my hand and kissed my palm. Then she continued, 'There are no guarantees in a war like this. Let's live for today and forget about tomorrow. We may not have another chance,' she cried.

'Sweetheart, what are you talking about?' I said taking her into my arms. 'I will keep you safe. We will be married just like we planned. I promise. You have always been so proud that you are a virgin. I want to wait for you. Well, actually, I don't really want to wait for you, but I will,' I said jokingly.

'Hold me, hold me tighter," she said. Finally, she pushed back and kissed me on the lips. 'You're right, of course. I don't know what's wrong with me. Sometimes, I feel such a sense of dread and I can't seem to shake it.'

'Well, now that we are both a little calmer,' I teased, 'we could fool around a little if you wanted.'

'Dirty old man! That's what you are! You're just a dirty old man!'

"Laughing at me, she started to run and I chased after her, never telling her that I had a feeling of fear inside me too."

***

Julia slammed down the "stop" button on the tape player and jumped up from her chair. "He wanted her babies, but not mine," she said slowly.

Pausing for a moment she looked over at Victor and said, "I'm not sure I can do this. I don't know if I can listen to this or if I'm strong enough emotionally to hear about his life. Actually, I'm not sure I give a damn what his life was like. What does he think telling me this will accomplish. Does he think it will make me forgive him for what he did? Well it won't! This damned tape will not change one thing for me!"

Victor said nothing as Julia sank back down into her chair and turned to stare out the window at the garden below.

***

Carmen was baking an apple pie in the kitchen. She felt it was important to keep her hands busy with all the commotion in the house. She had almost fainted when the doctor had shown up looking like he had already passed on to the next life and, when he left, she could tell that he was very upset. Then later, Victor had come into the kitchen and asked her to make some tea for him and Julia. He was white in the face and she wasn't sure if he was going to make it back to the study with the tea.

When she asked him if he was okay, he hadn't even heard her he was so deep in thought.

Pounding the dough for the piecrust harder than she probably needed to, she raised the rolling pin, gazed at it for a moment and then started her attack again. She wondered what the next crisis would be. Not *if* there would be another crisis; she knew better than that now. It would only be when.

As she thought about what might be going on in the adjoining room, she slammed the dough down again and went back to work with her rolling pin.

"I hope you get whatever it is that is troubling you out of your system and you don't take it out on me," a voice said behind her.

Whirling around with the rolling pin in her upraised hand, Carmen squealed in fright. "Alejandro," she said, realizing it was the foreman of the ranch, "you scared me!"

"I'm sorry. I didn't know how to warn you so that you didn't end up cracking me upside the head with that weapon you have in your hand," he chuckled as he looked at the sight she made with flour in her hair and on her cheeks and nose.

Flushing, Carmen turned back to her work, "Well, what do you want? No, don't tell me, a flying saucer has landed on the ranch and you are here to tell us that all the cattle are gone, along with all the men and all the horses and......"

"Whoa...., Carmen, calm down. What are you talking about?"

"Oh," she said turning around and brandishing the rolling pin at him, "I suppose you think that something like that couldn't happen? Well, nothing would surprise me. Not anymore! Now," she paused, "I have work to do, so what do you want!"

Standing there mashing his hat in his hands he mumbled, "I was wondering if I might come by later and have a cup of coffee and a piece of that pie you're making, if it survives."

Carmen smiled and then turned. He was a fine looking man. A little old, she told herself, but a fine looking man. Blushing, she looked away and said, "I'll think about it, now get out of here!"

Pushing his hat back onto his head, he nodded and quietly left the room. Once outside, he took his hat off and with a loud whoop he flung it into the air. Inside the kitchen, he heard Carmen's laughter.

Chapter Thirteen
On the Beach
Anzio, Italy – 1944

Lieutenant Robert Walker thought he might be dead. It was completely dark; his eyes were open, but he couldn't see.

"I'm blind! That must be it. I'm blind! Oh no," he thought, as panic seized him when he realized that he was alive but all he could see was blackness around him.

There was dirt in his mouth and he could not get his breath. Something heavy was lying across his body. Reaching out he thought he felt someone's hand …it was cold and wet. As he continued to move his fingers along the arm he found that it was attached to a body lying across him. He clamped down on his jaw and held the scream in.

Opening his mouth to breathe, more dirt fell in and he started to choke.

"Where am I?" he thought, afraid to speak out loud.

He panicked again and tried to move out from under the weight that was crushing his chest. Pushing against the body, he realized that someone's leg was lying across his left shoulder. It was wet and sticky with something and there was no foot attached, just gore and bone. The wet of it was dripping and soaking the left side of his shirtsleeve. Grinding his teeth, he choked back his sob and tried to stay calm.

They were dead…he was in the ground with men who were dead.

He was buried alive!

"The Germans have buried me alive! Oh, God, no!"

He tried to calm himself and assess his situation like they had taught him at the Citadel. It had seemed much easier in training. Of course then, you just never believed anything like this would happen to you. Trying to gather the thoughts that were flying around inside his head like mad hornets, he tried again to focus on what he knew.

He knew he was injured, the pain in his left leg and foot raced like fire up and down his body each time his heart beat. He couldn't stay here much longer the oxygen was running out, so no matter what the cost he had to try to get out. That was first.

Moving himself slowly, he pushed and pulled at the dead men. Fighting the dirt and the bodies, he moved as silently as he could as he tried to dig himself out.

He was terrified, so terrified he wanted to cry.

He bit his tongue so hard he could taste the blood in his mouth. He was choking on the dirt and the gore.... he couldn't breathe. Were they still out there, could they hear him, did they know he was alive? Every muscle in his body was trembling and jerking.

After what seemed like an eternity, he was able to pull his head out of the dirt and gasp his first breath of air. Trying to move slowly, he lifted his head and listened. He couldn't hear anyone moving around. Taking a chance he moved a little more until he could see above the hole he was lying in. Looking around him he saw that the earth was smoking as if it had been on fire. Everywhere there were bodies and vehicles that had been blasted by the artillery the Germans had thrown at them. The sky was black with smoke and there was an eerie silence.

There had been two divisions that had landed at Anzio in hopes of surprising the Germans and outflanking their line. Most of those two divisions appeared to be dead. He did not see any Germans, only dead GI's. His men...his men were dead. The anger welled up in him. Somehow the Germans had known. His men never had a chance. Someone had screwed up!

Fighting back his anger, he lay very still, holding his position, trying to calm his breathing, but he still did not hear anyone. Pulling himself up and dragging his bad leg behind him, he crawled out of the hole onto the battle-scarred ground. Trembling and shaking, he vomited again and again as he let the horror of what he was seeing sweep over him. It appeared that everyone was dead...everyone but him.

Where were the Germans? He needed to get out of here, to try to find his unit and see if anyone had made it out.

But first, now that he was out of the hole, he needed to check on his injured men. Then he needed to find some medical supplies. The pain in his leg and foot was so bad he could hardly bear it.

He started crawling from man to man to see if anyone might have survived. There was no one. Shaking with exhaustion and fear he continued his search, losing hope that anyone else might have made it through the ambush.

As he crawled forward to another man, he realized it was the medic. There was no doubt that he was dead, one entire side of his face was gone. Fighting back the nausea, he searched the medical supplies looking for morphine. Finding an ampoule, he broke the seal and stabbed the needle into his leg through his pants. Lying down, he felt the drug move into his system. When the pain had been reduced to a level he could stand, he crawled on his belly, staying close to the ground, to continue his search. That was when he noticed that his ears were ringing loudly. The flash of fire and then the concussion of the blast that had thrown him in the air was all he could remember and it must have affected his hearing. He couldn't hear any sound. Hopefully, the Germans were all gone and he would make it out of here back to some of the other men.

He had been lucky; he knew that. The bodies that had been lying with him in the ditch and all the others were men who would not be going home again. They were his men...he was their leader. Sobbing now, he continued to search the craters that pockmarked the landscape from earlier artillery rounds. No one was alive; the craters were all filled with dead men.

The morphine was taking hold and he couldn't go on. Crawling up under one of the few standing jeeps that had come off the ship with them, he hid himself the best that he could.

As the pain left him and he started to drift, he thought of his mother and how she would suffer if he died and he didn't come home like he promised. He was so afraid - afraid that he would never keep his promise to her and would die here alone.

Then he thought of all the mothers of all the men who had laid down their lives today. Tears rolled silently down his cheeks.

Lieutenant Robert Walker was only twenty years old; and as he fell asleep, he knew only one thing. If he lived through this war, his life would never be the same again. It would be forever changed by this day; this day and the bodies lying all around him on a devastated beach in Anzio, Italy.

Chapter Fourteen
Cassino, Italy – 1944

Click

Julia turned the recorder on and Roberto's voice filled the room once again.

"Less than four weeks later," he continued, "the Allied forces sent over two hundred planes to bomb the Abbey of Monte Cassino, which stood on the massif above our town. Saint Benedict had built the monastery in the sixth century and it was considered a most holy shrine. The Allied forces believed that the Nazi's had set up outposts in the Abbey so they dropped leaflets from the plane, like thousands of large snowflakes, saying 'Against our will we are now obliged to direct our weapons against the Monastery itself. We warn you so that you may now save yourselves. Leave the Monastery at once.' We were not at the Monastery but it didn't help; the people in our town had nowhere to go. The Allies learned later that there were no Nazi outposts in the Abbey but the damage was done.

"As the Abbey was destroyed, only the cell and tomb of Saint Benedict survived, our town was hit again and again by the shelling. We were being obliterated in a cloud of flame, smoke and shattered stone. Every day we faced a landscape that resembled hell.

"My mother had always been a small woman with a fragile constitution. The trauma of the bombing and the constant reports of another neighbor dead or a friend losing a limb had finally taken its toll. About two weeks after the ferocious bombing of the Abbey, she fell ill. Our water supply was low and we were almost completely out of food. My father was bereft and would not leave my mother's side, so it was left to me to try to remedy our desperate situation.

"I knew that each day American fighter-bombers dropped brightly colored parachutes with canisters of ammunition, food and water to the

Allied soldiers who were isolated on the slopes surrounding our town and leading up to the Abbey. I had determined if I waited for a very windy day, that I might be able to watch for the landing and secure at least one of the canisters for my family.

"We sat in the light of the dying fire that burned in the fireplace of my home. As I placed fresh wood on the coals, the young girl I would soon marry spoke to me, 'I will go with you. It is far too dangerous for you to go alone. Besides, you will need help to carry the food and water back.'

'No,' I said emphatically, 'You will not go. It will be far more dangerous for me to have you with me than to go alone. I can move faster without you.'

'Roberto,' she pleaded, 'please listen to me. This is crazy! You cannot do this alone. I will not let you go by yourself. I am going! Please, don't fight me on this.'

"So we argued back and forth throughout most of the night. I knew her family needed food and water, too, but I felt that if I could go out several times each week, I could bring back enough for both our homes. Finally, in the early morning light she agreed that I would go alone.

"The place that was my destination was at a point not too distant from our homes. I had played there as a young boy, using it for my hideout away from the other children. I had built a small shack from old pieces of board in the shelter of old trees and underbrush. It was almost completely hidden from view in all directions and offered a place to hide if my plans did not go exactly as I planned.

"She helped me prepare several empty bags and some tools that I would need to dismantle the large canisters that were dropped. I would only take what we initially needed, hide the rest and return for it later. I dressed completely in light clothing, hoping to blend in with the snow that hung on the trees and coated the mountain ravines. I left in the semi-darkness with the thought that I could get most of the way to the shack before the sun came up. Once I was able to get the provisions into hiding, I would wait until dark to start my return. She and I kissed deeply and pledged our love before I walked silently into the snow-covered hills.

"I had walked only about a mile when I heard someone behind me. I ducked behind a small outcrop of rocks and waited. I saw her as she came creeping up from the last tree she had attempted to hide behind. She had followed me!

114

"Cursing silently, I waited until she was along side the place where I lay in the snow, then jumped up and grabbed her from behind, placing my hand across her mouth so that she could not scream. She fought me with a strength I never knew she had and it was all I could do to hold her.

'Stop! It is only me, Roberto.' 'Stop fighting me,' I hissed, holding my mouth close to her ear. 'If I let you go, do you promise not to make a sound?'

"When she nodded her head, I released her and dragged her to the ground behind the rock. 'What the hell are you doing here?' I demanded, trying to speak softly but strongly enough so that she would understand how unhappy I was to find her here, especially since we had agreed that I would do this alone.

'You scared me to death, Roberto. Couldn't you have let me know that you were there without making my heart stop! I thought you were one of the enemy soldiers.'

'And well I could have been,' I hissed. 'What are you thinking about walking around out here alone? Have you lost your mind?'

'Roberto, let's not fight. I am here now and there is nothing you can do. Now you will have to let me help you. Let's just go do it and get back!'

"Looking back at that morning, I realize that I made the wrong decision and a fatal mistake when I decided to let her stay. I should have gone back and tried another day but, since we were almost to my place hidden in the hills, I decided to go on.

"Cold wind and snow swept the jagged crags as we moved on toward our destination. It was one of the worst winters ever in Italy, with the mud wet and sticky during the day and hard like a diamond in the freezing nights. We fought our way through the bitter cold, hiding when we could.

"As we crossed through a small, cratered valley, we found the bodies of two dead Allied soldiers - scavenger dogs were tearing at their throats. Crying out, she slid behind me and held my coat up to her eyes. Pressing her face into my back and trying to stay in my footsteps, she let me lead her. Stopping a short time later she turned to me and said, 'Oh Roberto, why? Why is there so much death around us? It scares me so.' She cried softly in my arms and I did not know what to say so I held her and tried to comfort her. Finally, we moved on. We had almost arrived at my boyhood hiding place when I thought I heard something.

"A voice.

"A voice speaking in English.

'Damn,' the voice said.

"Dragging her behind me, we ducked down. My heart was pounding in my throat. It appeared that someone had found my tiny shack. Fear rushed through me. Could we turn around and get back? Did they hear us?

"Pressing my finger against my lips, I instructed her to be quiet as we started to back away from where the sound of the voice appeared to be coming from.

'Well, well, well,' a voice boomed right behind us. 'What do we have here!? Hey Walt, look what I found!"

"As we turned in fright, we saw an American soldier with a gun aimed at us. He was big in the way that men whose ancestors come from Norway are big. He had blond hair that was cut very close to his head and massive shoulders and legs.

"Another man approached us from the side, also carrying a weapon. This man was even bigger than the first. He stood at least six and one half feet tall, a giant of a man. Where the first man was blond, the man named Walt was swarthy-looking and had piercing blue eyes. With his coal-black hair and coloring he could have easily been mistaken for a southern Italian if it weren't for his size.

'Aieeeee... Chi...hua...hua!' he shouted. 'What do you have here? No stinkin' Krauts... no sireee. No couple of Heinies, no way. You found us a couple of Eye...talians! Whoooeee!... and one of those Eye..talians is real pretty too,' he said as he jerked her out from behind my back.

'Let her go,' I yelled as I pushed him away from her.

'Private Broderick, get a grip on him, will you,' commanded the man named Walt who still held her by her arm. The blond man pushed me back with his rifle and left it pointed against my chest.

'Back up! Don't be stupid! We are not going to hurt you. *Capisce*?' he said as I staggered back.

"The dark man jerked her scarf off of her head and all her beautiful hair spilled out in waves across her face and down her shoulders.

'*Mama Mia*,' he whispered stroking her cheek, 'you sure are beautiful, little one.'

'Don't touch me, you pig!' she spat, knocking his hand away.

"Grabbing her by the back of her head and pulling her toward his face he said, 'Ah, a little spit-fire too, huh? *Bella! Bella*! Yes, you have done good Broderick. You have made my day!'

116

"I could understand only parts of what they were saying and fear washed over me when I realized the dark one's intent. Lunging at him, I knocked the gun away that the blond man had against my chest and hit the dark man hard with my shoulder, forcing him to let her go. As he flailed his arms to try to keep his balance, the blond man struck me on the side of my head with his gun. As the blackness swam over me I crumbled to my hands and knees. My head was ringing and I couldn't see. I struggled with all my might to fight against the wall of darkness that surrounded me and the pain that caused great beads of sweat to pour from my body.

'Roberto, Roberto, no…no. You have hurt him. Let me go,' I heard her scream.

"I tried to focus my remaining energy in my legs, but I could not stand. Somehow she got away from them and threw her arms around me.

'You have hurt him! He is bleeding, you bastards!' she screamed. 'Roberto, Roberto," she sobbed. 'I love you. Please…help me. I'm afraid.' Tears were streaming down her face. I tried to speak but the words would not come. Placing her fingers against her lips, she kissed them and placed them on my lips, in the way that we sometimes said goodbye.

"Before I could hold her she was ripped up off the ground and slung over the dark man's shoulder.

'No-o-o' she screamed in a high-pitched wail. As I tried to get to my feet the blond man placed his boot in the middle of my back and forced me flat against the ground. Then he placed his rifle against my left ear. My head was turned away from the shack, so I could not see what the dark man was doing to her. I cried out in anguish as I heard her repeated screams.

'Watch him, private, I'm gonna take our little wild one and have some fun with her. I hope she's a real fighter. I love it when they scratch and bite. Do you want to play sweetie? Sure you do,' he said as he walked away with the screaming girl.

'I don't know, man," the blond man said after him, 'I'm not sure this is a good idea. They're just a couple of kids. I think we should just let them go.'

'I don't care what you think. I'm tired of this war and I need a little fun. You can have her after me. Now watch him,' he commanded, pointing at me.

"She was fighting and screaming as I struggled against the blond man's boot, I cried out in anguish. The next blow from his rifle knocked me unconscious."

Click

* * *

Lieutenant Robert Walker and Sergeant Tony Ramosa had heard the screams. They were situated behind a rock ledge and were edging forward to determine the cause.

Walker had awakened on the Anzio beach and heard groans coming from one of the craters. After pulling the dead men away, he had found Ramosa dazed with a mean head wound that stretched from eyebrow to eyebrow and across one full side of his face. Walker had wept with joy at finding another person alive. He had wept with relief because he was no longer alone.

After Walker cleaned and bandaged Ramosa's head wound, the soldier appeared to be okay physically. However, sometimes he would stop and stare at nothing for a long period of time then, blinking, he would come back to reality. Walker knew that emotionally Ramosa was close to going over the edge, just as he was. The horror of being buried in the pit and all the death around him had left a blank look in his eyes.

Ramosa tore strips of cloth from the dead men's uniforms and tended to Walker's foot after cutting away his boot. His movements resembled a spastic scarecrow and his hands trembled uncontrollably as he worked. From that day forward to the last day that Walker saw him, Ramosa never spoke a word to anyone. It was as if all the words he would ever speak again in his lifetime had burned in the flames and died and were buried in the craters alongside his fellow soldiers.

Using his rifle as a makeshift crutch, Walker had hobbled over to a jeep that Ramosa had been able to start. They had been headed to find other friendly troops and to get medical attention when they had heard the screaming. Earlier, they had come across a squad of German soldiers and had barely escaped being noticed when they abandoned the jeep and huddled on the ground, half buried, behind a mound of snow. Now they were taking no chances.

Crawling on the ground to avoid any further injury to his foot and to conceal his movement, Walker edged his head around a large rock. He saw a soldier standing in front of a ramshackle wooden building. He was one of theirs, a GI. There was someone on the ground directly in front of the soldier who appeared to be a young boy, a civilian. The boy's face was turned toward them and it was covered with blood. Walker could not tell if he was alive or not. He could hear a woman screaming in Italian and the voice of another man coming from inside the lean-to.

"Private, you should feel this. She's so tight, young and tight. Oh, man, I don't know how long I'm gonna last. This little bitch is so sweet... Ahhh... Yes, fight me. Come on! Fight me," he taunted her, "fight me!"

"Hurry up, man," the other soldier hissed through his teeth. "Hurry up! I think I heard something. Come on man, let her go!"

"You're gonna love this one man. I promise you. Just hang on! I'm almost done."

"I'm telling you to get out here. I think I heard something. Do you understand? We need to get the hell out of here. Hurry the fuck up! I'm freezing my balls off out here. Let's go!"

The soldier outside the small shack was pacing back and forth, sniffing the air like an animal trying to find the scent of the enemy. He held his gun up ready to fire.

Walker slid to the other side of the rock abutment and pulled himself up to a standing position while Ramosa angled in from the other side. The soldier had his back to Walker so he did not notice him. Very calmly and quietly, Walker said,

"Put the gun down, soldier, and step away from your weapon."

The soldier's face paled as he whipped around to face the voice. Without thinking he aimed the gun and fired at Walker. His bullet missed. Walker's did not. The soldier died in a pool of his own blood.

"What the hell is going on out there?" a voice inside the shack said. When he appeared in the doorway, he had a young naked girl in front of him. He was holding his left arm under her throat. He had a large shiny knife in his right hand and it was pressed under her chin.

I will never forget her eyes. They were large and dark, filled with fear and pain. I didn't know her age but she looked very young. I glanced at Ramosa, whose face was filled with hatred. His jaw was clenched so tightly he was almost purple in color.

She had been beaten in the face. One eye was completely swollen shut and purple tinged; her lip was cut and bleeding. Her skin was almost blue from the cold and she was shivering uncontrollably. There were small puckered bloody marks on her breasts and stomach. At first I could not tell what those marks were and I was filled with disgust when I realized that they were bite marks. He had bitten her repeatedly with such

119

force that she had bled. Her inner thighs were also covered with blood and it ran down her legs onto her feet. My heart was crushed.

Ramosa and I trained our guns on him. "Let her go," I said hoarsely. "Drop the knife, let her go and step back."

She begged me for help with her eyes. "Don't let me die, please help me," her eyes screamed.

"Hey, Lieutenant, you want to try her out?" he grinned. "She's a real hellcat and tight...Whoooeee! Is she ever tight. Here, she's yours. I'll give her to you."

"This is an order, soldier! Let her go, drop the knife and step back!" I shouted.

"Hell, I ain't gonna let her go. What's one little Eye..talian gonna matter. No one's gonna know and no one's gonna care!"

"I'm giving you a direct order, soldier. You're facing a court martial. Don't make it any worse. Now step back! Do it now, soldier!"

She was struggling against him now, panic sweeping over her face. Somehow she knew.

Laughing, he said, "She ain't gonna tell nobody if she's dead!"

Before either one of us could react, he slashed the knife across her throat and tossed her aside and onto the ground. Shaking from exhaustion and the image of her eyes - the way the light left them when he ripped the knife across her throat - I screamed, "Drop the knife, put you hands behind your head or I'm going to blow your fucking brains out, scum!"

With one fluid movement he threw the knife and it lodged in my shoulder. Ramosa and I both fired at the same time. The soldier was dead before he hit the ground.

Using my last bit of strength, I hobbled over to the girl. Ramosa was already there holding her in his arms and crying piteously. Her eyes were blank and she was staring out at something we could not see.

"There is nothing we can do," I said, "she is gone. Let's find something to cover her with."

Ramosa went to the shack and found her coat. Covering her gently, he came to the place where I had fallen to the ground. As he pulled the knife from my shoulder, I screamed. For the second time that day he took strips from a dead soldier's shirt and made a compress and pressed it into the wound. Then he wrapped me the best that he could to prevent any more bleeding. He looked at me when he finished bandaging my shoulder, and at first, I thought he might speak. I could see the emotions warring in his face and the gratitude in his eyes. When he squeezed my hand, I knew it was his way of thanking me for trying to save the girl's life.

"See about the boy, Ramosa.....see about the boy," I whispered.

He was alive but unconscious. His head wounds were serious but he would survive. Ramosa set about trying to waken him.

A squad of American troops found us a short time later. I was in pretty bad shape by that time. I had lost a great deal of blood and my vision was blurred with images swimming in and out of my sight. The commander got the story from me since Ramosa still could not speak. The sadness and the pity he felt for me was marked across his jaw, as he clenched and unclenched his teeth, grinding them together, when I told him all that had happened during the last eighteen hours. The look on his face was almost all I could bear, so when I finished talking and he turned and looked at me, I refused to meet his eyes.

For a few moments he examined my foot and shoulder and did not speak. Finally he said, "Son, you're probably going to lose your foot. I'm sorry. Sorry as hell for it all," he finished as he gazed around at the carnage.

I turned my head away and let the tears fall. "A foot?" I laughed. "A foot? I'm going to lose a foot?" I laughed hysterically. Then I broke down sobbing. They couldn't understand. They didn't know that I had lost my soul in the eyes of a dying girl or that my shattered heart was left on a smoking beach in Anzio. I was just a shell now. During the last eighteen hours...I had lost me.

***

Click

"When I regained consciousness," Roberto continued speaking, "the first thing I noticed was the sound of many voices. Dizzy and disoriented, I tried to raise my head from the ground.

'Be still,' a young man said. 'Take it slow. Lie still for a few more minutes.' He was speaking to me in Italian but I could see that he was one of the American soldiers. 'You are wounded but you will be fine if you just take it slow,' he continued.

'The men,' I mumbled since my tongue didn't seem to work, 'the men, they took her.' The world tilted and blurred as I tried to get up.

'They are both dead. Do not be afraid. They won't hurt you now. We are here for you and we will help you get home. Just rest for a while until the dizziness goes away.'

'Where is she? Please tell me. Is she all right? The dark man he was hurting her. Tell me… tell me…..,' I cried as my speech failed me.

"A man, who didn't look much older than me, came forward, using a rifle for a crutch. He was an American and he was injured. Lowering himself down beside me on the ground, he looked at me and his eyes were filled with tears. It was then that I knew. Howling in anguish, I rolled violently from side to side. 'No, no, no, please God not her. Please……no…,' I begged.

"After a while I asked to see her. 'First,' the wounded soldier said, 'you need to know what happened to her so that you are prepared.' Softly, he told me all he knew while the other soldier interpreted in Italian.

"I lay on the ground in the freezing cold wishing that I had died instead of her. Why? Why? Why? was all that I could think of. She was so sweet and innocent. Why her? Finally, when I was able to stand, they took me to her.

"She was covered with her coat. Pulling it down, I looked at her tiny sweet face and dissolved in a fit of grief so strong that I thought my heart would crack in two. Holding her broken body, I screamed out her name. When I saw the wound to her beautiful throat and all the marks and blood on her body, I was filled with a hatred so strong that I could feel the fire from it burn a path across my heart. Laying her body down, I staggered away a short distance and vomited repeatedly. Then I sank down to the ground and lay there whimpering from weakness and despair.

"When I could finally stand again, I went to her body and placed her into her coat, then gathered her up into my arms for the long walk home.

'Wait,' the soldier who had spoken to me in Italian said, 'let us help you. We will take you wherever you need to go.'

"I did not answer him; I just turned with her body in my arms and looked at all their faces, one man after the other, so I would never forget any of them. They were my enemy, they had brought great pain and suffering to my country, they had killed my brother and now they had taken the girl I loved. Hatred bubbled inside me as I spit on the ground and turned my back on them.

"When I started to walk the several miles back to her home, the soldiers followed me. Even the man named Walker, who was injured, refused to ride in one of the jeeps and he hobbled after them trying to keep

122

up. After a time, I saw two of the soldiers stop and make a sling, from the two dead men's jackets, and place him in it so that he wouldn't have to walk. Staying back a respectful distance, they thought they paid honor to my loss and my pain. I hated them and wished them all dead with every step I took.

"On my journey back, the grief, exhaustion and the pain in my head would drive me to my knees where I would collapse against her body. Each time I fell, the soldiers would stop behind me and stand with their helmets removed while the snow, which was falling steadily, covered their bare heads. Time would pass – I don't know how long – and finally I would struggle to my feet, holding her broken body against my chest, while my limbs trembled violently and the tears froze to my cheeks and mixed with the blood from my wounds. When I would start to walk again, they would place their helmets back on their heads and follow me.

"It seemed like an eternity passed as I fell and stood and groped and cried, and they watched silently, but finally I entered her village. Somewhere, it seemed to come from a great distance, I thought I could hear the villagers calling to each other to come and see. When I noticed they were pointing behind me, I turned and saw the soldiers standing in formation. Raising their arms in unison they offered me a salute and, after holding that position for a moment, they turned on their heels and walked away. The wounded soldier who had been placed in a sling, and who I now realize probably saved my life that day, held his salute until the troops passed out of sight.

"After the last man could no longer be seen, I turned and stumbled. As I fell, I heard a great rushing wind roar through my head. Several of the men who had gathered to watch, ran to my side and offered to carry her. I shook my head to say no, so they helped me to my feet. Staggering to gain my equilibrium, I walked on.

"Her mother was the first to see us. The sky was filled with her high piercing shrieks when she realized that her daughter was dead. I'm not sure how I managed to keep walking. The roar had changed to the sound of several trains pounding across tracks, which ran inside my head, and I could barely see, my vision was so blurred. Her father was suddenly in front of me and as I lifted her lifeless body and placed her gently into his arms, the blackness engulfed me and I plunged headlong into oblivion.

"I don't know how long I slept but I had no dreams that I could remember. When I wakened I was lying on a small cot that had been placed next to a warm fire in the kitchen of the house. My head was pounding again and flashes of red and white lights streaked across my eyes as I rose from the makeshift bed.

"I found them in her bedroom. They had washed her body and dressed her in a clean white nightgown. The destruction to her face was marked by dark purple bruises that stood out in stark contrast to the rest of her skin that appeared to have been bleached of all color. The covers were pulled up to her chin so the terrible wound to her neck was not visible. Her hair had been washed and arranged on her pillow. Her father was seated in a chair beside the bed and he was stroking her hair, lifting the strands and letting them slide through his fingers.

'It's okay, baby. Don't worry. Mama and Poppa are here now. No one is ever going to hurt you again. You rest now, we won't leave you,' he said over and over.

"Her mother was completely calm now and sat on the floor next to her husband's chair with her hand on his thigh and her head resting against his leg. She did not speak.

"I noticed the white dress that was hanging on a dress form in her room. Clouds and clouds of white material inter-laid with what appeared to be thousands of white seed pearls is the image that was left in my memory that day. Even now, after all these years, I can close my eyes and still see that dress. The dress she had hand made and that was to be worn on the day we publicly declared our love before God and the church. Like me, the dress stood silently; waiting for a wedding that would never be.

"Her father noticed me standing in the doorway. 'Come to me Roberto, my son, come to me,' he said softly. Kneeling down beside him, I looked directly into his wife's eyes. I don't believe that she could see me. I had seen animals that had died with their eyes wide open and they had the same look. Turning away from me, she stared back at her only child who lay dead on the bed. She had told me many times that she couldn't wait until we were married so that we could give her grandbabies to hold; grandbabies that would look just like her beautiful daughter. Now, all such dreams lay broken and dead just like her only child.

"Her father took my hands in his and said, 'Thank you for bringing our baby home to us. You have our eternal gratitude. We are ready now to hear what nightmare has brought this pain into our home. Please, if you can, tell us what you know. We want to hear it all.'

"As I told the story, stopping when the grief caused me to be unable to speak, I saw him visibly age. The twinkle and the fire he had always had in his eyes just faded away. Her mother did not look at me or comment through the whole telling of it.

"When I finished he wiped the tears from his eyes and pulled me to him and, placing his head upon my head, we wept together. Finally, he faced me and said, 'You are my son now just as you would have been if you would have been married. All that I have is yours. All my land, all my wealth, I give to you. When we are gone, it is all yours. Roberto....., Roberto......,' he stopped unable to speak. 'My wife and I cannot give you our daughter now,' he paused again, choking on his tears, 'but we give you our hearts.' As he said this, his wife turned to me and placed her hand across her heart. In a symbolic gesture of taking it from her chest, she placed her hand in mine. Her father did the same.

'Now, my son, there is nothing you can do here for now. You need to go home. We have heard that there has been heavy bombing in your area. Go now and see about your family.'

"And so I did. They stood in the doorway and waved goodbye as I walked away. It would be the last time that I would ever see them.

"Later that night, after I left, they poured gasoline and kerosene all over the house. Then while her mother lay on the bed beside their only daughter, her father leaned over and kissed the cheeks of both of the women that he loved more than anything in the world. Then he sat down beside them and struck a match.

"I was weak and injured so it took me a while to travel the distance back but as I neared my home I started to run. All at once I was overcome with a desire to see my parents' faces and to feel their arms around me. When I crested the hill above our place I saw that all that was left of our home was rubble. Fires were still burning here and there among the roof beams and partially standing walls. Our neighbors stood a safe distance away watching. Screaming for my mother and father I ran toward the crowd and what was left of my home. Two of the men blocked my path.

'No, Roberto. It is no use. They are gone. We have tried to go in but the fire is too hot. There is nothing anyone can do,' one of my father's best friends said as he stood with tears falling unashamedly down his face.

'Let me go,' I yelled as I struggled in his arms. 'How do you know? They might still be alive. I have to get them out!'

'No. Your father made it out but when he didn't see your mother he ran back in. We tried to stop him. When he found her we heard him screaming her name over and over and then a few moments later we saw him with her burning body in his arms. As he tried to get out, the remainder of the roof fell in and they were trapped beneath the large beams. There have been no sounds since then.'

There was a long empty space on the tape as Roberto paused, then he spoke directly to Julia saying, "Julia, you must forgive me but I must stop for a moment for I am overcome by the emotions I felt on that day."

After a time he continued to speak. "There is something that you need to know; something that will help you to understand a piece of the puzzle that I left you. You may wonder why I haven't mentioned the name of the girl I loved. I left it out intentionally. You may have guessed by now………

Her name was Julia."

Click!

***

Julia stopped the recording. She doubled over in her chair and started rocking herself back and forth. I went to her chair and kneeling down beside her, pulled her off into my arms. I sat down on the floor with my back to the wall and held her. All she said was, "That's why he named me Julia. It was her name."

As I sat there, holding her, emotions I could not define left me shaking. Roberto had named her after the girl who had died when he was just a boy.

The woman I was holding was not named Julia!

Was her name Elizabeth?

What have you done Roberto, I thought? She loved you for almost twenty years of her life.

What have you done?

Chapter Fifteen

It was several days before I joined Julia again in the study to continue listening to Roberto's tape. During that time she had started getting up at dawn and running several miles before breakfast. When she arrived back at the hacienda she would be soaked in sweat. After pulling off her running shoes, she would sit at the edge of the cliff looking out over the pampas before she came in to eat.

I wondered then, as I have wondered many times in the years since, where all that courage was hidden in her body. She was then, and still is, the strongest, most courageous woman I have ever known. The tragedy of her life is one that few of us could have endured. Ah...but there is so much more to tell.....so much you don't know.

***

Click

Roberto's voice seemed weaker now and over the next several days, as we listened, you could hear the difference as his illness took its toll. I was filled with pain for the boy Roberto had been and what he had had to endure. But it was still unclear to me how this all tied to the woman I knew only as Julia, and she wasn't talking. I would be devastated by the time I learned the truth about her life.

"My life was over and I did not want to live," Roberto said weakly. "I believe now that it was only my hatred for the Americans and my desire for revenge that kept me from taking my life during the month following the death of Julia and both of our parents. My neighbors would find me wandering the streets at all hours and would take me home with them. After feeding me, they would offer me a bed. Sometimes I would stay a night or two and then I would wander off again until another neighbor would find me and take me home.

"One morning when I awakened, I found Father John sitting on the stoop outside the house where I was staying. He was a man of average height with a slender build. With his very black hair and deep blue eyes he was considered very handsome. Or so I had heard the village women and girls say when they were pondering why someone so desirable had chosen to be a priest.

"Smiling up at me from where he was sitting, he motioned for me to have a seat beside him. Doing as he asked I sat down and he put his arm around my shoulders. 'Roberto,' he started, 'I am sorry for your pain and suffering. This war is a terrible thing, but you cannot let it break you. There is a purpose and a reason for your existence. Your survival after all the terrible events you have endured is a miracle. I know that you do not believe this now but it is true and you must go on.'

"Pausing a moment he continued, 'Julia's parents have left all that they owned to you. Her father brought a large metal box to the abbey with instructions that it and all its contents, plus all of their land and their winery, were to go to you if he and his wife were to die. As you know, they took their lives later that same day. I blame myself for not being there for them when they needed me the most.' Pausing, he took his arm from my shoulders and crossed himself murmuring, 'May God have mercy on both their souls'. Then he continued, 'Between your inheritance from your parents and now this gift, you are a very wealthy young man.'

"The young priest sat silently looking out into the distance as he absently rubbed his hands up and down his black trousers. 'Your father's brother, your Uncle Gino, lives in Argentina. I have written him on your behalf explaining your situation. I have a letter I received from him today. He is most anxious for you to come to live with him. You are his last living relative since the recent death of his wife and baby daughter during childbirth. The news of your father's and mother's deaths has hit him very hard at a time when he was feeling very lost and alone. I will leave the letter with you so that you can read it yourself. It is a very emotional writing so wait until you are ready before reading it.'

"Turning to face me, he said, 'Roberto, maybe together you and your uncle can both find the strength to go on. Maybe you can help him live and he will not be so desperate. Maybe by helping him, you can find the peace and the healing that you need so that you too can go on with your life. I think you should go. I will miss you as I miss your parents and Julia and her mother and father and all the others I have lost from my little flock of lambs.'

128

"Looking away from me, I saw the tears form in his eyes and I saw the pain that he suffered because there was so little he could do in a world that had gone mad. It was a short time before he fought back his emotions and could speak again.

'This is a terrible place now. It is almost as if God has forgotten us and left us with no hope of being saved. You should go. I will help you.'

"Standing up, he smiled down on me and said, 'Think about it, Roberto. There is nothing here for you but painful memories. Go and start a new life somewhere far away from here; away from all of this.' As he spoke he waved his hand in a wide circle taking in the land in all directions. 'Come to me at the church at any time if you decide you would like to go.' Placing his hand on my head he spoke very softly, almost in a whisper, 'I will pray for you'. Then he turned and walked away.

"After reading my uncle's letter, I went home that day, back to the place where I had run and played as a small child. The place where I had been loved as some children never are loved, by parents who thought the sun and the moon rose in my eyes.

"Standing in the midst of the blackened ruins, I said goodbye. Then I went to Julia's home and did the same.

"I went to Father John the next day. Dressed as a young priest, I was able to move across the borders with him and finally arrived in Spain. We traveled mostly by boat and sometimes on foot. What appeared to be huge sums of money would change hands and then another fisherman would take us to the next port or another farmer would allow us to ride on his cart to the next town.

"In Spain, I left the priest to continue the rest of my journey to Portugal alone. I had not spoken to him during the long and arduous trip. Even when he hugged me goodbye on our last evening together, I could not speak. As he prepared to leave he asked that I pray for him and that I support the Roman Catholic cause when I prospered, as he was sure that I would prosper greatly. I could only nod to indicate my promise, then he turned, waved back over his shoulder and walked away.

"I arrived in Argentina after a very long ocean voyage that lasted almost three weeks. I had been seasick most of the first week and had only barely gained my sea legs when we docked. My uncle Gino was there to greet me. He was a large man like my father and he wept and squeezed me so hard that I almost fainted. Yelling to everyone he knew, my uncle told them, in a form of Italian that was interspersed with Spanish, that I was his nephew; and wasn't I a fine looking man; and shouldn't they all be so lucky to have such a fine looking nephew and on and on. He did this while slapping me on the back so hard I would almost fall, or by squeezing me in his massive arms and choking the breath out of me while swinging me in wild circles. I had to smile, in spite of myself, he was certainly exuberant and I could not help but like him.

"It was a strange land that I made my new home. Icy mountains and flat rolling grasslands marked the terrain of my uncle's ranch in Cordoba. Animals I had never seen roamed this beautiful and lonely landscape. All in all, I found that it suited me.

"I started out working in the vineyards, which was natural since that is where I had worked since I was a small boy, while my uncle worked his cattle ranch. Somehow between the work, the long sunny days watching the grapes grow and his worrying about me while I worried about him, we made a life together.

"Sometimes the pain of losing Julia and my family would become too much to bear and I would leave and wander the pampas, camping out at night under the stars with just a blanket for cover and my horse for company. My uncle would always wait a few days and then, under some pretense or another that I was needed back at the vineyard, he would find me and bring me home.

"It was months before I really started to speak again, but he never questioned it, and somehow we managed to communicate without my words, during that dark time when I wondered, from day to day, if I would just be able to keep breathing in and out. Often, I would find him sitting on the porch of my cabin when I arrived back at the end of the day. I would sit beside him while he told me stories about my father's and his lives when they were only boys, or about his wife and the baby they had wanted so much, and how much he had loved her gentle ways, and how much he missed her laughter even now.

"As time went by and I grew into a man, I never tired of Uncle Gino's stories; stories that helped me heal. Over time, I would sometimes speak of my life before coming to Argentina. Only once did I finally manage to tell him about that horrible day when my life was shattered. When I was finally able to speak those words to him, I felt the weight ease a little off my heart. The pain, at last, became easier to bear.

"Over the years we fell into an easy rhythm. It was during the time of Eva and Juan Peron and the bloody wars in 1973 that my Uncle Gino became ill. Within a few months he was dead and my world was rocked again. It had been twenty-nine years since that day in Cassino and I was now forty-five years old. I had never married and very rarely dated, so my uncle's death left a huge void in my life. Since I was the only living relative, all my uncle's wealth became mine. When I moved into the great house on the *estancia*, my loneliness slowly increased.

"Each morning while drinking my coffee, I would read all the international newspapers from front to back. I had investments of my own and now with my uncle's, world news was crucial to my overall future planning. It was in late June, several months after my uncle's death that I first saw you.

"There was a picture of you in the New York Times. You were standing and holding a small baby girl in your arms while holding the hand of a young boy who looked like he might be about four years old. Your husband stood beside you. I hated him immediately. He represented one of the pompous, supposedly God-fearing, Americans who had stolen my life from me.

"Your beauty stunned me, as it still does to this day, but what struck me the most then was your absolute resemblance to Julia. You were the same height and build and, though you were older, you had the same hair, eyes and face. At first, but for only a moment, I thought that Julia had somehow survived and that she wasn't really dead. I tore the article from the paper and started carrying it with me wherever I went.

"The more I looked at your picture, the more obsessed I became. Julia and I would have had children. Why should this American man have you and his children when I didn't have either? Why should he have the love of a beautiful wife? Hatred and envy drove me deeper and deeper into despair.

"Your name was Elizabeth Grant and you were thirty years old. Your husband, David Grant, was an advisor to the U.S. Trade Commission. You and your children, Alexandria, aged six months, and your son Brian, who was three years old, were to accompany David to France where he would participate in a trade mission with the French government. The article went on to say that you would be leaving for Paris, France in early August, which was about five weeks away.

"During the next two weeks, I stopped eating and I could not sleep; the rage and the anger ate away at me night and day. Thoughts of you drove me mad. I relived Julia's death over and over until I was manic in my obsession for revenge. About three weeks before you and your family were to leave for France I made my decision. The Americans had taken Julia's life. I would take yours!

Click

***

Julia stood and started pacing the room. Her hands were clenched at her sides and her face looked like a storm was crossing it. Suddenly, she ran to the fireplace and grabbed up the poker and started swinging it. Screaming, she broke the lamps and smashed the tables while sweeping everything off in a violent motion that sent broken glass and splintered wood flying. Victor sat still and just let her do it. When Carmen ran into the room after hearing the commotion, he signaled to her that she was to do nothing to stop Julia. When she finally grew tired and dropped the poker, Julia bent over at the waist and started to laugh. Carmen and Victor were frozen in place.

"God, that felt good!" she said. "I'm sorry, but that felt so damned good, I can't believe it! I think I will go for a run now before I really go amok and do more damage than I have already done. But, I have to admit that it really, really felt good! You know Victor," she said turning to me, "you might want to try this poker thing, because it's just not good to keep all that stuff pent up inside. Sometimes you just have to grab up the old poker and just let it rip!" Suddenly she was shrieking with laughter. Then her face crumbled and she walked rapidly from the room with her fists pressed against her lips

***

Julia ran and ran, pushing herself harder, pounding the ground relentlessly; pushing herself beyond her limit. She didn't want to think. Finally, her legs would not support her any further and she could not go on. Collapsing to her knees, she tried to breathe. Her lungs felt like they were on fire as she struggled to take oxygen in. Trembling and jerking, she rolled over onto her back and tried to calm her racing heart.

She was in anguish and her tormented mind would not let her rest. What about my children, she thought? Do they believe that I'm dead? How are they? Are they healthy? Are they happy? The questions swirled in her mind. Placing her hands across her eyes, she scrubbed at her face. The emotions of loss and the pain of remembering were slowly breaking her. Ever since she had seen the picture from the newspaper that Roberto had kept all those years, and the memories had come flooding back, she had been slowly breaking apart.

Fear was the worst part. She was fifty years old and she was so afraid, she could hardly function. Her children did not know her and probably did believe she was dead. She had been gone from their lives for twenty years. Roberto was not her husband and he was dead now and she was alone. And what about David, the man who had been her husband and the father of her two children? He was probably remarried by now and believed that his young wife was dead.

"Oh, David, David, how are you?" she said out loud wishing she could see his face and tell him that she was alive.

Then she thought about her parents. Were they still alive? They would be old now if they had lived. Would they even recognize her if they saw her? Would she recognize them?

There was so much to think about but the thoughts of her children pushed all the other thoughts away and she was suddenly swept back in time to the smell of baby powder and pink chubby cheeks and baby skin that was as soft as velvet. The power of these feeling caused a wave of agony to roll over her. Oh, how she wanted it all back! She wanted those years that she missed as they were growing up. She wanted to hold her babies again. "Damn you, Roberto, damn you, I want my babies back!" she moaned as she pounded her fists on the ground beside her.

Then she cried. She cried for their little hands and feet and the way they smelled and Brian's tiny voice when he called her mommy and all those tender moments when she had held them in her arms and rocked them each to sleep. She cried because it was all gone and she would never get it back.

Victor stood silently in the shadow of a tree and waited. He understood part of it now and his heart was broken for her and the family she had been forced to leave behind.

When Julia wore herself out and cried herself to sleep, as the sun was starting to dip toward the horizon, he went to her and lifted her off the ground into his arms. When she stirred and started to protest he whispered to her, "No, Julia, let me be your legs this one time, let me walk for you. Let me carry you and your burden down the road so you can rest just for a little while. For a few moments you don't have to carry it alone. Let me take you home. Let me help you."

Julia heard his soft reassurances spoken in whispers and, because she had no more fight left in her, she let go and went back to sleep.

***

Late that night, Julia slipped into the study with a cup of hot chocolate in her hand. She had expected to find the room empty and she intended to finish listening to the tape alone, but when she entered she found Victor sitting before a small fire drinking a glass of brandy.

"What are you doing here, Victor?" she asked very softly.

"Waiting for you."

"You knew I would come?"

"I knew you would come," he replied.

As Julia sat down next to him in a chair opposite the fire, Victor thought about how much he loved her. He loved all that she was; her beauty, her grace, her strength and so much more. He watched her through hooded eyes as she sipped her drink. He was madly in love and it was hopeless. It always had been. He tried to purge her from his soul. But even the suffering and guilt that he felt because he wanted her, that forced him to leave Argentina while Roberto was alive, had not stopped him from wanting her every day more and more as the years passed. Passion? Yes, he acknowledged to himself, that was certainly a part of it. But, she aroused him even when she was sitting silently, not moving, as she was now. It had always been a painful cross to bear.

Most of the time, when he came into her presence, he would back out of the room he had just entered and say something stupid - like he was in a hurry to get somewhere, or he had forgotten something and needed to go find it. Or, worse yet, there were those times when he had to sit and hold something over his lap, while he blushed and tried to distract her attention from his bulging trousers. He smiled softly to himself. Yes, she had made his life very complicated. But, he loved her and there was nothing he could do to change it. She thought of him just as a friend and he would take her friendship, if that were all he could have. Julia's voice interrupted his thoughts.

"Victor," she said, "why do you keep trying to save me? Why do you care so much?" Without waiting for an answer, she continued, "You have been a guardian angel to me over and over. I want you to know how much I appreciate all that you have done for me and to tell you that I love you for it. You are a wonderful man and someday a woman, a very, very lucky woman, is going to be blessed to get you for her husband. I pray that you are showered with happiness and love for all that you have done for me."

Victor did not speak. She did not know that her words had cut him to his soul. As Julia looked at him, she noticed for the first time how gray his eyes were and that you could see tiny flecks of black scattered throughout his iris and then she noticed his mouth. His lips were full and looked so soft; shaking her head she continued to speak, "Do you remember the night of the funeral when you dragged me back from the cliff?"

"You mean the night of our mud fight? The night you showed me just how good your aim was with a mud ball?" he teased.

"Yes," she laughed, "that night."

"Yes, I remember," he said softly.

"I'm sorry. I'm sorry I acted so badly. I know I caused you enormous worry then. I know that you are still worried, but I don't want to die anymore. I....I......," Julia choked back her tears.

Victor set his drink down on the table next to him turned and took her hand into his. "Julia, please don't say anything. You don't owe me, or anyone else, an apology. You've had to endure a great deal. Besides, what red-blooded man would not enjoy rolling around in the mud with you?" he laughed as he winked and rolled his eyes suggestively.

Julia smiled at him. Tears were hanging like diamonds in the rims of her eyes. Trying to change the subject, Victor asked, "By the way, young lady, have you been raiding the kitchen?"

"What?" Julia said, not understanding for a moment what he meant. When he indicated her cup, she wiped absently at her eyes and said, "Well, no, not really. I happened to notice that Carmen was awake and working in the kitchen so I went in to tell her some of what was going on with me. I felt like I owed her an explanation for my actions after tearing the study apart today. It was a very emotional talk, as you can imagine. You know how she worshipped Roberto. I left many details of the story out, but even so, we ended up crying together. After that she insisted that she make me a large cup of hot chocolate to make me feel better. And, even though I didn't want it, I didn't have the heart to refuse. I was barely able to convince her that I didn't want the large piece of pie that she also wanted me to eat." Laughing she added, "I swear, if she bakes any more bread, cakes, cookies or pies, there will be no space left in our kitchen!"

Victor laughed too. "Yes, as far back as I can remember, she bakes up a storm every time there is crisis in the family or she is upset about something. She flings flour everywhere and it looks like the middle of a snowstorm there is so much white dust flying around the room. And, of course, Carmen never seems to notice that she is also covered from head to toe with flour and looks like an apparition springing up out of the mist. It can be pretty damned frightening," he chuckled.

Julia laughed. "Yes, that is a very good description of 'Our Lady of the Flour' who now resides in our kitchen and is intent on baking until every room in the house is filled."

As they laughed together, and then sat quietly sipping their drinks, there was a peace between them that covered the room. Finally, Julia sighed and said, "Victor, I need to finish this tape. I need to find out about my children and my family. It is the only thing that gives me the strength to go on. But first, I want to release you from your promise to stay with me. I know how much you loved Roberto and I know how hard this must be for you. I can do this alone if you want to stop now."

"No, Julia. I need to know. I want to understand what happened, so that I can reconcile the man I thought I knew with the man that I obviously didn't know. A man, it seems, who was capable of incredible cruelty," he muttered softly. "I would like to stay," he finished.

"Of course," Julia said, "but you must understand that the remaining story will be very difficult to hear. I only remember some of it and I know that it could shock and disturb you. You must prepare yourself for the emotional toll it will take. I am trying to be strong but even I don't know how I will react once I know the whole truth.

"You have done so much for me, Victor, and I can't expect you to keep saving me and dragging me back from the edge. You have been acting as if this is not tearing you apart, but I know differently. You must remember that I have known you a very long time and I see your true feelings no matter how much you try to hide them."

Oh, Julia, Victor thought, if you only did know my true feelings. How I long to take you in my arms and hold you next to my heart and never let you go. How I would never hurt you, or deceive you, if you were mine. How much I wish I could wipe away all the pain and betrayal from your eyes and make you laugh again.

Of course, he said none of these things and answered, "It is true that I don't know what comes next and yes, most of what I have heard has been confusing and painful. But I will not leave you to face this alone. I have no delusions that this will be easy, but if there is going to be a firestorm or a walk into hell that results from listening to the remainder of Roberto's tape, then let's do it together."

Julia smiled at Victor and then she leaned over and kissed him on the cheek before turning away. "Okay," she said, "if that's what you really want to do. I just want you to know that you are my champion and my hero."

Victor watched her as she walked to the tape player and he wished for more; so much more.

Chapter Sixteen

Click

Roberto's words, sometimes spoken in a whisper now, flowed out into the room.

"Over a period of many years, I had arranged for my family home in Cassino to be rebuilt. It was a beautiful place and although I visited Italy several times a year, I never stayed long since the memories gave me no rest when I was there. Most of the neighbors who had lived near our home had died during the war or had moved away, since the city had been almost completely destroyed by the bombing. As a result, my home was not only quiet and restful but it was also secluded. Large olive and pine trees surrounded the main house and they offered cover for my comings and goings. There was also a rather substantial out-building where I kept various gardening tools and a small tractor.

"I had ample room for the van that I bought to use in your abduction.

"The temperature in August would be brutal, but I planned to keep you in the cellar below the house where it should be more comfortable. I had not thought about what I would do after this but I knew I would never return to Cordoba. In the back of my mind, I believe I had accepted that I would take my own life once you were dead.

"I arranged for everything I would need; black clothing, black ski mask, drug filled syringes to subdue you, a bottle of chloroform, a large army-issued silver knife, food, water and a special double lock for the cellar door. I actually whistled while I set it all in motion. The demons that had haunted me for all my life were finally set free and went gleefully about their work and left me alone. I was happy for the first time in many years and slept each night through. My private yacht, which I had used for my trip from Cordoba, sat idly by with a small crew who waited for my return to start our voyage home. They didn't know that this time I would probably not return.

"The day before I was to leave for Paris, when all my preparations were completed, I went to the land where Julia's home had stood. It was a beautiful sunny day and I longed for the Italy of my youth when I was surrounded by all the people I loved. My loneliness was so tangible I could taste it and it left a bitter taste in my mouth. Nothing mattered anymore. Soon it would all be over. Just a few more days I told myself, trying to find comfort in that thought.

"I stood looking at the land that lay silent beneath the clear blue sky and I marveled at the large, rolling meadow of wild flowers that grew and blossomed in abandon where her home used to stand, and then I smiled. At that moment I knew that the land understood death and loss so much better than we ever could. Each year the earth paid homage to Julia, by bringing forth hundreds of bouquets of flowers to lay at the place where her soul had found its final rest.

"The gentle blossoms bent and swayed with the whisper of the wind and I was lost in sadness for all that had been taken from me so many years before. I cried for her that day; a deep wailing that came up from the depths of my soul; a pain so horrible that it tore apart any resolve I might have had to turn back. Sometime later, when the sun was only a soft, reddish glow on the edge of the horizon, I promised Julia again that I would avenge her and all of the others in our family that had lost their lives at the hands of the Americans. Then I left for France.

Chapter Seventeen
Paris, France - 1974

"I arrived in Paris a day before you and your family. I had learned that you would be staying at the *George V Hotel* on the *Champs Elysees*, so I rented a suite at the *Hotel des Tuileries*, on *rue St.-Hyacinth*. It was a small but luxurious hotel several blocks away from you, but still within walking distance. It is said that Marie Antoinette's first Lady-In-Waiting had formerly owned the property and that Louis XVI had stayed there with the Queen. Since this particular hotel was one of my favorites, I had been a frequent guest over the years and had become friendly with the staff. They would not find it unusual that I was in Paris for a few days.

"Not knowing what to expect or how I was going to accomplish your abduction, I decided to follow you as you moved about the city. Twelve fat avenues made up what was known as the star (*etoile*) of the *Place Charles de Gaulle* and the *Arc de Triomphe* was located at the center. Your hotel was adjacent to the busiest avenue of the *etoile,* the *Champs-Elysees,* which moved an enormous amount of vehicles filled with travelers and sightseers each day. Airline offices, car showrooms and bright, light shopping arcades dominated the upper end of the avenue, but there was also the *Lido* cabaret, *Fouquet's* high-class bar and restaurant, several cinemas, and outrageously priced cafes, so there was something for everyone. The other avenues that made up the central portion of the *etoile* were filled with huge apartments that were empty most of the time since their owners, usually royal, banished royal or just very rich, were out of the country vacationing at their other residences around the world.

"Paris was a city teeming with people and antiquity and one that I usually loved to visit. This time I found I could not enjoy it, but I saw that you did. You smiled as you walked with your nanny, who pushed your young daughter in her baby carriage, and your son, who you sometimes carried when he became too tired to walk. I enjoyed those days as I followed you and tried to find a pattern in your routine.

"It was a very rare occasion when you were actually alone, which made my planning more difficult and I worried about how I would make it all work. There was only one constant that I noticed after following you for several days. Each morning, after kissing your husband goodbye on the steps outside your hotel, you would go to the *Parc de Monceau* with your children. If this held true, I felt I might be able to take you and escape very quickly from the city since the park was in a wonderful location with large avenues leading away from it. The *Boulevard Courcelles* bordered it on the north and the avenue *Velaquez* bordered it on the east. The park had a roller-skating rink and plenty of room for children to play, as well as gardens with antique colonnades and artificial grottos, so there were many trees and vegetation for cover.

"In this park, many of the people who were at the heights of finance in France had been pushed in their carriages by their nannies when they were infants. I wondered if you knew about this when you arrived and your nanny pushed your young daughter in her carriage, while you and your son played together and explored the gardens. The times I watched you walk hand in hand with your son, while holding your baby daughter in your arms, made me feel some emotion I could not describe. There was an ache deep inside me that would cause me to turn away for the day and return to my hotel. I would have to give up my silent vigil shadowing your steps as you wandered the city, peeking into the shops or stopping to buy an apple that you shared with your little boy, because something painful would twist in my stomach and I could not stand it.

"I did not realize the depth of my feelings, until one morning several days later when it rained. I stood in the soaking downpour for hours wishing and hoping that you would come to the park, as if those two emotions would make you somehow miraculously appear. On the one hand, seeing you each day filled the vast emptiness I felt deep down inside me, while on the other hand it caused me great pain, but I needed to see you. So, I just stood there silently with the rain pouring down my face as the passerby's huddled under their umbrellas and looked at me as if I were a madman, which of course I was.

"The next day, when the rain had stopped and I arrived at the park, you were there. I was so excited to see you that my heart started to pound in my chest and my hands started to shake, as I took my usual spot on the park bench, where I would sit and pretend to read the paper each day, while surreptitiously watching you. My hands were trembling so badly that I thought you might notice the way my paper was jerking and grow suspicious but you didn't seem to notice me, you were so caught up in teaching your son to fly a kite.

"After you had the kite high in the sky and it was circling slowly, you allowed your son to hold the string in his tiny hands. A few moments later a strong burst of wind pulled the string through his fingers and the kite lifted and spun away. When he cried you hugged him to you tightly and carried him in your arms to the swings, and although I could not hear the words you said to comfort him, he finally quieted.

"He sat in your lap with his back against your chest while you held the chain of the swing with one arm and him with the other. Your bare legs hung down and you pushed the two of you back and forth with one foot. Sometimes you would reverse, lay back in the swing, and push hard which would cause you to spin in circles. Your son started to laugh and giggle as you twirled him around and around. As you leaned further and further backwards, your long hair would brush the ground and you would laugh with him and it would light up your entire face.

"Your body was painted with the shadows of moving leaves that flickered and danced as the sun and the wind played hide-and-seek between the branches of the trees. I could have stayed there forever looking at you, I was so lost in the picture you made and in the kaleidoscope of emotions that washed over me and made me feel faint. When you both were very dizzy, you stopped the swing and attempted to run hand in hand to the pond. You were like two drunken friends and I smiled as you lurched crookedly from side to side. Finally, you fell down on the grass and held hands as you looked up at the sky. Seeing and feeling the love between you and your son, I almost changed my mind and turned back from what I had planned. But… as you know…I didn't.

***

"I checked out of my hotel the next day and spent the day wandering the city. I did go to the *Parc* later that morning, but I avoided you and your children and went instead to a small art gallery, the *Musee Cernuschi,* which was located in the park, but far enough away from you that you would not notice me. It was a favorite gallery of mine; one that I visited whenever I was in Paris. A wealthy banker had bequeathed it to the state after nearly losing his life for giving money to the wrong side in the war. It was a small gallery, but it was filled with ancient Chinese art that was breathless to behold.

142

"When I left the gallery, I continued walking through the city and I filled my day with the sights and sounds of the Paris that I had grown to love. When it grew dark, I went to Doctor Fernandez' home, which was closed down for the summer. I had asked him if I could keep a car at his residence since it was so difficult to find parking in the city. He had readily agreed and even offered me the use of his beautiful chateau, both of which he would not have done if he had known my real intentions.

"I had made the decision to take you the next day if you came to the park as you usually did. It killed me each time you went home to your American husband. He didn't deserve you. I would leave him your children but you were mine!

"There was no going back now; I had to do it because I had to have you. You were mine and you belonged to me and I would have rather been dead than to let you go. So, I stayed awake all night that night preparing the van for your unwilling passage and then working out the route that would take me out of Paris and back to Cassino. The drive would take between twenty to twenty-four hours since it was over nine hundred miles and I would have to try to stay awake for the long and stressful journey.

"Since I had never driven this distance without sleeping at least a few hours, I decided to prepare dark, thick coffee in the morning before I left for the park. I also knew I would have to keep you quiet until I got out of the city and across the border into Italy, so I placed a bottle of chloroform and a handkerchief in the pocket of my jacket in order to sedate you.

"The border between France and Italy was not guarded but I didn't want to take any chances that you might cause some disturbance that might alert someone to your presence in the back of the van. This might happen if you were just tied up but still conscious. It was unknown to me how long the drug would keep you asleep or how long you could be asleep before it became dangerous to your health; little things for which I did not have any back-up plan.

"However, mistakes or not, now that I had made the decision to commit the crime, I was in a frenzy of anxiety for morning to come. I can tell you that I never thought about the fact that if I failed I would end up dead or in prison for the rest of my life. Nothing mattered; I had to have you; you were mine.

"I went to the park early the next morning and parked the van close to the area where you and your son played most of the time. It was near a large pond and your little boy was always mesmerized by the antics of the frogs, so both of you spent a great deal of time sitting very still, close to the edge of the bank, watching the frogs leap back and forth among the lily pads. The spot was hidden out of the direct sight of your nanny and usually it was deserted by the other early morning Parisians, those individuals usually preferring the jogging paths and the strolling carriage lanes. I did not know exactly what I was going to do or how I would manage to get you to the van, but as it turned out, it was easier than I expected.

"I had just found a place on the grass and was sitting sipping my coffee and pretending to read my paper, when you arrived with your son's hand clutched firmly in yours. You were dressed in a simple white cotton dress with white sneakers, with no socks, and your hair was unbound so that it swirled and swayed as you walked. There was a white soccer ball in your hands and you and your son were having a lively, animated conversation. There was a large grassy area to the left of the pond where I supposed you intended to play ball. I was dismayed since I did not know how this change of events would affect my overall plan.

"When you looked up and saw me sitting on the grass, I could see you hesitate and start to walk away. I almost jumped up to run after you, but instead, I calmly waved, said good morning in French and indicated with a flourish of my hands that you would not bother me if you played with your son. These gestures somehow reassured you, so you began the game by kicking the ball softly to him while he chased after it with his little legs and attempted to kick it back. His kicks were rather erratic and you were sent running this way and that, back and forth across the grass.

"You never looked more beautiful than you did when you yelled your encouragement to your little boy each time he kicked the ball straight. Or when you held your hands up to your face, to cover your smile, when he missed the ball entirely, lost his balance and tumbled to the ground. I watched you secretly, by peeking over the top edge of my paper, afraid to breathe too hard, afraid I might miss my opportunity. Thankfully, it was not very long before that opportunity presented itself to me in the form of a ball that flew past me when you kicked it a little too hard.

"Your son raced after it as it headed toward the street and you started to run after him screaming his name and begging him not to go out into the street. When he was close to me, he stumbled and fell and I pushed myself up from the ground and scooped him up into my arms. He was frightened and surprised by my grabbing him and he began to struggle, pounding me with his little hands and crying for his mommy.

144

"When you ran up to where we were standing you held out your arms and said, 'Shush, Brian, it's okay. Mommy is here, hush now.' You were looking at me strangely as if you sensed danger. Speaking to me in French, you said, 'Thank you very much but please put my son down.' When I did not do as you asked, I saw a flash of fear in your eyes. 'Please,' you repeated as you stepped closer to me. When you approached another step closer I said, 'Certainly, I'm sorry' and I placed him on the ground at my feet.

"As you stooped down to take him in your arms, I grabbed you from behind and placed the chloroform over your mouth and nose. As you struggled - you were much stronger than I had anticipated - you pulled your face away from me and moaned, 'Run, Brian! Go to Nanny! Hurry, baby……..'

"But, by this time, I had you again and the chloroform was stronger than your will to get away and your body went limp. I ran to the van with you in my arms, opened the door, placed you inside, slammed the door and then jumped in and drove away as quickly as I could; trying not to draw too much attention to myself. As I looked in the rear view mirror, I saw your little boy standing there with a stricken look on his face and I could see him mouth the words, 'Mommy! Mommy!' Then he turned and ran away as fast as his little legs would carry him back toward your nanny, who had just come around the grove of trees that protected me from view.

"Adrenaline caused my heart to slam against my ribs and I began to shake violently, so it was difficult to concentrate on my driving. I was elated and could not believe my good luck. I had done it! You were mine now! That is all I could think about.

"As I was congratulating myself, I suddenly felt cold and fear pierced my heart like a shard of glass. What had I done? Was I crazy? The world was going to be looking for me and I was going to be caught. How could I possibly think I could get away with this? You were an important man's wife and they would leave no stone unturned in their search for the madman who had done this horrible thing. I should take you to the nearest safe place and leave you on the side of the road. But, first I had to get away from Paris. That seemed to make sense to me, in my demented state of mind, so I decided to leave Paris and then let you go.

"It was almost three hours later before I heard you moan. Those three hours had seemed like an eternity. I had looked over the back of the seat and in my rear view mirror at least a thousand times trying to see if you were still breathing or if I had killed you. Several times I had considered stopping and leaving you beside the road where someone could easily find you, but I couldn't make myself do it. What if someone found you and did you some harm? It would all be my fault for leaving you helpless and unconscious.

"When the irony of what I was worried about finally hit me, I began to laugh and I laughed until tears poured down my face and I became hysterical. After my laughter died, I started to cry as the horror of what I had done swept over me. I felt like I had fallen into a black cloud and had been hit by a lightning bolt. My nerves were jumping inside my skin, bright lights kept leaping across my vision and I was drowning in a rain of panic and tears. I stared up at my face in the mirror and I was surprised to see a man of normal appearance looking back at me. Somehow I thought that a madman with an evil, sick, tortured soul, a man who could take a young, helpless woman against her will and submit her to terror, would look like a hairy beast with fangs who howled at the moon.

"As I cried, I knew that what I had done to you would not settle any score or mend any tear in my heart or bring me any peace. And…I was desolate.

"However, as quickly as these emotions ran through me and as the storm in my soul raged on - you must remember that I was truly mad and like all mad men my thought processes were a tangled web – it was only a few moments later when I began to feel differently. It all happened when I stopped the van, in the shade of a huge stone pine tree at the edge of the roadside, out of view of the traffic, in an effort to regain control of myself. After walking back and forth for a while, I opened the van door and looked at your sleeping face and a feeling of warmth and peace flowed over me. Like a purge it ran through me and it pushed all the pain, sorrow, guilt, shame and any common sense that I had left, down and out of my body.

"You were lying on your back with one arm flung up over your head. Your legs were slightly splayed and, because your dress was twisted and thrown up over your waist, I could see the edge of your white lace panties. I tried to stop myself from what I did next but I was too dazed by your stillness, your beauty and the fact that you were unconscious and therefore you could not resist me.

"There was tremendous power and euphoria that came from knowing that I could do anything I wanted. So, I moved my fingers slowly up along your long, silky legs and under the edge of the lace. As I ran my fingers back and forth, touching the soft mound of hair and feeling the

146

heat that came from the center of you, I became fully aroused.   Taking my hands away, I unbuttoned your dress and began to explore your body.

"You were beautifully made. Your olive complexion, pink nipples and the black patch of hair between your legs made you a voyeur's dream. You smelled like the air after a morning rain and it was all I could do not to take you at that moment. But, when you cried out softly, I pulled back, rearranged your clothing and walked away from the van. I could smell your musk scent on my hands and I wanted to plunge inside you and lose myself in your hot wetness. I struggled with myself, fighting back the demons, and in the end I found that I could not rape an unconscious woman.

"But… I wanted to.

"I paced the perimeter of the van and I thought about my situation. I knew that it wouldn't be long before you were completely awake. So, after I knew I was in control again, I took a rope and tied your hands behind your back, after rolling you over onto your side. Then I bound your feet. I did not gag you since it would be some time before we reached the border and the roads we would be traveling were fairly desolate.

"Having to touch your body again, to tie you, however, took its toll. I was trembling all over when I finally started to drive again. It was almost two hours later when you spoke to me from the back of the van.

'I have to go to the bathroom,' you said.

"Your voice had startled me out of a near death experience since I was almost totally asleep at the wheel and headed toward the edge of the road, which had a steep drop several hundred feet down. I turned to look at you and you were staring straight into my eyes.

'Okay,' I said. 'It will only be another few minutes before I can find a place to stop. It will have to be outside somewhere and I will have to help you with your clothes because I will not untie you.'

"You blushed and turned away. You did not speak again until we stopped. I wondered what you were thinking and how afraid you must be.

"I pulled off into a heavily wooded area where it was secluded and out of anyone's view from the road. 'I will untie your feet so that you can walk,' I said as I opened the van door. 'Do not try to run or I will hurt you and I will never untie you again. Do you understand?'

"You nodded yes, so I motioned for you to walk in front of me. I was carrying my knife to threaten you but I knew I would never use it even if you tried to escape. After we had walked into the tall grass a few feet away I asked, 'Would this be okay?'

'Yes, but could you please untie my hands?' you asked.

'I'm sorry. I cannot. But I will help you.'

"As you stood very still, I placed the knife against your abdomen and pulled your dress up and stuffed it into your neckline. This left you naked from the waist down except for your underclothes. As I knelt in front of you, I could feel you trembling beneath my hand. I looked up at your face but you had turned away. Very slowly, I pulled your panties down and told you to step out of them. I could feel your hesitation but after you complied, I pushed the knife further down your body near your groin. Your were truly shaking now as I took my free hand and ran it up and down the insides of your legs. 'You are so beautiful,' I said, but before I could continue I felt a hot stream of liquid rain down on me. Yelping, I jumped backwards and scrambled to my feet.

"When I finished wiping my face and I looked at you, the muscles in your neck were straining from your anger. 'Don't you ever touch me like that again or I will kill you,' you hissed through your teeth. There was no doubt in my mind that you would, if you could. I smiled at you and this only made you angrier, but I loved your spirit. This was exactly what my Julia would have done.

"Jerking your dress back down, I placed your panties in my pocket and said, 'You won't be needing these anymore and if you try that again I may not stop the next time you ask me to. Now get in the van!' With that, I roughly pushed you forward and after you were back in the van, I retied your ankles.

"After we had pulled back onto the highway and driven for a few miles, I remember quite well the sun was starting to fade from the sky as your words shook me to the core saying, 'Are you going to kill me?'

"Startled, I hesitated before I answered you. I could hear your voice trembling and I could feel your fear and, although my heart broke for you, I could not lie.

'I don't know,' I said.

'Are you going to rape me?'

'Probably.'

'Will you ever let me go?'

'No.'

"You were very quiet for a moment and then you said very, very softly, 'Why are you doing this?'

"And I answered without pause, 'I don't know anymore.'

Chapter Eighteen
Somewhere in France - 1974

Elizabeth came awake slowly, climbing through a smoky haze. She could not lift her arms because they were too weak and they were tied behind her back. She remembered the man, so she tried to lie very still with her eyes closed so that he would not know that she was awake. The drug he had given her, plus the movement of the van that she was lying in, was causing her stomach to roll. As she fought the nausea, she prayed she wouldn't be sick. She needed to think and plan but she was so frightened that she could hardly breathe.

Even with her eyes closed she could still see his face in vivid detail. She could feel him grabbing her and feel the fear that crippled her when she knew that she was losing consciousness and that she couldn't fight him anymore. Until she managed to escape, she would try to memorize his face and everything about him so that when she was free, she could help the police find and capture him.

She knew that his hair was very dark and that he wore it a little longer than most men did, that he was tall and broad shouldered and that most people who happened to meet him would consider him handsome. She was confused about what he had done to her; he had seemed so nice. Why? What did he want? Fear caused her to grimace.

Forcing herself to relax, she looked around and noticed that her son was not with her in the van. That probably meant he had gotten away. Before she had lost complete consciousness, she seemed to remember that the van was moving and she was alone. She prayed that she was right.

Because her wrists and ankles were tied, she was starting to lose her circulation in her arms and legs. She needed to go to the bathroom and she needed a drink but she was afraid to speak.

Fear was causing her teeth to chatter. She tried not to cry but the tears squeezed out from under her eyelids and ran down her face onto her neck and into her hair. She wanted to live. She wanted to see her children and her family again. "Please let me live. Let someone find me and take me home. Don't let me die. Please.....," she prayed as the tears poured from her tightly closed eyes.

Chapter Nineteen
New York City -1993

Rosita stood at the altar of the old Saint Patrick's Cathedral. She was dressed in white, which was certainly blasphemy under the circumstances, and she was not listening to the ceremony. Looking down, she smoothed her white linen suit and thought about what had brought her to New York.

For several years she had taken acting lessons. No one but her parents had known. They thought it was just a young girl's foolish daydream so they smiled, gave their approval and opened their purses and paid the astronomical fees without a word, never realizing how intent she was on actually becoming an actress. Those years she spent in drama school were part of a plan she had to make Victor notice her and fall madly in love with her when she finally became a famous star on Broadway.

Those dreams all crashed and burned but the skills she gained during that time were going to pay off for her. First, by winning a small role in a very popular soap opera and, secondly, here today when she would play the hardest role of her life, the blushing bride.

She had auditioned and been accepted for the part of Gina in the soap opera, "Another Day", which was one of the longest running shows on television. It was a small part but she was already getting more lines and walk-ons since her fan mail had become almost as large as the reigning queen of the show, Lauren Prescott.

Lauren and Rosita had taken an instant dislike to each other; each for their individual reasons, Lauren because Rosita was beautiful and very talented and Rosita because she wanted to take Lauren's place and was ready to do anything to get it and Lauren knew it. Lauren had been with the show for almost twenty years and had grown up on television while her fans watched. But at forty-two, even with the benefit of plastic surgery, she no longer looked the part of a young woman. As such, her role was becoming more and more the part of a matronly, older woman.

Lauren hated it but was smart enough not to let the producers know. They had added Rosita to the show, in almost the same part that she had made famous years before, and Lauren understood that her position was now threatened by this new arrival on the set.

During the first few months, a bitter war developed between the two of them that was fought behind the scenes as they sized each other up and the battle lines were drawn. Rosita had to be very careful and never let her guard down. Many times she did not receive the script changes that Lauren had made and Rosita was forced to adlib the entire scene that she played with the older star. The first few times this occurred, Rosita was so angry that she thought about going to management to complain. But, she didn't and, much to her astonishment and to Lauren's chagrin, Rosita somehow always played her part perfectly, knowing instinctively what to say or do, while the viewing audience fell madly in love with her and her character. Everything Lauren had tried so far had backfired and she hated Rosita now with a burning passion. Rosita, however, wasn't worried because she had learned that management knew what was going on and had taken a hands-off approach and left her to deal with it on her own. So far she had done so beautifully.

Rosita's thoughts drifted back to the ceremony where the priest was droning on and on about how love was eternal, blah, blah, blah. She wished he would just get the damned thing over with. As she glanced at the man who would soon be her new husband she was surprised to see that he was actually very handsome. She wondered why she had never noticed his tall frame and broad shoulders; then she shuddered. He had made love to her many times or at least he had thought they were making love. She had acted out the part, whimpering and pretending that it was the most wonderful thing that had ever happened to her. Not that most women wouldn't find him a wonderful lover. He was incredibly endowed and took his time trying to please you, but of course, it all made her sick to her stomach. She couldn't stand him touching her and after today she wouldn't have to go through that anymore! Of course, like most men, he wouldn't understand and would probably have his feelings hurt but she didn't care. He would just have to get used to the fact that his wife was never going to sleep in his bed again!

Rosita's train of thought was interrupted when she realized the priest was speaking to her.

"Excuse me, I'm sorry. What did you say?" she said softly with her eyes downcast.

153

The priest smiled, thinking that she was like so many other brides before her; probably just a little nervous. He cleared his voice, "I said, will you have this man to be your lawful wedded husband, and with him live together in Holy Matrimony pursuant to the laws of God and this state and will you love him, comfort him, honor him, and keep him both in sickness and in health, and forsaking all others keep you only unto him so long as you both shall live?"

Rosita smiled brightly at both the priest and the groom, who was beaming from head to toe, and said, "Why, yes... yes I will!"

Chapter Twenty
Cassino, Italy – 1974

Click

"It had been almost three months since you had become my unwilling guest and my obsession," Roberto continued. "You were everything I had ever hoped to find and more. When you walked, taking long purposeful strides, it made me think of the times I had seen the world's top models on ramps in Paris or New York. Of course you were oblivious to your beauty and grace. I was completely enthralled by the way your eyelashes brushed your cheeks when you lowered your eyes, the way you moved your hands whenever you spoke and your soft sigh when the breeze would blow the smell of the flowers over you as you strolled in the garden. I was very happy, but all was not well.

"The first few months, you tried to make the best of your situation. But as each day went by, I could see the despair you felt just by looking into your face. The fire that used to burn so brightly in your eyes was growing dim as you realized that there was no escape and that no one was coming to rescue you. This realization was choking out your will to go on, and I was causing it.

"I knew about the picture of your family that you hid beneath your mattress. I wanted you to keep it because I believed it brought you some comfort. I could see now that I was wrong and the picture would have to go. Through it you were clinging to your past life and you needed to realize that that life was gone forever and that I was never going to let you go.

"You had made some progress, but it was very slow. Once in a while you still insisted that your name was Elizabeth when I called you Julia. Most of the time now, instead of immediately correcting me, you would stop to consider before you answered and I could see your confusion as you tried to cling to the name Elizabeth. I spoke to you hundreds of times each day and always I called you Julia. I think you grew tired of trying to correct me and sometimes it wasn't worth the effort, so you just let it go. Other times I could tell you were not sure what your real name was.

"Each day I would allow you ample time for bathing and you always took all of your meals upstairs in the main dining room. You seemed to enjoy this very much. The evenings were cooler now, as the months of fall came and winter approached. So, after dinner, we would walk the perimeter of the garden or sit and talk quietly until late into the night. Those were magic times for me and the longer we were together the more I fell in love.

"At first, you would beg me to let you go and you would promise me almost anything in return. But now, as the days gathered upon themselves and you grew more despondent and afraid, you didn't ask me anymore and most of the time now you refused to speak to me when we were together.

"Each night, when you thought I had locked you in and gone upstairs, I would close the door but I would not go up. Instead I would sit at the top of the stairs. I prayed you would not cry, but each night you did. I sat through the long hours, until you cried yourself to sleep, wishing it could be different and that you could find some happiness with me. After a while I would go and stand by your bed and look at you while you slept. I wanted you as much as I have ever wanted anything, but I didn't just want you sexually. I wanted your love. For this reason I could never force myself on you. Watching you sleep, I dreamed of a lifetime together, but I didn't know what to do to break your hold on your past life.

"Over the many days, you grew thinner and more fragile. Your skin lost its lovely dusky glow and you became very pale. I could see your veins under your skin, particularly those that throbbed in your temples. I cursed myself for what I was doing and I tried to make myself give you up and let you go, but, I was deaf to what my heart told me.

"Other times, more sane times, I knew that I was a monster and that you could never love me and that I should set you free. When you cried about your children and begged me to let you go back to them, I suggested to you that we could always have more children together. But before the words had barely left my mouth, you had screamed at me that you would rather be dead than to ever bear my child. So, I knew I would have to let you go. The thought of it caused my heart to ache, but I could see you wasting away before my eyes as you gradually lost your will to live. I could not let you die. If I couldn't break your hold on your other life, I would have to let you go to the place your heart was yearning to be ... back to them.

Click

Chapter Twenty-One
Cassino, Italy - 1974

She had to get away. He was mad; completely mad. He kept calling her some name;......what was it? Julia? Yes, that was the name, Julia. She had tried many times to tell him that her name was Elizabeth and that's what she wanted to be called. But he just ignored her. She was growing more and more confused, feeling lost and disoriented as her hold on reality started to stagger and weave from the weight of her fear and her continued captivity. Sometimes she wondered if she had made up her other life and really did belong to this man as he kept insisting that she did.

He kept demanding that she forget about her family; she didn't think she ever could, but things were turning upside down in her mind and sometimes she was unsure of what was real and what was not.

Her children and husband were all that she focused on as the days of her nightmare continued but she didn't know how much longer it would be before he broke her and she would start to believe what he wanted her to believe. If it weren't for the picture that she kept hidden under her mattress, she was afraid that she would forget who she was altogether. She had removed it from her wallet that she had kept in her dress pocket and hidden it knowing that he probably wouldn't let her keep it.

The photo was taken about two weeks before they had left for France. It showed her very handsome husband, David, with little Brian standing beside him holding his hand. She was holding their small baby daughter, Alexandria, in her arms and everyone was smiling.

Sometimes it looked like it was someone else's picture that she had chosen randomly from their photo album and decided to carry around with her so she could pretend they were her family. She had touched their faces so many times, trying to feel them through the paper, trying to make them real, that their images were starting to fade just like her will to go on was fading.

Roberto was his name and he actually thought that they could have a child together! When he had first spoken to her about his crazy idea, she had screamed at him telling him that she would rather die. He didn't seem to mind and just smiled at her and went on calling her Julia. It was all making her crazy and last night she had seen just how deeply and hopelessly she had fallen into the trap he had laid for her.

For the past several months, he had starting touching her. After her bath he would make her put on a silk robe and would not let her have her clothes. At first she tried to fight him but she was no match for him so now she didn't try to resist.

Sometimes, they would sit out on the deck and at other times, depending on the weather, they would sit in a chair in front of the fireplace. Always he made her sit astride him straddling his lap with her legs on either side of his, facing him. Then he would pull the robe off her shoulders. At first she had tried to hide her body from his view but he was too strong and he told her that if she didn't let him do what he wanted to do, he would rape her.

He would take his time touching her breasts, running his hands up and down her body. Then he would kiss and lick her nipples while placing his hand between her legs. As he held his hand there tightly against her, he would kiss her cheeks and suck on her breasts while telling her that she was beautiful and that he would always love her, cherish her and never harm her in any way. She could feel his erection and trembled with fear that he would lose control and take her even though he promised each time that he wouldn't. She could feel his barely-controlled lust and she was torn between shame, for the way he made her body feel, and her hatred for him.

Other times he would make her take off the robe completely and she would just lie in his lap while he told her about his life in Italy and Argentina. She felt sorry for him when he explained why she would replace his Julia who had died so long ago, but when she tried to explain that what he was doing was not right, he would hold her gently and place soft kisses on her temples and continue to speak.

Every night when her eyelids would start to droop, he would say, "Go to bed Julia, my love, you grow tired. We will speak again tomorrow," and she would grab her robe and hurry away to her bed saying a prayer of thanks that she had escaped again.

But that was until last night; last night when she had fallen into the pit and become trapped.

She was astride him with her legs spread and he was touching her, playing with her nipples, kissing her neck, when he placed one of his fingers inside her and started to move it in and out. He had never done that before and she stiffened and tried to pull away. He spoke to her gently saying that she should not fight him; but as she arched her back to get away from him, he touched her on the nub of her sex while continuing to force his finger in and out of her. Hot and cold shudders ran through her as she bucked against him, her senses paralyzed by her burning need. She felt something she had forgotten that she could feel – longing! As if he had given her an aphrodisiac, her body awakened and she lost control. She had rocked against his hand seeking her release, pressing her breasts to his face as he ravaged them with his mouth. She begged him not to stop. Then she climaxed in a wave that swept her up and caused sensations so strong that it was almost painful. As her body calmed, and she realized what she had done, she burst into tears while he held her tightly.

"That was beautiful, Julia. You have made me very happy. You are so beautiful and you have just opened yourself to me. Don't cry. It's normal that your body would react this way after all these nights and what I have done to you. Go now, go to bed before I lose control and break my promise to you."

She had thrown on her robe, her face burning with shame, and had rushed down to her room. She was a whore! She had betrayed her husband and her children.

In a rage, she had torn the room apart, throwing the books and lamps breaking and destroying everything she could get her hands on. Finally, after she had ripped the room apart, she threw the covers from her bed and flung the pillows against the walls. Then she fell to her knees and began to cry hysterically.

The truth was hard to face but when she looked into herself, what she saw was very clear. She needed him.

She needed someone to make her feel alive again. She was like a junkie who needed a fix. Nothing mattered; she would do anything for the few moments of oblivion when the pleasure carried her away and she could forget. She was desperate with a madness that left her feverish and out of breath. She had no shame. You could have held a gun to her head and she knew that she would have still done what she did then.

160

She crawled onto the bed. There were no sheets or pillowcases, so she was lying on a bare mattress on her back. She spread her legs apart and threw her arms out at her sides, like a sacrifice. She knew he would come and when he did, she would not resist him.

He was fully dressed and he spoke softly to her as he made love to her with his hands and his mouth, never taking for himself. She didn't remember how many times she climaxed, her body feverish and ready for more as each time he managed to drive her further up the road to sexual madness. She had never known such ecstasy or wantonness. She begged him for more and more and he complied, giving her pleasure so intense that she would sometimes feel faint.

When she was exhausted, she turned onto her side while he sat in the chair by the bed holding her hand and stroking her hair as she fell asleep. During the night she awakened once and he was still there watching her quietly as she drifted back to sleep. In the morning he was gone.

She had to get away. She knew that she had crossed a line, a line of no return, and soon she would answer to the name, Julia, and she would do anything he wanted her to do. She could not let that happen. He was handsome and desirable and as evidenced by her actions the night before, she was in more danger now than she had ever realized. She would lose more than her life; if she stayed she would lose her soul.

She was completely dependent on him and that frightened her. Several weeks before he had left her a note on the stairs saying that he had gone to town for supplies and that he would be back in the late afternoon. By ten o'clock that night he had not returned and she was frantic with fear. She was locked in. She would be left here to die and no one would ever know. What if he were hurt in an accident? What if he just drove away and left her here? Who would know? Who would rescue her?

When he returned some time near midnight, she almost threw herself into his arms she was so relieved to see him. He had been drinking and his eyes were very red. He explained that he had stopped to have a few drinks and was very sorry to be so late in returning. She had missed him desperately.

She was becoming attached to a man that was her mortal enemy. She had heard of the "Stockholm Syndrome" which had earned its name in the early 1970's when several bank employees in Stockholm, who had been captured during a robbery, had been placed in a bank vault by their captors. Although they had been held in the vault for several days, during

161

that time, the captives bonded with their captors. Then, as further evidence, there was the video of the kidnapped heiress Patti Hearst, after she had changed her name to Tanya, which showed her holding an automatic rifle, standing in a bank wearing a black wig and screaming, "Get down on the floor or I'll blow your mother-fucking heads off!"

She knew it could happen and she did not need any further proof that captives could bond with their captor, allow themselves to be called by another name and then be brainwashed to believe their captor's demented ramblings. She had to do something!

The tiny hatch marks she had scratched onto the cellar wall each night when the sun went down, told her that it had been almost 165 days and nights since he had brought her here. She knew that no one was coming for her; that she was probably presumed dead by now. It was time - time to try. And if she didn't succeed, then she didn't want to live anymore.

She had made other random attempts to escape but each time it seemed he read her mind and was one step ahead of her. But, after last night, she knew how to do it. She would remain in control and she would seduce him. She had seen him watching her last night, his lust marked by his clenched jaw and the stark pain on his face from not allowing himself a release. Somehow tonight, when they were both naked and when he least expected it, she was going to escape; even if it meant killing him. There was no time left now. The die was cast and whatever happened tonight, it would end here, because it was almost too late.

Chapter Twenty-Two
Cassino, Italy - 1974

Click

"I had decided to let you go," Roberto whispered, "and having made up my mind, I had fully prepared myself for the long prison term, that I was sure would be the end result of a trial, where the jury, who would be appropriately incensed over my horrible crime, would ultimately read their verdict and then throw the book at me.

"There were candles on the table and I had cooked a special meal, thinking that it would make a soothing backdrop for telling you that I was going to release you and let you go back to your family.

"Last night had been heaven and hell all wrapped up in one. I had seen your inner being. I had touched your spirit and danced with your soul. Each time passion ripped through you and you reached what we call *piccolo morte*, the "little death", I saw you clearly. Not the beautiful, naked, erotic creature that lay like an offering across the bed, but the essence of you.

"What I saw was a woman so beautiful and pure of heart that it broke my resolve to hold you any longer. I was not worthy of you. To make you mine I would have to kill everything that made me love you. You were like a flower and I had taken away your sun and your rain and now I was pulling off your petals one by one. So, that night I was going to take you wherever you wanted to go, get you safely back to your family, and then I was going to turn myself over to the police.

"After I was satisfied with the table and my preparations, I lit the candles, unlocked the cellar door and walked down the steps. My mood was festive and I was eager to see you, knowing that this would be our last night together.

"I kept you locked in whenever we were not together. So I had remodeled the lower floor in a way that would allow you ample space and

163

light so that you would not find it too confining. The room was very large and open. It was painted in a delicate shade of peach so that the light from the windows, situated at the very top of the walls surrounding the room, although crossed with bars, would bathe the room in a warm glow.

"There were large Persian rugs scattered throughout the room and fresh-cut flowers adorned every table and flat surface. At one end of the room there was a large four-poster bed draped with white netting and filled with numerous large plump pillows that were covered with white lace filigree that matched the white lace bedding.

"At the opposite end was a seating area that consisted of an overstuffed couch and two armchairs that were covered with a pastel floral pattern. Beside this, along one entire wall, I had built floor to ceiling shelves that I had stocked with every type of American fiction and non-fiction book I could find. A small cherry wood armoire for your clothes, a table and two chairs - in case you chose not to spend your meals with me - a dressing table and stool, plus a small water closet that did not contain a shower, finished out the room. It had taken most of the day to repair the destruction that was a result of your anger the previous evening.

"I was surprised to find you waiting for me with a smile on your face and the smell of good perfume floating in the air. You were wearing one of the dresses that I had bought you, which you had always adamantly refused to put on. It was more of a shock since I had never seen you in anything but the dress that you wore when I kidnapped you from Paris, a robe or naked.

"Each night you would wash the damned dress by hand and hang it to dry. Most mornings it would still be wet and even though I encouraged you to wear something that I had bought for you, you always refused.

"You were beautiful. The dress was a white gauzy material with a long sweeping skirt. The neckline was low so it showed an ample amount of your bosom. You were obviously nervous about this because even though you kept smiling at me, your hand would inevitably reach up and tug at the neckline every few moments in an effort to cover a few more inches of your cleavage. I knew I was staring but I could not help myself.

"You were acting so strangely and looking back, I think that if you had known what my real intentions were that night, things would have turned out very differently than they did.

"Finally recovering my voice, I told you that you looked very beautiful. You smiled and moved closer to me. I explained that I had made a very special dinner and that I had a surprise for you. A wonderful surprise that I felt sure would make you very happy. But you just smiled at me again and moved even closer. I wasn't sure what to say or do, so I just stood there mesmerized by you and your body heat that I could feel even with the distance still between us.

"When you were almost touching me, you abruptly pulled your dress down to your waist. Your breasts spilled out from the material and you took my hands and rubbed them over your nipples. I was stunned and I stood there motionless as you continued to rub my hands over your body.

"Regaining my composure, I stepped back from you and croaked, 'No! Get dressed, Julia, and do it now!'

"Instead of obeying, you dropped your dress to the floor and stood before me, naked and lovely - so erotic and sexy that I grabbed for you and began to kiss you with all the passion that I had been struggling with night and day. In my delirium, I actually thought you had changed your mind and really wanted me, but when you stiffened when I tried to lay you down, I understood. I let you go and turned away.

"As I paced back and forth, I told you to get dressed. You cried while you did what I asked. I have to admit that I watched you wishing things could be different between us, wondering if I weren't making a mistake by not having you at least one time. But, I gritted my teeth and finally you were dressed.

"You were sniffling and sitting quietly on a chair at the foot of the bed when I pulled up your mattress and took out the picture of you and your family that you thought was hidden from me. I wanted to tell you that I was going to release you and send you back to your family, but before I could speak you flew at me, punching me blindly, kicking and screaming, 'Don't touch my babies! You bastard! Don't you ever, ever touch my children!'

"I should have just given you the picture but I was so caught off guard that I didn't even realize that I had the picture in my hand as I tried to defend myself. When I moved to get away from you and made an attempt to deflect your blows, you grew more violent and screamed louder. 'Give....me.... back....my.....babies! Give.....them.....back! I'll do whatever you want just don't take my babies! Give....them......back!!!'

'Julia stop! Stop!' I kept shouting as I tried to grab your arms and hold you. You were so enraged that nothing I tried worked. You were completely out of control, hysterical and didn't know what you were doing. I wasn't going to be able to control you without hurting you, so I jerked away from you and ran to the stairs, thinking I would get out and wait until you were calm and we could speak rationally.

"I had almost reached the top landing when you lunged at my back, nearly toppling me from the stairs. As I turned toward you, you gouged your fingers into my eyes and pain roared through my head. Without thinking, I pushed at you and grabbed my face with my hands.

"I heard you scream. Then I heard your body hit and you were silent. At first I could not focus my sight because the pain was unbearable. My damaged eyes were tearing but I stumbled back down the stairs groping desperately along the floor as I tried to find you in the area where I thought you had fallen.

"You were lying so still, when I finally managed to see you, that I thought at first that you were dead. My heart was pounding so hard that I could hear it in my ears and I had to listen to your chest several times before I could hear your heartbeat and determine that it was yours and not mine. Your pulse was weak but you were alive.

"You were lying crumpled onto your right side and there was a dark pool of blood on the floor around your head. I knew I shouldn't move you without something to support your neck and back so I ran up the stairs and out to the shed. In there I found a piece of wood that was long enough and narrow enough to act as a stretcher; and going back down into the cellar, I gently moved you onto it. Then I tied your body down with several lengths of rope. But, no matter how I tried, I couldn't move you up the stairs without putting you in further danger of injury.

"I left you in the cellar, went upstairs and grabbed the phone, placing a call through the marine operator. I was eventually patched through to my yacht and when I reached my captain, Miguel, I asked him to leave the boat and come to me at once. He did not hesitate before saying that he would do so immediately. It took several hours for him to travel to my home and I was desperate when he finally arrived. If he thought anything about the condition of my eyes or if he wondered who the young woman was, he never said a word and just went about the task of helping me lift you up the narrow staircase to my bedroom.

"We left you on the board and, after placing you on the bed, we cut your clothes off. Your right hip and shoulder were badly bruised but they did not appear to be broken. Your right arm, however, was broken in two places and you were bleeding profusely from your head wound. Miguel assisted me as I cut your matted hair away so I could see how bad it was. There was a very large bump and a jagged three-inch cut behind your right

166

ear. I had done some stitching over the years when animals were injured and I hoped my skills would be good enough to at least stanch the flow of blood. After shaving your head, I started to work with trembling hands. You never moved as I closed the wound or when I set your arm.

"Without proper medical supplies, I did as well as I could but I knew you needed a doctor. After setting Miguel by your bed and telling him not to leave until I returned, I went to phone Argentina.

"It had been almost six months since I left Cordoba and when I heard my friend Cesar's voice on the phone, I had to choke back my tears. Trying to stay calm, I explained that there had been an accident at my home in Cassino and that my wife had been badly injured. When he started to ask questions, I told him I would explain everything when he arrived.

"Quickly, I ran through the fall from the landing when you missed a step, how I didn't believe it was safe to move you and that I didn't trust any of the local doctors. He promised to be on the next flight out of Buenos Aires and I hung up. I had to lie to him because he might not have come. I would tell him everything, all of it, but first he had to help you.

"I relieved Miguel and showed him where he could get a few hours rest. It had been many hours since you fell and it would soon be dawn. The candles on the dining room table had burned themselves out and the food I had prepared had long ago grown cold.

"I sat with you and I was filled with despair for the pain that I had caused you. You were injured and could possibly die from those injuries. I had driven you to the point of desperation and all that had happened to you was a direct result of your trying to get away from me. As you lay there, silent as death, I vowed that I would somehow make this all up to you. If you would just live, I promised that I would repay the debt I owed to you and your family.

"It took almost two days for Cesar to arrive and during that time I never left your side. You never wakened and you never moved. I was crazy with grief by the time the doctor saw you for the first time.

"He was concerned about your lack of response during his exam and agreed that I had done the right thing by not moving you. My stitches were a mess but he decided that they would keep the wound together and because of the location of the injury, it wouldn't matter if you had a scar from my lack of expertise. Your arm, however, would need to be reset and placed in a cast. I was glad you were unconscious during this procedure for it caused me to gnash my teeth while he put the bones back correctly.

"After he finished and felt that everything that could be done for you had been done, he sent me to shower and rest. When I awakened several hours later, still bleary eyed from lack of sleep, we went out onto the patio so that I could tell him what had happened as I promised I would.

"I made the story up as I went along. We met in Rome and fell instantly in love. You were on an extended vacation and had decided to live in Italy for a while so you were looking for an apartment. You were a single woman, with no children, who had never married. You had no living relatives since your parents had been killed in a car crash when you were a young woman. You had been in that same crash but had been spared, receiving only minor injuries.

"I did not know much more than that. It was a whirlwind romance; we married while in Rome, and had come back to Cassino for our honeymoon. We had been here several months and had planned, during the next several weeks, to return to Cordoba and make it our home. Your were climbing up the stairs carrying sheets from the bed when you lost your footing and fell the entire length of the staircase to the floor. The rest he knew.

"This seemed to appease his curiosity and I could tell he was genuinely happy that I had found someone to love. His concern for you was evident but he assured me that he would do everything in his power to help you recover.

"Cesar never connected the woman in the bed to the woman who had been kidnapped so many months before, even though I learned that it had become international news and your picture appeared in the paper for several months afterward.

"With your head shaved and your thin, gaunt appearance, you did not resemble that woman any longer. Besides, Cesar thought I was an honest, law-abiding man and he would not have ever considered me capable of something so dishonorable, or criminal, as the abduction of another person.

"I had him completely fooled. Several times I started to tell him the truth but decided against it. I wanted him to stay focused on you and not be blind-sided by what I had done.

"Six days after you fell, you moaned and opened your eyes. Cesar and I were both in the room. Looking around you asked in a weak voice, 'Where am I?'

"I could not speak I was so elated to find you awake, so Cesar answered. 'You are in Cassino, Italy. You have had a bad fall so you must lie very still. Do you remember the accident?'

'No,' you murmured. 'No, I don't remember.' Then you slipped back into unconsciousness.

"Over the next week, you would waken for short periods of time, drink a little fluid and go back to sleep, but you never spoke again. Cesar was encouraged by your progress and tried to still my anxiety as I paced and grumbled about how much time it was taking. I just wanted you well again. I wanted you awake and talking. But, most of all, I wanted you out of bed so I could see for myself that you were going to be okay. I was haunted, night and day, as you lay there so pale and still.

"It was almost another week before you woke and spoke again. You were in the middle of a conversation with Cesar when I stopped outside the door.

'Is he a good man?' you asked hoarsely.

'Oh, yes!' Cesar replied as he redressed your wound. 'Your husband is a wonderful man. I have known him since he was a boy and I would trust my life to him. You are a very lucky woman.'

"My heart was pounding in my ears as he continued, 'Your name is Julia Bertinelli, you are thirty years old and your husband is Roberto Bertinelli. You are newlyweds and this accident has made Roberto very anxious. Don't worry, your memory will return in time. Now rest and get your strength back.'

"As you fell asleep, I motioned the doctor out of the room and asked him how you were and why you couldn't remember and how long it would last. He explained that you would grow stronger as the days went by and soon you would be able to resume a normal life. However, you were suffering from post-traumatic amnesia that is sometimes caused by a serious blow to the head.

"You might or might not ever recover your memory of events that happened prior to the fall or even the fall itself. You would be confused and possibly irritable while you tried to regain your memory of events that could be lost forever. Your mind would be fragile and you could be prone to periods of extreme moodiness or abject depression followed by bouts of crying. It could be something as simple as a smell that might trigger the release and bring forth the flood of memories that were locked up in your subconscious, or you might never remember.

169

"Cesar left during the next week saying that he had done all that he could do and that I could help you as you regained your strength. Besides, he said, he should return to Argentina, where he would announce our marriage and have the *estancia* prepared for our arrival.

"I never told him the truth about you.

"It was only many years later, after you had fallen from your horse when she bolted, that he started to question what I had told him. You were pregnant with the only child we had ever been able to conceive and the fall caused you to lose the baby. You were devastated because you wanted a child so badly, but when Cesar told you that you would never conceive again, you fell into a deep depression that lasted for months.

"It was during his exam after the baby was lost that he learned that you had been pregnant before and had delivered at least one child. When he confronted me with this, I told him that he must be mistaken that I knew that you had never had any children. He told me that the damage to your body did not lie but I wouldn't listen and put him off. From that day on, he knew something was not right about you and me, but he did not know what it was.

"I believe it was a curse that fate placed against me that caused you to lose our child. I had taken your children from you and I was never going to have one of my own. This was the only time in the twenty years we spent together that I almost told you the truth and sent you home. The pain you suffered over the death of our baby tore me in two because I realized how much you loved your children.

"It was only after my illness was diagnosed that I finally told Cesar the truth. He was horrified and threatened to go to you and to the authorities if I did not do so immediately. I asked him to give me until after your birthday party and he agreed, but he did so reluctantly. It was after the party that I gave him the tape that you are listening to now, and asked him to listen only after my death. I know that he felt like an accomplice to my crime but please believe me when I tell you that he never knew what I had done and should not be blamed.

"But, to go back to that time in Cassino, let me continue. After Cesar left Italy, and Miguel went back to my yacht, I spent all my time with you. It was spring now and the air was cool and the countryside beautiful. So, as you regained your strength, we would take short walks and we would talk while holding hands. It was during your second month of recovery that you had the first of the many spells that would haunt you over the

170

next twenty years. You cried day and night for three days and would not leave your room.

"During those days, I paced the floor outside your room growing more and more despondent and afraid, afraid that you would remember. You see, I had decided that since you didn't remember, I shouldn't tell you and, maybe after you were better, we could go to Cordoba and have a life together. Forgetting my pledge to you, I prayed you would never remember who I really was and what I had done.

"It was during one of our walks late in the evening, when you stopped, dropped my hand and walked away from me. As you stared off into the distance, I resigned myself to losing you if that were the direction in which your long silence was headed.

"Turning to me you said, 'Roberto, are we really married?'

"I paused before I answered. Afraid to speak, I looked down at my feet and jammed my hands into my pockets. After a short time I said, 'Darling, why do you ask?'

"You were looking straight into my eyes and your face was flushed from the exertion of our walk. You were so beautiful with your huge doe eyes that you made my head swim. Your hair was only about one inch long, which only accented the beauty of your high cheekbones and the lines of your face.

'Because we don't sleep together, and my clothes are downstairs and yours are upstairs, and there are two bedrooms and... don't we g-g-get a-a-long?' you forced out in a rush of words, stammering at the end.

'Oh, my darling, my silly, silly darling,' I whispered as I pulled you into my arms. 'Of course, we got along. Have you looked at how many clothes you have? There was no way that all of them would fit upstairs so we decided to use the smaller closet upstairs for my clothes and the one downstairs for yours. Besides we were just newlyweds and you were still a little shy around me, so it gave you some privacy whenever you dressed.

"As for the two beds, we slept downstairs when the weather was hot because it was so much cooler. And, young lady, you have been very ill and I did not think it would be wise to sleep with you in case I hurt you when I turned in the bed. Also, I did not think it was appropriate for me to ask for my husband's rights while you were recuperating."

'Roberto,' you sighed into my chest as I held you gently against me, 'You are so nice, I wish I could remember you.'

'Julia, my darling, we have a whole life ahead of us to make memories. Glorious memories; memories that we will cherish. There is a whole world out there to explore, let's not look back. Come with me to Cordoba, my love, and let me show you how wonderful it will be. I will love you and care for you, I will never leave you or desert you, and I will be there for you at any time, day or night. Come go with me, let's take an adventure together.'

"You stopped me by placing your fingers against my lips and I was rushed back in time to that day when the other Julia had done the same thing to me before she was ripped out my arms. I knew that this symbolism was an answer to my torn heart and that you were meant for me. As you continued to rub your fingers gently against my lips, your touch burned me and a fire rushed from my mouth to my loins.

'I have a suggestion, Roberto. How would you feel if I asked you to marry me again? We could do it here in some small church. I know that you probably think that is silly, but that would make me feel really married and then I wouldn't feel so…so… shy about …' you struggled to finish.

"I stopped you with a kiss that left me reeling from desire and love for you. 'Julia, of course, I should have thought of it. That is a wonderful idea. I would do anything for you. I would marry you three or four times if that would help.'

"It didn't matter to me that the very least of my sins would be standing in a church taking vows while you unknowingly committed bigamy. I was in love and for a while, it didn't matter if it were only a day or a hundred years, you were going to be mine and I was going to be yours.

"So, two days later we were married at the small cathedral in Cassino. It had taken me all of that time to get a fake passport and identification for your new name, Julia Rosselini, which of course was the name of my long ago love. I thought it was rather poignant that we were married in the same cathedral that I had expected to be married in twenty-eight years before. The priest had changed but as the ceremony began, I stepped back in time and became that young boy again, a boy filled with love and wonder as he faced the woman he had waited for all his life.

"You were shy and soft spoken during the ceremony, as we pledged our vows to each other. When I placed a chaste kiss on your lips at the end of the priest's prayers of blessing for us, my heart leapt with joy when you kissed me back.

"Our wedding night was a night of wonder. You were nervous at first and I was gentle because of your shyness and your delicate physical

172

condition. But what a night it was. To describe it takes many words. It was a night of healing, a night of rapture and a night of beginnings. It was a night that transcended the earthly pale and led me to heaven. It was a night when an angel's kiss caused the man I used to be to fall away as our souls and bodies were united as one.

"Ten days later we left for Cordoba and the priest's blessings must have been very strong for I was blessed with twenty years of loving you."

Click

Chapter Twenty-Three
1974

Click

Roberto started to speak again after a long pause, "Julia, I would like to be able to say that if I had it all to do over again, I would not do what I did to you, but that wouldn't be true.

"I remain unrepentant.

"I believe that you and I were destined to be together and only through some twist of fate did you become another man's wife. You were the love I had waited for all my life, so I am not sorry for making you mine.

"I do regret taking you away from your children. I know how much you loved them and I am deeply sorry for all the years that can never be replaced.

"Since the days when we left Cassino, Italy and arrived in Argentina, I have had a man working for me, a detective. I hired him to keep track of your children and your husband and to make sure that they never wanted for anything. Your husband was very successful, so money was never an issue. For over twenty years, this detective has been clipping all the news articles that involved your family as well as taking photographs of all special events. He has, in general, been creating a chronological file that highlights all the years while your children were growing up.

"There are pictures of your daughter's dance recitals and volley ball games, prom pictures and birthday parties and the same for your son's soccer games and football trophies. I have donated anonymously to your children's schools and various sporting and dance groups and watched over them to make sure they were healthy and happy.

"You will receive all the photos and newspaper clippings soon. I have contacted the detective, his name is Joe McGuire, and he will bring them to you and introduce himself. He has been a loyal friend as well as an employee and I hope you will be kind to him when you meet in spite of what I have done.

"I know all of this is small consolation for what you have lost, but I hope you will find some happiness looking back at their lives and that it will fill up some of the empty places in your heart. Maybe then you can forgive me just a little.

"Julia, I never thought that you would ever go back to your family because I believed we would grow old together. Now that I will be gone, I urge you to go back and reunite with your family. Your son has graduated from college, your daughter is in her junior year, your parents are alive and well and, although your husband remarried ten years ago, I believe he would welcome you back with joy.

"You are young and beautiful and you have a whole new life still waiting for you to live. Maybe the time I will spend in hell will be lessened by a day or two if you can find happiness again with those you loved and left behind.

"I have destroyed your life as it was and I know this is true," Roberto said in a whisper. "But I hope you can consider our life together just a short detour along your life's pathway and know that you have years and years left in which to reclaim part of what I stole from you and your family.

"I must go now, I grow weaker each moment and my strength to continue is gone, but I love you, Julia. Now, I face eternity knowing that I will face it without you and I am not afraid. I will meet my God and accept my punishment for my sins and I will stand tall and not tremble. For loving you and having you by my side was heaven and, even though I will now walk into hell, I will do it with a smile upon my face, because you were worth it my sweet, sweet, Julia, my darling, my love and my life.

"So, it ends for the two of us for now, but I will wander through the nether life crying for your embrace and longing to see your smile and this will be punishment enough. Forgive me if you can and know that I was lost from the day I first looked into your beautiful eyes. And now, my love, until we meet again, ...goodbye."

Click

Chapter Twenty-Four
1993

Carmen and Alejandro were sitting quietly on the veranda watching the sun go down on the pampas below them. She smiled as she thought about the new feelings that she had for this man and how they had grown without her knowing how they started. He wanted to marry her and she was thrilled and terrified at the same time.

He was a widower and she had never married. That alone was enough to make their union somewhat precarious. Also, all she knew and seemed to remember anymore was her life here working for Roberto and Julia. She had always taken care of them and they were her family now. With Roberto gone, she wasn't sure what would happen to her position or to the *estancia* that she called home.

She didn't feel like she could ever leave Julia, especially now after Roberto's death. Once she was married, although they hadn't discussed it, she assumed that Alejandro would want her to move out of the main house. So, she was caught between her new love for this wonderful man and her love for Julia who was like her daughter.

It was wrong, she knew it was, but she had listened outside the study door for hours at a time while Roberto poured out his story. Her heart was broken for her poor Julia, but at the same time, she understood Roberto's obsession and could not hate him for it. He was a wonderful man and he had worshipped and adored his wife. She could find no fault with his actions during their years together.

Of course, it was a horrible thing that he had done and she was shocked that a man as gentle and compassionate as Roberto could have even considered committing such a crime. How Julia would survive all of the pain would be something that only time would tell.

So, she was torn. Torn between her feelings that ran for and against Roberto as she sorted through what she had learned from the tapes and what she had seen over the past twenty years. Torn because of the sadness and sorrow she felt for Julia and the obligation she felt to be there for her and to help her through all of this. And finally, torn by her growing love for this old man at her side and what to do about it.

Chapter Twenty-Five
Cordoba, Argentina - November 17, 1993
9:00 P.M.

Julia stepped out of the shower and started toweling herself dry. She had spent over an hour soaking but had not been able to clear her mind or relax. As she reached for her robe she began to smile.

Roberto's blue extra large robe still hung on a hook next to hers. She remembered his surprise when they bought the two and she had told him that she wanted an extra large also, but she wanted it in white. He used to tease her when she wore it, saying that he couldn't find her under all that fabric, then he would pounce on her and start tickling her until she begged him to stop. Then they would make love sometimes for the first time or, if after their bath together, a second time. Afterwards she would curl up in her chair by the fire and he would take the seat next to her and they would discuss their day together.

She missed him so much. Even with everything she now knew and all that he had done, she still missed him. The memories suffocated her sometimes as she struggled for breath and her tears fell like rain. Sometimes, she thought she might drown in her pain. Every day she went through the motions of living, but she felt nothing anymore but her grief over losing a man that she should hate.

Julia pulled herself back from the hurt and started to briskly dry her wet hair with the towel. Out of the side of her eye she saw the boxes and turned away trying not to think about them. They had been delivered three days earlier and she knew they contained the pictures of her family that Roberto had told her to expect. She had been trying to ignore their presence because she didn't feel well enough to open what could be a "Pandora's box" full of heavy emotions.

The boxes had been accompanied by a thoughtful letter from Joe McGuire, the detective, explaining that he had been instructed in a letter from Roberto to send these items to her, that he was sorry for the loss of her husband and that he was available by phone or fax if she ever needed anything.

She wondered what he must think about her and Roberto. Did he ever wonder why her husband had kept a secret watch over an American family? Did he ever put it all together and learn that she was the woman who had been kidnapped so many years ago?

Probably not, she thought. Anyone who ever met Roberto would hardly believe that he was a criminal.

Julia went into her room and sat down on the floor, cross-legged, resting her elbows on her knees. Cupping her face with her hands she stared at the boxes.

She was a coward. Yes, it was hard to admit, but she was a coward. The pictures inside these boxes were tiny moments in time that had been captured by the flash of a bulb and imprinted on celluloid. Most people save their pictures so that they can remember the moment and go back in time and feel something they felt the day they took it.

She had no point of reference to tie to the events. Since she was not there, a picture of her daughter's first steps would not bring back memories of how long they had waited for the day to come, if she stood up and started walking unexpectedly; forcing them to run for their cameras before she sat or fell back down, or if she cried once she realized that she was not holding on to something. She had all these memories of Brian's first venture from crawling to standing and finding out that his feet were made for something besides sticking into his mouth.

Her children didn't know her. They had grown up without her and she wouldn't be in their memories either. They were adults now and she could only remember them as babies. She hardly knew her baby daughter since Alexandria had only been three months old when Julia had been ripped from her life.

It would do no good, she argued with herself, to take these pictures and try to make herself feel a part of their lives. When she looked at them as they grew from a baby to a pre-schooler, a high school graduate, a prom queen, a football star, a college graduate and finally someone old enough to fall in love and marry, all she could feel, under the circumstances, was as an outsider looking in. The staggering loss and the horrible pain of anonymity that she would feel because she was no one in their lives would be too much to bear.

So the boxes sat there unopened and she sat there staring at them wishing she weren't such a coward, because she really wanted to see what was inside.

But she was afraid.

Chapter Twenty-Six
Missoula, Montana - November 17, 1993
6:00 P.M.

Alexandria sat in the big Chevy Suburban and thought about what had gotten her to this point in time. Her parents had tried to warn her about running with the wild kids, but she hadn't listened. She thought they were cool, they were fun, they were outrageous and, what did her parents know anyway. They were so old they couldn't possibly be in touch with the kids of today. Now, because she had ignored their warnings, she was going to die.

Vicky and Beth were scared too and she could see Vicky's mouth moving as she repeated her "Hail Marys" and "Our Fathers". They were really nice girls and it was too bad because they would never have been in the truck if it hadn't been for her. Neither one of her friends would have ever associated with this group, but she had talked them into it. Now, their deaths would be on her head too.

At first the three of them had talked about the wreck they were probably going to have and had decided that they were probably in the safest seat for the impact. There was only one problem with that theory. The truck was old and used just to move firewood, so it didn't have any seatbelts.

But now, she knew they were going to die. She had told her friends so and they had cried harder. They were going too fast and the roads were too dangerous, and she could feel it, something told her this was it! The end.

One of her new friends, Dana, one of the most popular girls in the group and one of the girls her mother had warned her the most about, was in the front seat wedged between three boys. She wouldn't have a chance when they hit.

A guy named Tom was driving. She didn't know him. He had graduated from the University of Montana two years earlier and he was a friend of Dana's. In fact it had been Dana who had pressured her into riding with her and Tom to Bozeman for the Grizzly/Montana State season finale.

She should have said no.

Besides the four kids in the front, she and her friends in the middle seat, there were five other boys sitting on the floor in the back. With the exception of Vicky, Beth, two of the boys and her, most of the kids had been drinking heavily and a few had talked about doing drugs prior to starting the five hour drive over the mountain passes.

She had begged Tom to stop and let her and her friends out but he had shouted back that they were just a bunch of grandmas and didn't know how to have fun. Then he had taken his hands off the steering wheel and the truck had lurched wildly from side to side, causing the three girls to scream in unison and start to cry. Everyone else was laughing and yelling, urging him on. Finally, he put his hands back on the wheel and told them to shut up because he wasn't stopping for anyone, that he was on a mission, and that a bunch of babies weren't going to stop him. Most of the kids screamed their approval, clapping and yelling. After that, the girls had held each other's hands and kept still.

It was dark in Montana as the days grew shorter and the ground was wet from a light snow that had been falling off and on most of the day. As it grew later and the temperature dropped, there would be patches of ice; there always were this time of year. She didn't know how fast they were going, but she knew it had to be at least eighty or ninety miles an hour.

They were on I-90 and she prayed that a highway patrol car would see them and pull them over. There was a lot of traffic headed to Bozeman and Tom was weaving in and out of cars throwing everyone from side to side in the truck. Some rock song she was sure she used to like, but would never want to hear again, was playing on the radio at a deafening roar.

She wondered how many other kids had been where she was now; realizing there was nothing they could do to change it, it was out of their hands. How many, like her, had wished they could go back in time, turn back the clock and wake up and realize it was only a bad dream? Then she thought about her parents. She hoped they could forgive her for hurting them this way

He was crazy, drunk and stoned out of his mind. She was only nineteen years old and in her junior year of college and she didn't want to die.

Chapter Twenty-Seven
Cordoba, Argentina - November 17, 1993
9:06 P.M.

Julia couldn't wait any longer. She tore into the boxes ripping them apart and dumping everything into a huge pile on the floor. They were not in albums so all the pictures and articles were loose.

The first picture she picked up was one of her daughter, Alexandria, in her high school graduation gown. My God, she thought, she is so beautiful. Alexandria was tall with long blonde hair the color of her father's, but Julia could see her own face as she looked into her daughter's eyes.

Julia started to weep from the joy of seeing her baby daughter all grown up and rushed to pick up the next picture. This one showed her daughter again standing beside a beat-up Volkswagen that was packed to the gills with clothes, ski poles, tennis rackets and everything else imaginable. She was waving at the camera and handwritten below the picture were the words, "Off to college".

There were pictures of her son, Brian, with his soccer trophies and another of him sitting on the ground in his soccer clothes, with his head bowed dejectedly, covered with mud. She wondered if he had lost the game. He was big, like his father but he looked so much like Julia that it was easy to see they were mother and son. His hair and eyes were hers and Julia was filled with love and longing as she ran her finger across his face, over and over again.

As she went from picture to picture, she saw Halloween costumes, Alexandria in her first tutu at a dance recital and her two children sitting on Santa's lap. Brian was smiling broadly, but the expression on Alexandria's face was precious as she sat there in her green velvet dress. She was staring up at the man in red with huge eyes and an astounded look on her face. Her lips had a curve to them that was somewhere between a smile and abject fear, although Julia thought she looked like she might burst into tears at any moment. She wondered what had happened that day and wished she could have been there to see it. Another picture showed Brian riding his first two-wheeler, smiling broadly into the camera. Both of his front teeth were missing and Julia started to laugh in spite of herself.

Pictures of her parents as they had aged tore her heart apart. If she could just hold them once more and feel their love and strength, if she could just go back in time and undo the pain they must have felt when they believed they had lost their only child.

The worst was the newspaper clippings of her husband and children standing by her grave at her memorial service. The article was dated over two years after she had disappeared. It was something her husband would have done. He would need to lay her to rest in a dignified manner.

Her daughter was dressed in a pink coat and hat, white tights and black Mary Janes and she had a huge smile on her face. She was clutching a small bouquet of flowers to her chest and appeared to be having the time of her life with her father and brother. She was so young; she couldn't possibly have known what it all meant. To her it was just another outing with her daddy and big brother.

Brian was tall for six years old and his face looked haunted. He probably still remembered the day his mother went away and never came back. He might even blame himself. Julia broke down for a moment and could not go on.

Finally, she went back to the article and looked at her husband, David. His face was ravaged with grief and it took her breath away to see how her husband and her son must have suffered prior to her memorial service while she was living in Argentina, lying in the arms of the man who had taken her away from them. Julia's gut wrenched with guilt and she thought she might be sick.

Stop it, she thought. There was nothing that could undo it and she could not beat herself up anymore. She was innocent. The priest had told her so repeatedly. She was not to blame and she had to let go of the guilt or she would not ever have her life back. So, she stood and walked to the window for a moment, trying to keep from screaming from the pain.

Julia was determined to finish so she went back to her task.

The pictures and newspaper articles of David's wedding to Lainie Montgomery, a famous TV reporter, six years after her funeral made her heart glow. She was a beautiful woman with red-gold hair and she was beaming with joy. Her dress was a long white sheath and she had white

184

roses twined into her hair. David was incredibly handsome in a black tuxedo and he was smiling, but the smile did not reach his eyes, which were still filled with pain. Julia moved on.

She hurriedly looked through them, rushing from one to the next, sometimes smiling, and other times crying, anxious to see them all. Finally, she lay down on the floor in the middle of the mess she had made. She piled pictures on top of her, as many as she could, covering her body, her face and her eyes until you could not see her beneath them.

She was filled with peace. They were all alive, they were well and they appeared to be happy now. She was blessed. They didn't know she was alive but it didn't matter anymore. They had adjusted to their loss and moved on. Her children were beautiful, smart, healthy and much loved. What Roberto had done had not destroyed them. David was remarried and had been for many years and he had finally laid her soul to rest. Her parents were alive but at eighty-six and eighty-three years of age they certainly didn't need the shock of her reappearance.

She would not go back. It would be pure selfishness on her part to interfere in their lives after all these years.

Lying under all the pictures, she was filled with sense of warmth, as if her entire family had come to her and was now hugging her. She could feel the essence of their lives and now she could let them go. It was a relief to finally make the decision she had been fighting.

She would not go back. She would stay in Argentina. She would ask Joe McGuire to continue sending her pictures of her family and it would have to be enough.

Chapter Twenty-Eight
Missoula, Montana - November 17, 1993
6:06 P.M.

Alexandria wouldn't remember it, but the accident happened six minutes later. They had just driven out of the canyon when Tom lost control of the Suburban. As the right front tire dropped off the roadbed onto the shoulder, the speed of the vehicle caused it to flip end over end throwing the passengers out the front and back windows with each revolution.

Later, because of the extent of her injuries, the doctors would determine that Alexandria was thrown out first and that her body was projected the length of a football field before it skidded to a rest on the shoulder of the road. It would be further determined by the amount of glass and cuts found on the back of her head, that she left the vehicle backwards through the front windshield.

The velocity of being thrown at such a high rate of speed ripped her out of her shoes. One of her boots would be found still in the van and the other along the roadside where the vehicle first left the roadway.

When she landed, her brain continued to move at eighty-five miles per hour then it slammed into her skull and caused an immediate brain hemorrhage. Like an orange thrown violently to the concrete, her spleen tore in half and the bottom portion of her liver was ripped off causing massive internal bleeding. Both hips were dislocated and both legs were pulled out of their sockets. She was near death when they found her lying on the darkened highway.

The driver, Tom, was thrown out next and later, when his blood alcohol level was tested at the trauma center, it would be four times the legal level and he would test positive for cocaine use. He would suffer severe head injuries and he would never fully recover.

Then all the other passengers were thrown out. They left the van at varying times and speeds as the van started to slow in its rotation. Dana

186

landed face down on top of Alexandria's body and because she went out last, she would only suffer a broken wrist. When Beth wakened she would not be able to move her head and would think that she was paralyzed. Her long hair would be lying under the right front wheel of the van when it came to rest. She would have a broken pelvis.

The highway patrolman who had chased them for less than a mile would say that the driver was weaving erratically before he left the road. He would also state that the scene of the accident would remind him of his time in Vietnam, with the sound of crying and screaming in the darkness, some of the passengers staggering around with blood pouring down their faces, and others lying deathly still on the ground.

Miraculously, no one would die that night and some of the victims would suffer injuries as minor as the loss of an earlobe or a broken collarbone. Alexandria and the driver would not be so fortunate.

She would be airlifted by helicopter to the trauma center, Saint Patrick, located thirty miles away in Missoula. She would be placed on life support because she would no longer be able to breathe on her own. When admitted she would be listed as Jane Doe, number one, and rushed to surgery. She would be in surgery seven hours before someone in the accident would identify her and a call would be placed to her parents in Alexandria, Virginia. The doctors did not believe that they could make it to Missoula in time.

Chapter Twenty-Nine
Cordoba, Argentina

Julia received the call about her daughter about 11:00 P.M. She was lying on the floor where she had fallen asleep while looking at the pictures of her family when Carmen knocked on her door to tell her she had an urgent call from Joe McGuire.

When she picked up the phone and said hello, he said, "I'm sorry to bother you so late and I'm not sure if you're still interested in the family back here or not, but I've been still kinda keepin' an eye on them. I've been doing it so long, it's a hard habit to break and well, I'm sorta attached to them now. Anyway, I've had some bad news."

Julia panicked and she held her breath as her heart started to race. Slowly, releasing her breath she said, "Yes, I'm interested."

"Well, it's the girl, Alexandria. She's had a bad automobile accident. I don't know all of the details but it appears that she is in bad shape. She's at the trauma center in Missoula, Montana where she goes to school. They've called her parents to fly back from the East Coast because they're so worried that she might not make it. I'm real sorry to bring you this kind of news over the phone, but I thought you might want to know."

Julia couldn't think; she felt like she was suspended in the air, then she heard the sound of glass shattering inside her head.

"Julia," he said. "Julia, are you there? I could meet you in Miami tomorrow night. I could go up there with you if you want. You don't have to go alone if you don't want to. Maybe I could help. If you call me with your flights, I'll be glad to go with you."

After a moment she replied, "Yes, thank you. You are very kind. I would like that. I'll make my arrangements and I will call you back as soon as I have confirmed my plans, and thank you again."

After writing down his number, Julia didn't hang up the phone; she just dropped it on the floor. Carmen followed behind her and placed it in the cradle.

"What is it, Julia? What has happened," she asked softly.

"It is my daughter, Alexandria. She has been hurt and she …," choking a little Julia paused then continued, "she may be dying………, I need your help."

"Of course, tell me what you need and I will take care of it immediately," Carmen replied.

Very calmly, with no emotion, Julia said, "I need to get a flight to Miami that will either get me in tomorrow night or first thing Sunday morning at the latest. I need you to call Cesar about my passport. My name is false, my birth certificate is false but, since I'm a naturalized Argentine citizen, will it work? I'll need a new photograph, at the very least, so ask Cesar to set it up. I don't care how he gets it done. Tell him I'm calling in all my markers. I need an appointment with my hairdresser first thing in the morning. Tell her it's urgent. Get me a drink, something strong and alcoholic. Leave me the entire bottle. Have one of the other maids come to my room and repack all of these pictures for me. Ask Alejandro to prepare my car so I can leave for Buenos Aires at a moment's notice." Pausing for breath she added, "Please go now and I will pack, and… thank you for your help."

Julia realized, at that moment, that she had always known that she would go, that she had planned every minute detail in advance, including changing her appearance so no one would recognize her. She was never going to stay in Argentina and give up her family. Her daughter's accident had only taken "when" she would go out of her hands.

* * *

Julia was out on the balcony of her room. It was a warm night but a storm was brewing. The wind was whipping at her gown and wrapping it around her ankles as she paced back and forth. She had packed her bags and put them outside in the hall. She was drinking her fourth scotch. She actually hated the taste but she needed something strong to help numb her feelings.

Stopping in mid-stride, she looked down over the railing at the stone patio floor that lay below. For a moment she thought about jumping. But she knew that if she did, with her luck, she would probably break her hip or her leg when she hit the hard stone below. Then, of course, it probably wouldn't heal properly and she would end up with a limp, forced to use a cane for the rest of her life. So, it probably was a stupid idea.

Victor entered her room as she was musing on her bad luck, after he had called her name several times and not received any answer. Walking further into the room, he called her name again and she said, "Victor, is that you? Come on in. I'm out on the balcony."

Victor stood in the doorway and watched her move back and forth. She was wearing a white silk gown that was low-cut and diaphanous. The force of the wind against her body was pushing the gown flat against her skin and Victor had to smile. It was obvious that she had been drinking, first because she never would have let Victor see her disrobed this way and second, because of the irregular steps she was taking while waving her arm that held her drink, wildly from side to side as she spoke. Victor smiled to himself, Julia was always breathtaking but, in her half-naked state, she was spectacular.

"I knew you would come, you always do. That's one thing I can count on if nothing else. Good old Victor will be there for me when trouble comes. Isn't that right, Victor?"

"Yes, Julia. I will always be here for you if you need me."

"And why do you do that Victor? Why do you give a damn about me, or what happens to me? Don't you have better things to do with your time than to keep hanging out with a woman who is fifty years old and half crazy?" Turning to Victor, she staggered from side to side, waved her arms and said, "You need to go back to New York and get on with your life. I don't understand why you stay here after all you know about us. God, it must just sicken you just to think about it." Turning away from him she walked to the banister and looked over it.

"How far down do you think it is to the patio below? If I jumped off would I kill myself?" As Victor gasped and moved toward her, she turned back to him. "Oh, don't worry, I won't jump. But, since you're here, there is one little itty-bitty thing that you could do for me."

"And what would that be, Julia?" he answered cautiously.

"How about going into the other room and bringing out that great, big, beautiful bottle of scotch that's sitting there and pouring me another drink. I'm feeling real thirsty right now."

"I would be glad to do that for you if you're sure you can deal with the way you're going to feel in the morning when you wake up. From the amount it appears you have been drinking, it could be a pretty grim sight."

Julia ignored him, "I guess you heard about my daughter? Of course," she answered without waiting for his response, "of course you did. That's why you're here. So....., now you know why I need another drink," she said, handing him her glass and walking away from him.

Victor set the glass down on the table on the balcony and came to Julia's side. "Yes, I heard about your daughter. What can I do to help?"

Julia turned back to him. The wind had started to pick up in strength and it was whipping her hair across her face as drops of rain started to fall. Pushing the hair out of her eyes, she said, "Victor, she might die! I don't even know her and she might die. I don't know if I can stand it!"

Victor pulled Julia into his arms. "Let me hold you. You're trembling. You need to put your robe on. Then we can sit and talk and maybe I can help in some way."

As he took her into his arms, he lost it. Looking back later, he would realize that this moment was when it all went crazy. At first he had tried to pull his body back a little so that his erection, which grew the moment he touched her, wasn't pressed up against her, but she clung to him and refused to release him. Groaning, he whispered, "Julia, I need..." but he never finished his thought because some power he could not control pulled him down to her upturned face and he kissed her.

Fire shot through his veins when he felt her mouth against his. At first it was a tentative kiss and he could feel Julia's hesitation but when he felt her respond, he pushed his tongue deep into her mouth and ground his body against hers as his blood pounded in his veins.

Then Julia pushed him away and staggered backwards, slipping on the wet tiles. She placed her fingertips on her swollen lips. He could see her confusion as she fought against the desire she felt and that he could see in her eyes.

"I'm sorry Julia. Forgive me. I took advantage and I'm sorry."

Julia just stood there staring at him, rubbing her hand over her lips. It had started to rain harder now and the wind was howling loudly as it drove great sheets of water down on them, soaking them to the skin and causing them to battle to maintain their balance.

Victor thought he saw Julia's mouth move but, if she spoke, the sound of a great thunder-clap, followed by a streak of lightening, tore the words out of her mouth and sent them spinning away with the wind and the rain.

The sight of her standing there, soaking wet, almost naked plus the taste of her that he still had on his mouth, caused Victor to lose control.

All the years he had wanted her came roaring up out of him and although he tried to clench his fists and grind his teeth to fight his desire, the beast within him would not let him turn and walk away. Not this time.

He grabbed at her roughly, ripping her gown from her body and crushing her against him, plundering her mouth with his tongue. Picking her up so that her legs straddled him around his waist, he pushed her violently up against the wall of the building. The heat from the center of her caused him to gasp as her naked skin touched his stomach and his erection that had pushed up, out of the top of his jeans.

Julia tore at his shirt, ripping the buttons off and then pulling at his jeans. She kissed his neck and chest, biting at his nipples and then she bent backwards so that he could lick and suck her breasts. The rain poured, slashing at their bodies as the wind drove it, yet they did not know it because, instead of the storm they heard the song that only wild animals can hear when they mate. It was a song of madness that is born and then rises up out of the heat of the earth. The siren's song was, and always had been, so basic, so seductive and so eternal that, like so many others before them, they were powerless to resist.

Victor couldn't wait any longer, so he took her with his pants still on. As he slid into her, Julia cried out, clinging to him, scratching and biting, begging him not to stop. He heard a roar in his head as he forced her to take more of him, slamming into her violently, making her give more back to him. He was hurting her. He knew it but he couldn't stop himself. He had to struggle to keep from losing it all together. He wanted this to last forever, he had died and gone to heaven and he didn't want to wake up.

Suddenly, Julia slapped him hard across the face, so he grabbed her by the hair and pulled her face up to his. Then he bit her lip until it bled and increased his strokes, pounding her harder and faster, grabbing her hair with his hand yanking her head back and forth as he bit her nipples. Julia threw back her head and laughed. Victor took that opportunity to sink his shaft all the way into her and she screamed with desire.

With Julia still wrapped around him, Victor walked into the bedroom and dropped her onto the bed. As the storm howled outside, he tore the remainder of his clothes off. He wanted to feel all of her.

Julia had rolled over onto her back after he had unceremoniously thrown her onto the bed. She was lying on her elbows watching him as he stumbled around the room in a crazy dance as he tried to remove his jeans and boots at the same time. Then she bolted from the bed in a dead run to the door, but he was too quick for her.

Grabbing her from behind, he said, "No, Julia. Where do you think you're going? We are far from done with this dance. What is it? You don't like the bed? Well, you just had to say so!" Then he threw her onto the floor and jumped down beside her. They tore at each other, rolling over and over, crying out as they struggled to feel more of the sensations that were driving them both mad.

Then she climaxed, which was good, since he didn't think he could last one minute longer. As she arched against him, he spoke to her, "Ah, Julia, Julia...," he groaned, "you are so beautiful, you are everything I ever dreamed that you would be. My God, you're incredible. But..., you're killing me, baby. You're kill...ing...me!" Then he joined her.

After a while, Victor rolled off her body that now was beaded with sweat and rain. He stood up and lifted her into his arms. Carrying her silently over to her bed, he lay her down and then sat down beside her. "Julia," he said, "I want to touch you. I want to feel your skin on the inside of your thighs and underneath your arms. I want to kiss your eyelids and taste between your legs. I want to rub my hands over your body and memorize the way you are made. Then I want to lick your feet. I want to watch the way your chest moves when your heart beats and kiss the pulse that throbs in your throat. Then I want to love you in all the ways a man can love a woman. I have waited most of my life to have you and I want you to let me know you, Julia. Let me know you completely. Because..., I love you."

"No," he said as she started to protest, "no, don't say anything. I know that you don't feel the same, but I have always loved you. I want this night, Julia. Just this one night. Please say yes. Let me make love to you," he pleaded.

Julia did not answer but she let him. He pushed her and pulled her this way and that and she almost screamed because he wouldn't let her touch him. She was a candle flame blowing in the wind and she was burning up. He took his time and when he had finally driven her to madness and back several times, he made love to her. Not the violent coupling of before, but slowly, beautifully. Sometime during that blissful encounter she gave herself to him completely, all her resolves to be faithful to a man who was gone were lifted, there was no guilt, only bliss, arousal and fire.

Julia was standing in her robe at the foot of Roberto's grave. It was still dark, but the sun would soon start its climb upward, chasing the moon and the darkness before it. There wasn't much time and she needed to make her peace with him before she left for America.

The ground was wet from the storm and Julia shivered. She had been standing here for some time, she didn't know how long, having a talk with Roberto. She had explained to him how she had made love with Victor and how it had been different than when she and Roberto had been together. Not the love making itself, but how she felt afterwards. That, she understood now that she had always held a piece of herself away from Roberto and that, subconsciously, she must have always known that he had seduced and betrayed her. So, although she had given him her body, she had never truly given him her soul. That, since she didn't have a frame of reference before tonight, she had never known that any thing had been lacking in their relationship. Something had happened to her tonight and she wanted Roberto to know that she thought she could go on now. Then she told him that she still couldn't forgive him for what he had done, but she would try.

Finally, she spoke to him about her daughter and her terrible accident. She told him about her fears that Alexandria might not live and that she would have to go away to America now and that she might not ever return to Argentina.

Then she leaned down and kissed his name on the gravestone and whispered, "Goodbye, Roberto."

A ray of light broke through the semi-darkness and the wind blew softly across her face and she felt Roberto's spirit move against her, then she heard his voice whisper softly.

Julia turned and ran quickly back to the house. She had to hurry. Her daughter, Alexandria, was dying!

* * *

When Victor awakened the next day, Julia was already gone. She had left a short note on the pillow in his room that said simply, "I'm sorry."

Victor placed the note against his cheek and smelled her perfume. He had hoped for more.

"Julia," he groaned as he watched the sun rise and send streaks of light across the horizon.